W9-BZP-217

EYE of the STORM

James A. Forrest

the Peppertree Press

Copyright © James A. Forrest
All rights reserved. Published by the Peppertree Press, LLC.

the Peppertree Press and associated logos are trademarks of the Peppertree Press, LLC.

No part of this publication may be reproduced, stored in a retrieval
system, transmitted in any form or by any means, electronic, mechanical,
photocopying, recording, or otherwise, without prior written permission of
the publisher and author/illustrator.

For information regarding permissions, write to:
the Peppertree Press, LLC., Attention: Publisher
4017 Swift Road, Sarasota, FL 34231.

ISBN: 978-1-934246-50-4
Library of Congress Number: 2007925097
Printed in the U.S.A.
Printed May, 2007

Dedicated to my family on the Florida Sportsman Fishing Forum; may there be many more cups of coffee.

Special thanks to my wife, The Muse.

CHAPTER ONE

The sunlight shooting through the fall leaves and branches acted like a strobe light in Jack Foster's eyes. He drove up the winding road unsure of his destination. But he was sure that the man he would meet for the first time was the killer he had been looking for; a killer who had managed to remain undetected several years since slaying a young mother and her child.

Jack slowed down as he came to the sharp turn that led to the entrance of the trailer park. It was a steep climb and the four-cylinder of the rental car whined as it strained to make the ascent. Once in the trailer park he pulled off and looked at the directions he had written down. He sighed as he set the piece of paper on the stacks of folders in the passenger seat.

There were three manila folders ready to burst with notes and photos, held together with two thick rubber bands. The folders doubled in size since becoming the responsibility of Jack Foster; the hard work of many detectives, forensic techs, and Jack for the past seven years was chronicled in those notes and photos. It was all that hard work that led Jack to this place; to this man.

Cherokee, North Carolina was beautiful this time of year as the leaves changed colors and fell from the trees. Nestled in the Smokey Mountains, it was an area that still struggled with the cruelty the white man's greed inflicted upon the Cherokee Indians. Jack found himself feeling a little guilty as he read about "The Trail of Tears" in the little museum. It told how, in 1838, the Cherokee Nation was forced to move out to Oklahoma. Of the 15,000 who began the treacherous journey, only 11,000 made it. The plaque showed a long, winding red line from North Carolina to Oklahoma; the path known as "The Trail of Tears".

He looked up and around at the rest of the artifacts on the walls, in glass containers, and hanging from the ceiling. Then he looked at the papers in his hand. One was a pamphlet for the Museum Of The Cherokee; the other was the directions to Gregg Merriman's trailer. Jack wasn't sure why he was hesitant to go to the trailer. He had worked on this case for almost one year. He had dedicated most of his time to solving this case.

Maybe it was the fact he was all alone up here. He had informed Lt. Victoria Creek, head of the Criminal Investigations Division and Cold Case Unit, that he had a strong lead and he was going up to North Carolina to play it out. Truth was, Jack knew he had found the killer. He also knew that as soon as he handed that information over, that would be it for him; they would hand it over to one of the full-time detectives and Jack would no longer be involved. Sure he would get credit, as he did in the past, but he had invested way too much not to get a crack at Merriman.

Jack stopped in the gift shop before leaving and bought a stone-carved bear for his daughter. He wrapped the plastic bag around the little bear and stuffed it in his coat pocket before heading for the car. He slammed the car door shut and gave a shutter trying to shake off the cold. This Florida boy wasn't used to it being cold in October.

The car started, he turned the dial over to heat and was rubbing his hands together when his cell phone beeped. He picked it up, disconnected the charger, and flipped it open. He hit the scroll button and saw that it was from his wife, Amy. Jack raised an eyebrow and shifted his head side to side and flipped it shut again. As he packed for this trip, they had a huge fight. He knew she was right about the amount of time he was spending on the case, but he also knew that once it was finished things would be much better. He thought about calling her to say he was sorry, but then again, what difference would another sorry make. He could not waste any more time, he just needed to finish this.

The silver rental car basically crawled as it idled through the streets of the trailer park. Jack drove by and around the single-wide trailer. The trailer was yellow, almost faded white with brown trim. He saw Merriman's rusted out Toyota pick-up parked along the side. The gravel popped under the tires of Jack's car as he pulled into the driveway. The warmth of the sun soothed Jack's face as he stood up out of the car. He looked back to the stack of folders on the passenger seat, paused, and then shut the door.

His cell phone in one, the plastic bag in the other, Jack walked with his hands in the coat pockets up the creaky wooden steps onto the covered deck along the side of the trailer. He rubbed the plastic bag in his hand and could feel the form of the little black bear. With a sweaty palm he popped the rickety screen door opened and knocked on the aluminum door, which had about a twelve-inch diamond shaped window in it. Nothing. He tried to look into the window but it appeared to have some sort of tint over it. He knocked again.

Jack had turned around to see the leaves fluttering to the ground when he heard the chain being slid off of the door. He turned just as the door was slowly being opened. With it open about six inches, Jack could see the pudgy, balding man behind the door. The man eyed Jack from behind his large round glasses.

"I'm looking for…"

"You're looking for me," the pudgy man interrupted.

"You are Gregg Merriman?"

"I've been expecting you," he said as he pulled the door open all the way.

Jack looked into the dimly lit trailer. There wasn't much to it; a couch, a small round dining table, and a small TV. The light from the TV danced around from a picture Jack couldn't see from his angle. The sound was barely audible.

"Well, are ya gonna come in?"

The ceiling felt like it was right on top of him. Jack was not a big man by any means, but he felt as if he was standing in a tin can. A 1980's tin can. He made sure that he always had one eye on Merriman as he looked around.

The door shut. Merriman walked over and dropped onto the couch. "So do ya have a gun?"

"Do I need one?" Jack asked as he pulled out one of the chairs from the wobbly dining table.

"How do ya know I don't have one?"

3

"You never used one before," he replied as he took a seat. He faced the chair toward Merriman. Jack sat with his hands folded and his elbows resting on his knees.

Merriman slouched watching the TV, "So where do we go from here?" he asked, never taking his eyes off the TV.

"How did you know I was coming?"

"My Mom told me," eyes still fixed on the screen.

"Your Mom told me she hadn't seen or heard from you for years."

"She lied," still staring.

Jack responded by nodding his head and looking around.

"So do ya wanna know why?"

Jack's eyes snapped to focus on him, "Are you going to tell me?"

He took a deep breath and let it fall out of his lungs "Sure," still focusing on the shifting picture on the screen.

Jack waited, but there was nothing but silence. He squinted his eyes and looked at the sloth lumped on the couch. Merriman was now a rough twenty-six years old. The hair on his round head had thinned and begun to recede. He had a little potbelly covered by a navy-colored t-shirt that was a size too small. Jack followed the worn pair of blue jeans down to his bare feet. From his feet, Jack's eyes darted back to the round glasses sitting on Merriman's round face. Jack's focus went from Merriman's fixed gaze to the dancing reflection of the TV on his lenses; then he turned to see what was so interesting on the TV. Jack's eyes grew huge when the picture came into focus. It was a young woman, maybe a teenager being raped. The camera jostled around as the rapist tried to hold it while he subdued the girl. Jack could feel his skin becoming hot with rage. Anger washed over his face and he snapped his attention back to Merriman, who had been looking at Jack.

"See, you look at this and you get mad. You get disgusted. You feel hate." He shifted on the couch to better face Jack. "My heart starts pump'n, too. But mine is rush'n with desire. I love to hear the screams; the begging. The more they fight, the more I like it. The more they beg, the more I want to do. It's a huge rush. A rush…"

"Of power," Jack said with a scowl on his face.

Merriman smiled and sat up. "Yeah, that's it, a rush of power," he nodded slightly with his sick little grin.

"Is that you?" Jack asked pointing to the TV.

"Does it really matter?" still with the smug smile. "That's not why you are here."

"Why is it I'm here then?" Jack said as he sat back in the chair.

"The Mom and the kid," he said as he turned his focus back to the horror unfolding on the TV. "Ya want me to go jail. Ya probably want me to get the needle."

Nausea boiled in Jack's stomach at how monotone and calm this piece of shit was. The needle? The needle was too good for him. Jack wanted nothing more than for him to suffer like Jennifer and little Lauren. No, he wanted him to suffer more.

Merriman sat and leaned in toward the TV, "This one screamed a lot. Made me so damn excited. But none of them ever screamed like Mrs. Seiberg," he said with a smile.

Jack jumped up from the chair causing it to crash into the table behind him. He took a step forward and saw that Merriman was looking up at him with a huge smile. *That's what he wants you to do.* He looked to the ceiling, took a deep breath and looked down to Merriman with his own smile.

"You won't get me that easy," Jack said as he turned to get the chair.

Merriman leaped to his feet and lunged toward Jack hitting him in the back. Jack fell into the table causing the piece of junk to collapse underneath him. Jack rolled onto his back and Merriman jumped on top of him, wrapping his hands around Jack's throat. He squeezed with all his might. His eyes wild and his face distorted with rage.

Knifing his hands through Merriman's arms, Jack broke his grip and then punched Merriman in the center of the throat. Merriman rolled off grasping his neck and choking for air. Jack got to his feet and kicked Merriman in the gut.

This is it! This is your chance! Kill him! Jack walked up to kick him again. Merriman was on his knees, one hand around his throat, the other in the air waving like a white flag. Jack planted his shoe against the side of his face causing his head to snap back; his broken glasses flipped to the ground. Merriman's body crashed onto the floor and he started to cry.

"I thought you were a cop," he cried.

Jack reached up and rubbed his throat. The fact that Merriman had his hands on him made Jack disgusted; he slowly paced around the pile of filth. He stopped by the TV. It was now on to another victim.

Merriman peered up at him. A slight trickle of blood ran down his face from where his glasses cut his temple, "W-w-what ya gonna do now?"

Jack's focus shifted from the dreadfulness on the screen to the dreadfulness on the floor. He saw a girl with red-toned skin and silky long black hair; Cherokee. She sobbed and begged him to stop. The more she begged the more the camera danced around. *More cruelty from the white-man's greed.* Jack reared back his foot and Merriman gasped as he jerked his arms up to cover his face.

Merriman whimpered as the TV came crashing beside him.

"You are going to tell me," Jack growled at him.

Still with his arms up, "What? Tell ya what?" Merriman asked jittery. Through the gaps between his arms he frantically watched Jack pace.

Jack came to an abrupt stop and peered down on him. "You are going to tell me why you killed them," he said slowly and deliberately through clenched teeth.

"I... I... I don't know. I don't know why."

Like a hawk, Jack plunged down on top of him. He snatched Merriman up by the front of his dirty navy t-shirt and jerked his face within inches of Jack's. "Don't lie to me!" Jack screamed.

Merriman's jaw hung open and his eyes jerked back and forth as he looked into Jack's hate-filled eyes. "I don't know," he whimpered in a low voice. Merriman dropped back to the ground as Jack released him. He kept repeating "I don't know" in a whisper as he curled up on the floor.

Jack stood up and looked to the ceiling and took a deep breath and released it as he looked down to the floor. He reached into his coat pocket and retrieved his cell phone. While he opened it, he pulled a piece of paper out of his jean pocket with the Cherokee County Sheriff's Department's number on it. While the phone rang in his ear, Jack pulled the plastic bag out of his pocket and unrolled it. He reached in and grabbed the little black bear. As he turned his hand over and opened it, he saw the bear broken in two on his palm. He shook his head, put the pieces back in the bag, and began explaining who he was to the person on the phone.

The long drive home was spent trying to get a hold of Amy. Between the unanswered calls, Jack ran through the events of the last year trying to figure out where it had gone. He ate, slept, and breathed this case for the past eleven and a half months and now it was over. And now he couldn't get in touch with Amy to tell her it was over.

Jack did as he was told and made his first stop back in town the Manatee County Sheriff's Office. After a short briefing with Lt. Creek and the Sheriff, a press conference was held.

The Sheriff finished with, "I'll go ahead and take a few questions."

The half dozen or so reporters started asking all at once and the

Sheriff blindly picked one.

"Uh, yes, this would be for …" He paused to read his notes, "… Detective Foster."

The Sheriff turned to Jack and relinquished the podium with a wave. Jack looked out to the blinding lights of the cameras and nodded in the general direction of the reporter.

"Detective Foster, how were you able to solve a case that had long eluded many of your colleagues?"

Jack looked back toward Lt. Creek who looked back at him with an inquisitive look. He turned back to the lights slightly squinting, "Yes, I'm unable to give any specifics of the case at this time. The arrest of this man was done through the work of all the detectives over the years."

A rumble came from the reporters again.

"Yes, but what did you do differently," the reporter yelled over the crowd.

Jack took in a deep breath and looked down at the podium. He could see where his hands left sweaty prints. He looked back out onto the tape recorders, pads, pencils, and microphones, "I just listened to my instincts." He could see out the corner of his eye Lt. Creek bite her bottom lip and look to the floor.

Every question, every handshake, thereafter, didn't happen to Jack; he watched it happen to a guy who looked like him. The whole time he was at the Sheriff's Office he felt like a spectator of himself. He wasn't sure if it was the euphoria or exhaustion from finishing the case that made him feel like he was in a fog.

As he tried to make his way home, his cell phone rang. Jack snatched it up in hopes of seeing "Amy Cell" or "Home", but instead, it was a number he had come to know from his investigation.

"Hello, Darrel," Jack answered.

"Jack… Uh… Thank you," Darrell Seiberg said through a dry throat.

"I did it for the girls."

A long, hard sniffle, "I know, but thank you anyway."

"You're welcome," Jack replied in a somber tone.

And the call was ended. Jack flipped the phone shut and wondered if Darrel Seiberg, husband and father to Jennifer and Lauren, would ever be the same again. Not only had he lost his daughter, Darrel was the long-time suspect in the murders of Jennifer and Lauren. The fact that he was separated from Jennifer and the first to find them was enough to fuel the suspicion. Especially for then lead detective Sergeant Vicky Creek. She became blindingly sure that Darrel Seiberg was the killer even after Jack had tried to convince her otherwise.

As the garage door lifted, Jack was confused as to why there was no car parked. He entered the house and called for his wife. No answer. He called for his daughter. No answer. As he walked into the kitchen he saw the stack of paper's on the island with a yellow sticky note that simply read "Jack". Jack's face was scrunched up and he shook his head as he tried to understand what he was reading. It was petition for divorce filed by Amy. He dropped the papers on the counter and made his way to their bedroom. He paused at the door to listen. All he heard was the eerie sound of loneliness. He dropped his head, shuffled into the room and collapsed onto the bed.

The trial had re-ignited the pain and misery of many people in the community. All the years after the murders of Jennifer and Lauren Seiberg and the yellow ribbons still hung on the light posts lining State Road 64 leading to the entrance of Pomello Park. Nestled inside of the upper-class neighborhood on a two-acre lot, was the still empty Seiberg house. The realtor sign in the front yard had been sun bleached so bad you had to be right in front of it to read it. The end of the trial brought a form of closure for most of those people, but for some, it caused suspicion when they learned that the killer was a then twenty-year-old neighbor boy. Still they chose this place to give a final farewell to the mother and daughter in hopes of moving on.

At the front of the driveway there was a brick mailbox that more resembled a shrine. Jack looked over the bouquets, cards, and stuffed animals and placed the photo of the mother and daughter that he had taken from the manila folders on the pile of flowers. "Rest in peace, girls," he said as he stood up.

Finding Gregg Merriman meant the end of the investigation, but the beginning of the fight. For Jack it was the beginning of two fights; one for Jennifer and Lauren, the other for his marriage. One ended in victory; the other did not. Trying to convince Amy that he was done was impossible with the time needed for the trial.

Jack looked over the cold and lonely house and sighed. Then he opened the folded papers in his hand and signed his divorce settlement. Jack walked away closing two chapters of his life at one time.

CHAPTER TWO

She tore through the Caribbean, sparing all but one life; and now Hurricane Lynn was churning hundreds of miles away from land in the Gulf of Mexico. But that didn't stop her from having an impact on the weather; which is what Jack hoped for. When he checked the weather report the barometric pressure was rising and that meant the fish would be going insane as the massive storm approached the west coast of Florida.

It had been two years since his divorce and Jack was trying just to make it through life without any more major incidences. He left the Cold Case Unit and turned toward his charter fishing business.

As Jack was tooling down the winding road of Riverview Boulevard with his flats skiff in tow; Eric Clapton's "Promises" was playing on the radio. He eyed the million dollar homes that lined the southern boundary of the Manatee River on his way out to go fishing.

Jack never really cared to be rich, but he did like where the rich lived. He would often wonder about living on the water as he made his trek to the 59th street boat ramp. How sweet it would be to be able to walk out your back door, hop in the boat, and head out. The houses were something to marvel at as well. Ranging from Tutor, to Craftsman, to Mediterranean, and Colonial, they were the best money could buy. Much different from the 1970's, stucco box Jack resided in.

Soon he was at the ramp which was even slower than the usual weekday traffic. Folks worried more about the foreboding storm churning in the Gulf of Mexico than fishing. Fine by Jack. Fewer people on the water meant more water for him, but it also meant no one was really interested in paying him for a charter either. Jack figured the storm would do just like every other storm that was predicted to hit the Tampa Bay area; veer off and nail some neighboring coastal area either north or south of them. Or the storm would take a full swing north and smash the costal regions of Louisiana.

Jack pondered the thought of Hurricane Lynn ravaging the salt marshes of Louisiana as he was launching the skiff into the water. It seemed as if the poor folks over there were always getting hammered and west central Florida always managed to escape. After all this time, Louisiana, Mississippi, and Alabama were still trying to get past the devastation of Hurricane Katrina. The last thing they needed was another storm to go smashing into them. He tied off the boat, climbed back into his truck, pulled the trailer out, and parked.

As he made his way back to the ramp, Jack surveyed the chop on the river; not too rough, but it would be a bit of a bumpy ride for his skiff. A Great Blue Heron stood on the concrete wall that supported the ramp and with its bright orange eyes, peered into Jack's boat. Jack tipped the bill of his cap to the heron as he climbed into the skiff. The heron swung its long bill around as it looked at Jack and cautiously took a couple of steps back. Jack hoped the bird was a good omen to the trip ahead.

The skiff rocked in the channel as he idled his way out. The chop clapped against the side of his hull causing a bit of salty spray to come over and mist Jack's face. He pulled his sunglasses off and wiped them on his shirt, then placed them on his face once again.

Jack lifted his face and inhaled deeply through his nose. The salt air filled his lungs and caused his heart to beat a bit harder. The smell was exhilarating to him and instantly cleared his mind to focus on the task at hand; catching fish.

Standing on the casting deck of his skiff, Jack flipped his lure, a nightglow DOA shrimp, up into the mangroves around Terra Ceia Bay. He glanced up to the blue sky; other than the decent breeze causing the clouds overhead to drift at a good pace, it was blank of the carnage that would fall upon the Florida coast in the days to come.

Jack slowly retrieved the plastic shrimp with a small pop every so often. Then he felt the thump and saw the line begin to move across the water. He leaned forward, reeled in the slack, and pulled back to set the hook. He saw the line cut through the top of the water as the fish made a run for the mangroves.

"Not today," he said to himself as he leaned back and cupped the spool to slow the drag and keep the racing prey away from the jagged oysters at the base of the stilt-like roots of the mangroves.

The fish turned, raced toward the open water and jumped out of the water in a fit of flips and leaps while thrashing its head side to side.

"Little Snook," Jack said as a smile came across his face.

He lipped the 26-inch linesider, gave it a look-over as he popped out the hook, slid it back into the water, and prepared to move on when something light green in the mangrove overhang caught his eye. Jack had an eerie suspicion about what it might be.

Jack hopped up on the poling platform and pushed the skiff up into the mangroves. He hopped down and made his way to the front deck. As he did, a slight breeze came off the water by the mangroves and right into him. He froze. At the very instant his eyes were making out the form in the water, the smell hit him. He recognized the smell right away; rotting flesh.

Jack slowly knelt down and lifted the branches for a better look. The crabs scattered as the sunlight came upon the body face down against the roots like a piece of driftwood. Jack turned his head to the side and took a breath. He stood up and looked up to the sun. He shook his head and made his way to the console, picked up his cell phone and dialed 911.

"This is the Manatee County Sheriff's Office. This line is recorded; what is your emergency?" said a female voice.

"Hey, this is Jack Foster."

"Oh, hi Jack! What's wrong?" she asked sounding a bit concerned.

"I've got a signal seven out on the water."

Jack was content living a simple life running his small charter business out of his home. At this stage in his life, all he really wanted to do was spend his time on the water and with his daughter. Time with his daughter was not as easy to come by, but it wasn't always this way.

He was living the American dream; pretty wife, beautiful daughter, nice job, nice house, car, truck, and boat. There really wasn't much for Jack to want. He had worked for twenty-five years with the Manatee County Sheriff's Office making Lieutenant in the jail. Jack retired at the young age of 45 and looked forward to going full force with his upstart charter fishing business. But he still had a voice in the back of his head driving him toward the reason he wanted to get into law enforcement in the first place; homicide detective. Jack was very content being away from the day-to-day politics. Now he found much joy in taking people out on the water in the chance that he might educate them about fishing and nature, and save some of Florida's coastal wildlife.

Jack had always struggled with the idea that his life-long dream of becoming a detective would be nothing more than that. So he began to do what he swore he would never do. He started showing up at the Sheriff's Office poking around the Criminal Investigation Division, which handled homicide investigations. Jack was just hoping to lend a helping hand and that is when he found the Cold Case Unit. It was perfect for Jack. The CCU was a group of individuals from different walks of life that worked on cases that had grown old and cold of any chance of solving. With Jack's background, he didn't have trouble getting into the unit. And there he made a name for himself. The cases were food for a craving that had long yearned inside of him. Jack could not leave them alone. They were like puzzles; puzzles of the human mind. Jack solved two missing children cases that were ten and twelve years old in his first year with the unit. Then he solved what many considered to be one of the worst homicides in the history of the county; the brutal murder of a mother and her five-year-old daughter in an affluent part of the county. That homicide had become the albatross for many a detective.

Jack worked furiously on the case becoming what many had considered obsessed; especially his wife. Jack's overwhelming need to solve the murders of the mother and daughter began to eat away at the time he spent with his family. His mind began to blur the line of separation between the deceased mother and daughter and that of his own wife and daughter. For Jack, it was as if he needed to find the killer to prevent this very same thing from happening to his family. The case slowly drove him into his own private insanity. And his blinding desire cost him greatly. His marriage of eighteen years came to an end. His daughter, now fifteen, lived with his ex-wife who became bitter for the way she felt Jack discarded them for the cases. She had dropped little hints of frustration. She pleaded with Jack to take a break, but Jack's mind was consumed with the prospect of solving the case. It wasn't until the day Jack came home and saw the divorce papers did he begin to realize how addicted he had become. The cases never brought him any closer to understanding the sociopathic desire to murder. Instead, his undaunted desire left his family shattered, so he decided to walk away from the Cold Case Unit.

With the divorce final and his departure from the CCU, Jack turned his attention to spending his time on the water surrounded by Mother Nature's grandeur. The water had always been a part of Jack's life for as far back as he could remember, so he found comfort on the flats catching fish or helping others do so; an escape from the evils that men do; until now.

Jack hung up the cell phone and scanned around to see no other boats in the area. He went back over and looked at the body once more. He noticed a bulge from a wallet in the back pocket. Jack carefully leaned down and slid the wallet out, the smell starting to get to him. He stood up quickly and took a couple of deep breaths trying to clear his nostrils of the wretched scent.

"Who do we have here?" Jack said as he opened the soaked wallet.

The picture on the driver's license shocked him. 'It can't be!' he thought. The man on the driver's license was Tom Underwood, a very popular guide in the area, and a friend of Jack's.

Jack dropped the wallet and leaned down again. He held his breath as he lifted the mangrove branches and grabbed the sleeve and rolled the body. It was Tom. It appeared he had not been in the water for more then a day. Jack let the shell of his friend rest back into the water. He stood up and walked to the back of the boat and gazed out onto the shimmering bay through a cut. He heard the roar of large motors and noticed the hefty Scarab cutting across the water with lights flashing.

It didn't take Jack as long as it took the driver of the Scarab to realize that it was too shallow for the large boat to get back to Jack. Jack stood there with a scowl across his face as he imagined a large trough cut through the sea grass from the large boat. He motored up and moved over to the Scarab.

The boat driver was throwing out an anchor and that's when Jack realized who the driver was; Deputy Matt Darby. Jack was not fond of Darby. He was a know-it-all who knew nothing.

"There's no way you're gonna get that thing back there, Darby," Jack yelled over to him as he made his way.

"Mr. Foster. You sure do have a way of finding trouble don't you?" Darby replied sarcastically. "What are you doing out here anyway? Don't you know there is a hurricane headed this way?" now sounding more serious.

Jack rolled his eyes as he eased up to the Scarab. "Hop on, I'll run ya over for a look."

Darby looked around and noticed that there was no sign of another deputy. "Well, all right. You know this one is gonna hit us. We are well overdue and I've been studying the Tropical Cyclone Strike Probabilities; we are definitely well within the range."

Jack didn't respond as he didn't share in either Darby's passion for hurricanes or his fear of this particular one.

As they made their way over to the body of Jack's late friend, Darby looked down and saw the soaked wallet.

"What is this?" Darby yelled. Darby was always looking for a way to shine. It never really happened for him, so any chance he got to bust on those that did, he took. "You're not with the Sheriff's Office anymore! You know you're not supposed to disturb the crime scene!"

"Shut up," Jack said as he put the skiff in neutral, and then killed the motor.

The smell bored into Darby's nostrils. "Whoa! Man, that's bad. Poor F'er has probably been here for a week!"

Jack made his way to the bow. "Check this out." He lifted the branches and once again the crustaceans sidestepped for cover.

Darby turned and heaved vomit over the side of the boat.

"I already chummed for bait, but thanks anyways," Jack said with a chuckle. "Besides, I think you're disturbing the crime scene."

Darby wiped his mouth on the back of his hand and turned with a glaring look at Jack. "Why don't we just go back to my boat and wait for the Techies to get here. You know, let the real detectives do their job."

"Whatever, Darby. You wonder why nobody likes you." And with that he started the skiff up and motored back to the Scarab.

'Who would want to kill Tom?' Jack thought as he made his way back down the winding road of Riverview Boulevard, now in the dark. His usual marvel at the stately homes that lined the road did not happen tonight.

His mind was subconsciously shifting into detective mode; his mind was hungry for answers. He was able to get a nibble for his brain before he left the ramp; who was working the case and the cause of death.

Jack pictured the conversation…

He heard a voice call to him as he wound the winch, pulling the skiff snug on the trailer.

"Well, Jack, it's been awhile. Can't say that this is how I thought we would meet up again," said Detective David Roberts as he shook Jack's hand.

Roberts was good detective and Jack liked him enough. Roberts showed no hesitation toward the notion of having someone who was never a detective come in and look at his stack of aging files. And in several of those incidences, it was Jack who had gone through Roberts' cold cases.

Though Jack didn't solve any of Roberts' cold cases, he liked the way Jack worked, the way he thought; like a real detective. And he treated him accordingly, which earned Jack's respect in return.

"I didn't think it would be this way, either," Jack replied as he shook the detective's hand, then adjusted the cap on his head.

"So you knew the victim?"

"Yeah, fellow charter captain. Good man. Can't understand why someone would want to hurt him, let alone kill him."

"How do you know it wasn't a boating accident?" Roberts asked as he looked over Jack's shoulder and watched the medical examiner load up the body.

Jack turned to see what Roberts was focusing on. "Well for one, Tom was a hell of a boatman, and he wouldn't put himself in any predicament like that. Two, no one reported finding his boat capsized or beached. And three, one of the techies told me there appeared to be a couple of gunshot wounds to the chest," Jack said as he turned back to the scribbling detective with a smile.

Roberts peered up from his pad and saw the smirk on Jack's face. "I don't think you had anything to do with his murder, Jack."

"I know you don't. Really, there isn't a whole lot I can tell you. Me and Tom were friends; not best friends, but pretty good friends. I don't remember him making any mention of somebody wanting to hurt him or anything like that." Jack paused to rub his eyes. "To tell ya the truth, it's been a long day and I really would like to get home. I still gotta flush the motor and clean up the boat."

"That's fine Jack," said Robert's extending his hand again. "If you do think of something, please give me a call."

"You know I will."

Jack walked over and opened the door to the truck and was getting in as Roberts called to him once again.

"Jack."

He turned and looked at Roberts.

"Any chance we might be seeing you around the office in the near future?"

"David, I think the days of playing detective are over for me."

Roberts took a couple of steps closer "I never thought you were playing," he said with a kind smile.

Jack smiled back at him, gave him a slight nod and got in the truck.

Did he in fact actually know something that wasn't obvious at the time? He was running through the possible scenarios that might have lead to Capt. Tom's untimely demise when someone behind him honked the horn. Jack snapped into reality and looked up to see the light he had stopped for was green. He hit the gas and gave a sorrowful wave. Now back in the present, something on the radio caught his attention and he reached over and turned up the volume.

"Landfall should be some time in the next couple of days," said the voice on the radio. "Everything points to Lynn making landfall in the Tampa Bay area, so I hope you folks out there are ready."

Jack had forgotten about the hurricane that churned in the Gulf of Mexico. Lynn was a category two hurricane that had the potential to be more depending on how she ate up the warm waters of the Gulf. Jack knew that they projected the storm to hit the Bradenton/Sarasota area, but it seemed they had been doing that with every storm that came into the Gulf.

CHAPTER THREE

ZCZC MIATCPAT2 ALL
TTAA00 KNHC DDHHMM
BULLETIN
HURRICANE LYNN SPECIAL ADVISORY NUMBER 20
NWS TPC/NATIONAL HURRICANE CENTER MIAMI FL
7 PM CDT FRI AUG 18 2006

...LYNN STRENGTHENS TO CATEGORY THREE WITH 115 MPH
WINDS...

A HURRICANE WARNING IS IN EFFECT FOR THE WEST CENTRAL
GULF COAST OF FLORIDA.
FROM CRYSTAL RIVER SOUTH TO VENICE...INCLUDING THE
CITIES OF TAMPA AND SARASOTA.
A HURRICANE WARNING MEANS THAT HURRICANE CONDITIONS

ARE EXPECTED
IN THE WARNING AREA WITHIN THE NEXT 24 HOURS.
PREPARATIONS TO
PROTECT LIFE AND PROPERTY SHOULD BE RUSHED TO
COMPLETION.

A TROPICAL STORM WARNING AND A HURRICANE WATCH ARE
IN EFFECT FROM
NORTH OF CRYSTAL RIVER FLORIDA TO APALACHICOLA
FLORIDA...AND FROM
SOUTH OF VENICE TO MARCO ISLAND.

FOR STORM INFORMATION SPECIFIC TO YOUR AREA...
INCLUDING POSSIBLE
INLAND WATCHES AND WARNINGS...PLEASE MONITOR
PRODUCTS ISSUED
BY YOUR LOCAL WEATHER OFFICE.

AT 7 PM CDT...0600Z...THE CENTER OF HURRICANE LYNN
WAS LOCATED
NEAR LATITUDE 25.1 NORTH...LONGITUDE 86.8 WEST OR
ABOUT 310
MILES...500 KM...SOUTH-SOUTHEAST OF THE MOUTH OF
THE MISSISSIPPI
RIVER.

LYNN IS MOVING TOWARD THE EAST-NORTHEAST NEAR 7
MPH. A GRADUAL
TURN TOWARD THE NORTHEAST IS EXPECTED LATER TODAY.

REPORTS FROM AN AIR FORCE RECONNAISSANCE AIRCRAFT
INDICATE THAT
MAXIMUM SUSTAINED WINDS HAVE INCREASED AND ARE NOW
NEAR 115
MPH... WITH HIGHER GUSTS. LYNN IS A CATEGORY THREE
HURRICANE ON
THE SAFFIR-SIMPSON SCALE. SOME ADDITIONAL
STRENGTHENING IS POSSIBLE
TODAY.

HURRICANE FORCE WINDS EXTEND OUTWARD UP TO 60 MILES
FROM THE CENTER... AND TROPICAL STORM FORCE WINDS EXTEND OUTWARD UP
TO 150 MILES.

THE MINIMUM CENTRAL PRESSURE RECENTLY REPORTED BY THE RECONNAISSANCE
AIRCRAFT WAS 968 MB...28.59 INCHES.

HEAVY RAINS FROM LYNN SHOULD BEGIN TO AFFECT THE CENTRAL GULF
COAST SUNDAY MORNING.

THE NEXT ADVISORY WILL BE ISSUED BY THE NATIONAL HURRICANE CENTER AT
10 PM CDT.

FORECASTER BARRETT

Jack pulled just passed the house and then backed the boat up along the side of it. He hopped out to unhook the trailer when a stiff breeze kicked up shaking the palms in his front yard like pom-poms. He paused and looked to the navy night sky. The sliver of a moon shone through fast-paced parallel, puffed clouds. Jack looked to the west in the direction of the Gulf of Mexico. He thought about his friend and wondered what else could go wrong. As Jack stared off into the dimly lit sky, a flash of lightning flickered off over the Gulf.

"Hmm..." Jack wondered.

He turned and went straight to work on cleaning the boat. He lifted the single-car garage door, entered it and pulled a dangling string attached to a 60-watt bulb. His eyes adjusted to light, he quickly started looking around the cluttered garage. Shortly thereafter, he appeared again outside the garage with a pair of motor flush muffs in one hand and a bucket with a short bristled deck brush in the other.

While the motor ran, Jack scrubbed the boat. His actions were automatic as his mind ran through feasible circumstances of Capt. Tom's demise.

With the boat clean and his gear stowed in the garage, Jack headed into the house. As he opened the door in the garage a voice called out to him.

"Well, Capt. Jack, what did you catch?"

It startled him, but he instantly recognized the voice.

"Oh, honey, I'm so sorry. I completely lost track of the time and day!" he said.

"That's all right, Dad. I just hung out here with Bear," said his daughter stroking the bobtail cat.

"Kat, you know you shouldn't stay here by yourself," Jack said in a concerned tone. "You could have called my cell or something. If I'm not here when your Mom drops you off, I could always go there and pick you up."

"Do you want to spend time with me or not, Dad?" Katelyn said. Bear hopped off her lap as she got up and gave Jack a hug.

"You know the answer to that; of course I do," he replied as he squeezed her tight.

She pulled back and looked at him inquisitively, then reached up and scratched the thin goatee on his chin. "What's with this?"

"Oh, just trying something new. What do ya think?" he asked as he began scratching it himself.

"Uh, no." she said matter of factly.

"Why not?"

"Dad, trust me, no."

Jack felt lonely at home most of the time so he tried to spend as much time on the water as he could; but nothing could fill the void he felt from the absence of his family. Nothing, but the times when it was his turn to have his daughter. And even though Katelyn Foster did feel betrayed by him, she still loved her father dearly and never missed a chance to be with him. Jack always made it a point, now, to make her his sole focus when she was there. Some of her fondest memories were of the time she and her dad were on the water. It was a common bond that was deeply rooted in them and Jack wanted to make sure it continued to be that way. He always planned at least one day on the water with her and she was always glad to go. It was also a sore spot with his ex-wife because their daughter was so much like her father; it was a constant reminder of him.

Katelyn was a tall, thin girl with flowing auburn hair. Her eyes were piercing aqua blue. She was strikingly beautiful for a young girl, which always had her father worried. She loved her parents very much, but always seemed to be a daddy's girl. This of course made Jack feel very good. She was also a very curious girl and asked a lot of questions. Not annoying questions, but deep, thought-provoking questions. She was always seeking an understanding to something or everything much like her father. Katelyn needed to know. Many of Jack's friends would often comment that Katelyn was like an old soul in a young girl's body.

While the two hugged, Bear came over and began to rub against Jack's leg. The stocky cat had a raspy, deep meow and oddly enough, resembled a bear cub. Jack bent over and began to scratch him behind the ear.

"What's up, buddy?" he asked and the cat started purring right away.

"Come on, Dad, I'm hungry."

"Hungry? Why didn't you just grab something to eat?"

"Because I thought we could sit and eat dinner together," she said as she poked him in the stomach.

They walked into the dated kitchen and Katelyn leaned against the counter with her elbows resting her chin in her hands. She looked up at the dome light in the kitchen and shook her head. The house looked pretty much the same as the day her dad bought it. There were the personal things that Jack had placed out and a couple of additions in furniture, but otherwise it was like stepping into a time warp that led to the 70's.

Jack opened the refrigerator and he pulled out a plate with fried chicken on it covered in plastic wrap. "Hope you don't mind leftovers."

"Nah, I'm hungry enough to eat a horse," she said with a wink.

Jack smiled and proceeded to heat their dinner.

Katelyn turned and looked at the bookcase standing next to the dining table. There were various books on the shelves. The fiction was separate from the nonfiction; other than that, there did not appear to be any rhyme or reason for their placement. On one shelf there were no books. Displayed in their place was an assortment of wooden puzzles. They all seemed to be completed. Some formed geometrical shapes and others lay dismantled as though the purpose was to take them apart as compared to making something.

She walked over and began to peruse the worn binders. She saw several of the nonfiction books dealing with homicide investigation techniques, criminal psychology, and crime scene investigations. Katelyn was torn by these books. She truly found the material fascinating, but also found them to be a reminder of why she has to visit her father instead of live with him.

She had pulled a paperback titled, "Endurance", and was flipping through it when the microwave dinged. Jack pulled the steaming pile of fried chicken from it and placed it on the table as Katelyn sat down in front of it.

"That's a really interesting book. It's an amazing story about explorers lost in Antarctica. It's unbelievable what man can do when he is forced to survive. You can borrow it if you want. Something to drink?" he asked.

"I've got a glass of water. It should be fine," she replied as she leaned over and put the book back on the shelf.

Jack set the glass down beside her plate and took a seat adjacent to her. He looked up at the puzzles Katelyn was admiring and thought how glad he was that she was there. One less lonely night working on a puzzle.

Katelyn picked a breaded drumstick off her plate and took a big bite. "So, is that book about the guys' eat'n the dead guys to survive?" she asked out the side of her mouth with a smirk.

Jack smiled and looked at her sideways. "No, it's about these men out in the freezing Antarctica on an expedition when their ship gets caught in a giant ice flow and is crushed. They're forced to live on the ice. The amazing thing is that they all survived."

"Did they have a locater device, like an EPIRB or something?"

"No, baby, this was back in the early nineteen hundred's. They didn't have VHF radios or any of the stuff we got today."

Katelyn perked up, "Well, how did they do it?"

"They banded together as a team. Together they were unbeatable."

"Hmm…" she responded with a raised brow and took another bite.

Later they sat at the kitchen table playing Gin Rummy. Jack told fishing stories that he had told before and Katelyn talked about some boy in her English class. Jack's insides turned like rough seas the whole time she talked about the boy, but he felt good to know that his daughter felt so comfortable around him. Jack's loneliness faded to the back of his mind, unlike the murder of Capt. Tom. Any break in the conversation brought

Tom's ghastly image back to the forefront of Jack's brain.

An old wooden wall clock struck midnight. Katelyn, in mid chuckle, turned to look at the wooden clock with its large brass swinging pendulum. She read the etching on the glass door.

Jack & Amy

Foster

Dec. 7, 1985

Jack refused to part with the wedding gift he received from his sister and brother-in-law. Katelyn let out a sigh and looked back at her cards. Then she folded them up and laid them on the table.

"Well, it's getting late. I'm sure you have something planned for tomorrow so I should turn in."

"OK, honey," he said not looking up from his cards.

She got up and walked over to him and kissed his forehead. Jack sat there quietly. Katelyn took Jack's tanned cheeks in her hands and turned his face up toward her. "I love you, Daddy." she said as she looked into his eyes.

Jack gazed into her beautiful, innocent eyes. "I know you do, honey."

She bent down and hugged him, "Get some sleep."

"I will, honey. See you in the morning."

Katelyn turned and headed down the hall to her room. Jack got up and filled a glass of water and started tidying up in the kitchen when he heard her getting ready in the guest bathroom.

"Goodnight, Dad," she called out to him as she made her way back down the hall.

"Goodnight, sweetie."

Jack sat back down at the kitchen table. He looked up at the old wall clock and sighed. He gathered the cards up off the table and straightened them into an even stack. He split the deck in two and shuffled them: zip! Then the cards fluttered together as he arched them in his palms.

Who would want to kill Tom? he thought as he sifted the cards back and forth. *Tom never really spoke of enemies.* Jack flipped the first card; the one-eyed Jack of Spades. He then set the next six cards in a row next to it. *There have been plenty of women in his life but none that Tom thought were the extremely jealous type.* He flipped the next card, Eight of Clubs, and laid it on top of the card next to the Jack and then set out the next five face down. *Maybe a business deal gone bad?* He laid the Queen of Diamonds down and then four more cards. *Move the Jack on top of the Queen.* Then he flipped the King of Diamonds and laid out the next three. Move *King to the empty spot.*

Jack finished laying the cards out for his game of solitaire and made whatever moves he could. He then pulled three cards off the remainder of the deck and flipped them over, Six of Hearts. *What is it about Tom that would make him a victim?* Three more cards and flip. *He seemed to be financially secure.* Three more cards; flip. *But then again, there are plenty of people who aren't, but are good at hiding it.*

The next flip revealed the Ace of Diamonds which Jack put above the other cards. *I wonder if Tom ended up mess'n with a married woman.* he thought with a raised eyebrow. Flip; Eight of Hearts, which he moved onto the Nine of Clubs. He flipped the last three cards in his hand, King of Hearts; no move.

"This ain't looking too good," Jack mumbled as he picked up the stack of cards.

He pulled off and flipped the first three cards in the stack revealing the same six of heart it did the first time. He repeated the act four more times showing the same four cards as before.

"Ten of Clubs," he grumbled. "No good."

Probably not robbery since he still had his wallet. He turned over three more cards leaving one in his hand; King of Diamonds. A scowl came across Jacks face as he looked at the played cards in front of him. He flipped the last card in his hand to see the King of Hearts once more.

"Suicidal King," he said as he examined the picture of the king holding a sword that appeared to be stuck in his head. "Well, I know what *wasn't* the cause of Tom's death."

Jack looked past the card to the bookcase across from him. He got up, walked over, and looked over the bindings. He tried not to look at the collection of investigative materials he had gathered over the years, but couldn't help himself. He followed the row with his index finger then stopped on one, laid his finger on the top off the binding and pulled out the book titled, *Crime Classification Manual.*

He set the book on the table and walked into the kitchen and refilled the glass of water under the faucet. He turned and looked at the book on the table and swigged the glass. His nostrils flared as he took in a deep breath. Jack grabbed a pad and pencil off the counter as he walked back into the dining room. He sat down at the table and opened the book. *Not gonna get much sleep tonight.*

Jack had released the starving beast he kept locked away for so long; his mind. Try as he might to entertain his brain with puzzles and the lot, nothing compared to that of a good mystery involving the human mind.

Jack worked with fervor for two hours, making notes he hoped that would make sense to him in the morning. And though he was not tired, he stopped because he knew he had to, for Katelyn.

As Jack walked past Katelyn's door, he paused and hung his head. He knew he should have been sleeping so he could give her his all, but his addiction was too overpowering. Guilt-ridden and wide awake, Jack climbed into bed. He closed his eyes and thought of the water. And eventually drifted to sleep.

The next morning Jack awoke to the smell of bacon. He opened his eyes in the half-lit room, stretched on the bed, slung his feet over, and sat up. A glance at the red digital numbers on the clock revealed it was seven o'clock. Jack took in a couple more whiffs of the bacon, stood up and shuffled into the bathroom.

Hair a mess, wearing a t-shirt with some faded to near nothing print and a pair of shorts cut from sweatpants, Jack emerged from down the hall. "Hey, sweetie," he said in the midst of a yawn.

"Well, you slept in late. I thought you got up earlier then this," Katelyn asked as she flipped a couple strips of bacon.

Jack took a seat at the kitchen counter "Yeah, I usually do. Must have been the good company last night," he said with a wink.

Katelyn smiled back at him. She poured a cup of coffee and brought it over to him, "What time did you get to bed last night?"

Jack sipped the piping hot coffee "Not too long after you." He watched her for a reaction. Had she known?

"Well, I'm glad to see you got some rest," she said as she placed a plate of eggs and bacon in front of him.

"Thank you!"

"One or two pieces of toast?"

Jack washed a bite of his breakfast down with another sip of coffee "Two, please."

"So Capt. Jack, what do ya have planned for today?" Katelyn asked as she rested her elbows on the counter across from him.

Jack looked into her eyes "Oh, I don't know. That storm is making the weather go nuts still and you know what that means."

"Fish are going nuts."

"Exactly." Jack scooped more eggs on his fork with a piece of bacon. "But if you would rather do something else…"

"Yeah, right," she turned to pick up the toast that had just popped.

"Where's yours?" Jack asked as she placed the toast on his plate.

"I already ate. I wasn't going to wait for you like last night."

"I'm really sorry about last night."

Katelyn was wiping off the counter "What was the deal last night? Did you have a late charter or something?"

Jack took another sip of the hot coffee. It felt good going down his throat. "Well, something happened."

"Yes, I gathered that, that's why I asked," she said looking at him sideways.

"Right. Look, you remember Capt. Tom?"

Katelyn squinted her eyes and looked up, "Capt. Tom, he's the one with the nice Hewes right? We've gone out with him a couple of times, haven't we?"

"Yeah, we have. He's the one that put us on the Cobia a couple of summers ago."

"Oh, yeah! That was a sweet trip! How is good old Capt. Tom?"

Jack brought his dishes to the sink and started washing "Well, that's it. Umm, Capt Tom is dead."

"Oh, my!" Katelyn gasped. "What happened?"

"It appears that someone killed him."

"That's horrible!" she said as she begun to dry the dishes.

"I know."

"But what does this have to do with you?" she looked at him puzzled.

"I found his body."

"Oh, Dad, that's terrible. Are you all right?" Katelyn turned and hugged him.

"I'm OK. It's just hard to believe that someone would want to hurt him. I can't think of any reason."

"Who knows why people do the things they do," she said as she put the last plate away.

Jack raised his eyebrows, "Very true."

"So I take it they don't know who did it?"

"Didn't appear that way. But who knows what they turned up last night. Detective Roberts is working on the case. He's pretty good, so I'm sure they'll find out." Jack took the last swig of coffee from his cup. The two stood silent for a minute. "I'm gonna go ahead and hop in the shower real quick. Then we'll go ahead and hit the water."

"Sounds good to me," Katelyn said as she plopped on the couch.

She grabbed the remote and turned on the television.

She was watching the Today show when she heard Bear's raspy meow at the back door. She got up to let him in when the phone rang. She snatched the phone up on her way to the back door. "Hello?"

"Ah, yes, is this Skinny Dip Charters?" asked a man on the phone sounding unsure.

"Yes, it is. I'm sorry. How can I help you?" Katelyn grimaced having forgot that her dad runs the business out of his home.

"OK, well, I would like to book a trip in two weeks."

Katelyn looked around for a pen and some paper when she came across a notebook and a pencil on the counter. "All right," she said as she flipped it open. And when she did, she saw the notes her father had made the night before.

Jack came down the hall rubbing his freshly shaven chin "So, should we pack a lunch?" As he came around the corner he saw Katelyn sitting at the table with the notepad.

"I booked you a charter in a couple of weeks."

"OK."

"But you'll probably be too busy being a detective to do it," she said as she tossed the notepad at him. "Are you working cases again? Is that it? You can't be here with me because you are too busy with the cases again?" Katelyn turned and started to storm out of the kitchen when Jack grabbed her shoulder.

"No! Absolutely not! Kat, I'm the one who found his body," he pleaded to her. Katelyn stopped and turned back toward him. Her eyes were welled up with tears. Jack pulled her into him. "It's not like that, Kat."

"Then what's it like?"

"Listen, I'm the one who found Tom's body. I had to hang around and answer questions. That's why I was late getting home last night. The notes you found, yes, I sat up last night and worked through some things in my head. This is an ongoing investigation. They already have detectives working this case. They don't need me."

"You don't understand. It's like another puzzle, that's all." He said motioning over to the puzzles in the bookcase. "It's the ultimate puzzle though; trying to figure out what makes someone kill."

Her face was expressionless.

Jack held her out away from him by the shoulders and looked into her eyes. "Kat, look at me. Our time is just that. I'm here with you and that's where I want to be. I can't tell you how it hurts me that things are the way they are. I know I screwed up and I'm not going to make that mistake again. The notes are just something I do; just another way to keep the mind sharp, that's all. Please, let's go fishing."

Katelyn wiped her eyes and studied his face "OK, let's go fishing."

Jack pulled her in and hugged her "I love you so much!"

Something her father said clicked with Katelyn. Though she had never worked on a homicide case, she did wonder what would make someone kill. She thought about the books on the shelves. She thought about the cases her father had solved and ones he never got the chance to. Katelyn was more like her father than even he knew.

Conditions on the water were not much different from the day before. Jack polled the skiff along the mangroves looking for the log-like shadows of fish submerged along the shoreline. Katelyn stood ready with rod and reel in hand.

"Kat, eleven o'clock, about fifteen yards. Looks like a nice red," Jack said as he crouched down on the platform.

Katelyn scanned the water in the area Jack described and saw the elongated shadow. Slightly crouched, she let her jig soar about five yards past with a sidearm cast. Then she popped it with a flick of her wrist. She reeled the slack and popped it again. This time the shadow turned toward the bucktail jig.

Jack watched with anticipation. "Do it again," he whispered.

She did, and together they watched the fish torpedo the lure. Katelyn pulled back on the rod setting the hook and her drag began to scream.

"Got it!" she called back to him.

Jack smiled as Katelyn worked the rod and reel. She was as good as any that he had seen on the boat. "All right," he answered and began to pole after the fish.

It was a nice redfish, above the slot limit, and put up a hard fight on the light tackle Katelyn was using. She had a huge grin on her face as she watched the trail of swirls appear on the surface from the pumping tail. Katelyn worked the rod and reel, lifting the rod tip and reeling on the way down. She managed to bring the bronze battler boat side a couple of times, but as the fish caught sight of them it took off on long runs.

With every zing of the drag Katelyn let out a howl of excitement.

And when Jack finally netted the beautiful fish, Katelyn saw that it was bigger then she expected. At thirty-seven inches, it was truly a brute and quite the prize on eight-pound test line.

After Jack snapped a couple of pictures Katelyn bent over the gunnel and held the tired fish in her palms. She moved the big red back and forth, pushing water through its gills. With a slight fan of its tail, it eased out of her hands and swam off. Katelyn washed her hands together to get the fish slime off. As she was getting up, something in a cut through the mangroves caught her eye. As she squinted, the yellow police tape became clearer.

"Is that where you found Capt. Tom?"

Paying attention to Katelyn fighting the fish, Jack had lost track of where they were at in the bay. He climbed back onto the poling platform and looked around "Yeah, that's it."

"Can we go in there?"

"Kat, why would you want to go in there? It's not like there is anything to see. They didn't leave stuff in there."

"I don't know. I just want to go in there."

Jack was intrigued with her curiosity "All right, if that's what you want."

Katelyn was so focused on the long rolling flaps of the torn yellow tape that she didn't see the Snook that spooked as Jack poled in. She cocked her head and stared at the skinny bright yellow arms of tape as they waved at her to go back. Her back quivered and she wondered what it was like for her dad to find the body.

"There was actually a branch that was hanging over the body, but they cut it off and took it. You really couldn't see him until you came up to about here." Jack stopped the gliding skiff.

Katelyn turned to Jack, "Dad, why would someone kill Capt. Tom?"

Jack shrugged his shoulders and shook his head.

"Who do think did it?"

"I don't know."

"But you could figure it out."

"Kat, just like I told you at the house, there are detectives who are working on this case already and they will find out who did this," Jack said as he began to turn the skiff around.

As they made their way back out of the cut, Katelyn sat on the front deck with her legs folded facing him. She lifted her cap off her head and pulled it off to the side to release her long hair that she had pulled through the back. "Dad, why did you want to be a detective?" she asked as she adjusted the cap and pulled her hair through once more.

Jack gave a good hard push and the skiff coasted. He scanned the water for the next spot to go. "I don't know, Kat. I've always wanted to do it. I've always wanted to know what made the criminal mind work. You know, like I told you; know what drives them to kill another human being." Jack made another long push. "It's one of those things that no one has ever been able to figure out."

Katelyn nodded and turned to look over the bay. A breeze blew by and it felt cool against her face. Secretly she wanted to be a detective, too. She wondered the same things as her father, but felt she couldn't talk about those feelings with her parents. Katelyn's curiosity stemmed from secretly looking through the file her dad had on the slain mother and daughter. At the time, the images she saw were gruesome and frightening, but over time the question of why someone would do such a thing began to grow inside of her.

The answer her father gave her was the one she thought she would give if asked the same question. The answer made her feel even closer to her dad, but it also scared her knowing what her father's obsession did to their family.

"Come on, Kat, get ready."

"Oh, right." She hopped up and grabbed the rod out of the holder and took her position on the front deck. She glanced over her shoulder at her dad. He was scanning the water as he moved the boat along, but she could tell his mind was focused elsewhere. "What are you thinking?"

"Uh, honestly?"

"Yes, honestly."

"I'm wondering how they are making out on Capt. Tom's case."

"We should go find out."

Jack snapped his head down to look at her. "What? Are you serious?"

"Yeah, I think I am."

Jack looked up and over the water. Katelyn had turned around, facing him for an answer. He made another long push with the pole. "I think we should just keep on fishing."

"No, really Dad, I want to go."

"Why?"

Katelyn just shrugged her shoulders. But Jack could see it in her face that she was serious.

He looked down at his watch. "Well, if were gonna go, we need to head back in now."

Katelyn stepped down and put the rod back in the holder. Jack raised his eyebrows and shrugged his shoulders. He hopped down and put the push pole in the holders on the gunnel. Katelyn came around and sat down behind the console beside him as he fired the motor up and they were on their way.

It had been over a year since Jack had been in the Criminal Investigation Division of the Sheriff's Office, but it seemed like yesterday as Jack walked through the doors with Katelyn in tow.

The CID was located in the middle of the 3rd floor, so the only windows were in the Lieutenant's office and the conference/break room at the end. There were no walls, just a few support columns and cubical offices. At the front of all the cubicles was the desk of Audrey Brooks.

"Oh, my God! Jack Foster as I live and breathe!" Audrey said as Jack and Katelyn stood in front of her desk. The frail old woman came around and gave him a hug.

"Audrey, my dear, I cannot believe you are still here! What is it now, thirty-five years?"

"Yes, it is and it is my last. I promise," she said with a wink.

Jack put his arm around Katelyn "Audrey, I'd like you to meet my daughter, Katelyn."

"Oh, my, you are just beautiful."

Katelyn blushed and looked to the floor, "Thank you."

"So Jack, what has brought you back to us? I heard David Roberts mentioning your name. Is everything all right?"

"Yes and actually, David is who we are here to see."

Just then Audrey's phone rang "Criminal Investigation Division, this is Audrey, how can I help you?" She motioned for Jack and Katelyn to head back.

Katelyn looked around as they made their way back to Roberts' desk. It was nothing like she pictured. In her head there were people bustling in and out, phones ringing, and people in interview rooms getting grilled. This was more like a business office, which was located in a dungeon. There were no windows visible from any of the cubicles that seemed to be built around the three massive columns that ran down the middle of the long open room. There were two doors at the end of the room; one for the conference room and one for the Lieutenant in charge of the CID.

The two found Roberts at his desk on the phone. He smiled, shook

Jack's hand, and then held a finger up as he sat back down.

"What do ya think?" Jack whispered to Katelyn.

She shrugged her shoulders and nodded as she looked around.

"All right, nice to see you back, Jack. And who's this?" Roberts said as he stood up.

"This is my daughter, Katelyn."

"Nice to meet you."

"Yes, nice to meet you too," Katelyn said as she shook his hand.

Roberts looked toward the back office, "Does Vicky know you're here?"

Jack looked towards the door that read "Lt. Victoria Creek", then slowly shook his head, "No, I don't think she does."

"You know if she sees you what she's gonna want."

Jack looked at Katelyn and then back to Roberts "Yeah, well, that's behind me now."

"If that's the case, then what are you doing back in here?" Roberts asked with a raised eyebrow.

"David, I was just curious how things were going with the Tom Underwood case."

"Oh, well, we've gone through his house and are looking at everything we've found," he said motioning to one of the many folders on his desk. "You haven't thought of anything have you?"

Jack shook his head.

"Yeah, well, I'm sure it won't take long to break this case open. I'm pretty sure once we get the examiner's results back, coupled with any info we get from interviewing acquaintances, we should be headed in the right direction."

"Sounds good to me. Well, we won't bother you anymore. I was just curious how things were coming and Katelyn was curious how things looked around here," Jack said as he wrapped his arm around her shoulders. Katelyn just smiled.

"No trouble at all. You know we really could use some help around here," Roberts said as he motioned to the stack of cases on his desk.

"Yeah, you look busy, but I'm enjoying my retirement," he said with a wink.

"Right. Well, it was nice meeting you, Katelyn." Roberts shook her hand and then Jack's. "I'll give you a call as soon as we know something."

Jack motioned for Katelyn to head down the hall. "Thanks, I would appreciate it."

CHAPTER FOUR

Hurricane Lynn started out as a small tropical depression in the Caribbean. As she curved upward toward Jamaica, she grew in strength to a tropical storm and became the twelfth named storm of the season. As she graced Jamaica's southern coast, she grew into a category one hurricane.

It had been a busy year and NOAA would not normally make it all the way to "L" on the list this early in the season. But then again, Lynn would prove not to be a normal storm.

Once past Jamaica, Lynn swung out past Cuba, but then she turned up into the Gulf of Mexico. Once in the warm waters of the Gulf, Lynn grew and intensified and became a category two hurricane as she continued on her curved path toward the west coast of Florida. About 250 miles off the coast of Florida, people really took notice of her.

Up to this point Lynn had managed to navigate the water, not making landfall or causing major structural damage, but she was responsible for the death of one fisherman who got caught in her churning seas. Lynn slowed down a bit as she loomed in the middle of the Gulf, which caused forecasters to worry because of the probability she would grow stronger. And she did, tipping the Saffir-Simpson hurricane scale and becoming a category three hurricane with sustained winds of 115 mph.

It was as if she had slowed down to rest and gain strength. Lynn's northeasterly movement almost came to a halt at 7 mph. She was eyeing up the Sunshine state for her point of attack.

"The track now puts Lynn making landfall anywhere from St. Petersburg to Venice," said the voice out of the television.

"I can't believe they are actually gonna get this one right." Jack said looking over the brim of his cup, then sipping his coffee.

It was six in the morning and it was drizzling outside.

"Again, there is a mandatory evacuation for all costal areas within this range. Lynn is a category three hurricane, which can be very dangerous…" sounded the television off in the distance as Jack walked over to the kitchen table and put his coffee cup down. He looked down the hall to the bedrooms. Still no sign of Katelyn. He walked over to a coat rack by the front door and grabbed a jacket.

The rain tapped on the hood of the jacket as Jack lifted the garage door and surveyed the weather. He turned back and looked at the disorganized mess in the garage. It was cluttered with the typical garage items. The one place that appeared to have some semblance of organization was the back corner where Jack kept his fishing tackle. His rod and reels were lined up against the back wall. There was a table setup with a vice for fly tying and other fishing paraphernalia in various bins with masking tape labels. He contemplated going over to the table and messing around, but an inner voice told him otherwise. Leaning against the wall shared with the house was some half-inch plywood in varying sizes. The sheets of plywood were cut to fit the different windows of the house. The previous owner had left the makeshift wood shutters and Jack had left them there for the past two years he lived there.

Jack grabbed a 14-volt DeWalt cordless drill, a hand full of Tap-cons, and a couple pieces of the plywood, and made his way to the front of the house. As he started putting up the wood he saw Katelyn sitting at the dinning table eating a bowl of cereal through the front window. She looked up at him, waved and smiled. A drop of milk crept from the corner of her mouth and she quickly caught it with the back of her hand. Jack smiled, waved back, and then proceeded to cover the window.

"Come on Kat, we need to go grab some stuff in case we get it bad from this storm." Jack said as he pulled the jacket off.

"Nothing like waiting to the last minute, eh, Dad?" Katelyn asked with a wily smile.

"Don't give me any crap, I've been busy."

"Oh, yeah, with what?"

"OK, so I thought it was going to go somewhere else. Hell, it still could. Either way we could use some food. I don't feel like eating out for the next two weeks."

Katelyn stood up from the couch and stretched for the ceiling "That's fine; I could use some things myself."

"I hope you brought your wallet."

"That's real nice."

It was still drizzling as Jack and Katelyn made their way out of the house and to the truck.

"Excuse me, Mr. Foster?" asked a young man holding an umbrella over his head with one hand and a tape recorder in the other.

'A frig'n reporter!' Jack thought. "Go ahead and get in Kat." He handed her the keys. "I don't have anything to say to you. In fact, you should know that I couldn't even if I wanted to."

"Mr. Foster, are you going to assist with the investigation of Tom Underwood's death?" the young man persisted.

Jack shook his head at the young man as he opened the door and slid into the truck.

"What did he want, Dad?"

"He wants to bother me when I'm busy try'n to get ready for this stupid storm."

"Was he asking about Capt. Tom?"

"He was trying." And with that Jack started up the truck.

The young man was still standing in the front yard looking at them as they drove away. Jack waved to him with a smart-ass grin hanging on his face. The young man reached into his pocket and traded the tape recorder for a cell phone.

"Hey, it's me. Yeah, I would say that he's working on the case. Either way, why take the chance?"

Jack and Katelyn drove a couple of blocks away to a Kash-n-Karry adjacent to Manatee Community College. The parking lot was half full. They hopped out of the truck and started for the door when the rain started to come down. Inside, there wasn't much left of the store as many of the shelves were bare.

"Kat, grab a cart and we'll just walk up and down each isle. If we see something, we'll grab it."

"Dad, is this going to be a really bad storm?" Katelyn asked with concern in her voice.

"I hope not."

Katelyn looked over the store. The fact that they were practically cleaned out made her question her father's decision to wait. She looked over to the lines and saw the people anxious to pay and get out. Katelyn could sense the fear in them as they hurriedly walked by. Then she looked to her dad.

There wasn't anything real distinguishing about him: Average height, medium build. She thought to herself that average pretty much described her dad physically. But the longer she watched him she was reminded that he was not average at all. He walked through the isles with such confidence and calmness. He picked up various items, looked them over, and either put them in the cart or back on the shelf where he got them as if it was any other day of shopping.

They got in line; two gallons of water, one gallon of milk, a package of Nutter Butters, some hotdogs, and some buns in the cart. He reached over, put his arm around her and gave her a little squeeze. She closed her eyes and leaned her head on his shoulder. She felt safe.

When they finally made it out of the store, the parking lot had far fewer cars in it and the rain had lightened up, but now it was the wind's turn to show. Jack looked and saw the truck. He also saw a Chevrolet Impala parked on the other side of it.

"I wish you would get something bigger, Dad. I hate having to sit with the groceries on my lap," Katelyn said as she pushed the cart along.

"Uh-huh." Jack focused on the car. He was looking at the driver and, as they came around the back, he saw the driver watching them in the mirror. Jack slid his hand down into his pocket and calmly pulled out his knife, a Spyderco Harpy. The blade curved like an eagle's claw and was razor sharp. Jack flipped it open with his thumb and held the knife down by his side. As they came along the passenger side of the truck, the man in the car attempted to open his door, but Jack kicked the cart forward ripping it out of Katelyn's hands. The cart rattled forward causing it to be caught between the door and the truck. In the same motion, Jack grabbed Katelyn by the arm and spun her to the ground behind the truck. He then advanced on the driver who was hurriedly trying to open the door and get out.

The driver was banging the door into the cart, his left hand wrapped around the frame of the door, his right clutching a Sig Sauer 226 pushing against the window. Jack reached the Harpy through the gap in the door way and ripped it across the driver's left hand, severing all the tendons in the top of his left hand. With his foot, Jack kicked the cart past the vehicles. The driver yelled and turned the gun on Jack, but Jack reached through with his other hand and grabbed the gun pointing it toward the window. The driver pulled the trigger and the gun fired, piercing the driver side window. The slide of the gun ripped back and forth gashing the palm of Jack's hand. Jack's hand cupped over the slide caused the expended cartridge to catch in the slide and lock it back.

Katelyn started screaming from behind the truck. Jack grimaced and then turned the blade of the Harpy to the driver's right wrist slicing through it. The driver attempted to grab Jack's arm, but his hand was useless due to the severed tendons. Jack continued to grasp the gun with his hand bleeding all over it, pinning it and the driver's hand to the steering wheel. He pushed into the cabin of the car planting his elbow into the driver's throat.

Katelyn got up and began to run back to the store yelling for help.

The driver began to beat his left hand against Jack's head in order to stop him from crushing his larynx. But now Jack was in a rage and continued to push as hard as he could into the driver's throat, pinning him to the center console. Then the driver went limp.

Katelyn rushed into the store and the few people left turned and just stared at her. She was crying.

"Please, somebody help my Dad!" She begged through her tears.

"Was that a gunshot?" a middle-aged cashier asked.

"Yes!" Katelyn screamed and she dropped to her knees.

Everyone stood as if confused and afraid. Just then the automatic doors opened behind Katelyn. She was kneeling, sobbing into her hands clutched around her face when he came in and knelt next to her.

"Kat, come on sweetie, it's OK," Jack said giving her a hug.

She looked up at him. He had blood on the side of his face and on his shirt.

"Daddy!" she sobbed and hugged him.

He stood up with her hugging him. He saw the onlookers trying to figure out what they were going to do. The clerk behind the service desk was dialing a phone.

Jack grabbed Katelyn's face and looked into her watery blue eyes. "Kat, we got to go! We got to get out of here!" He took her by the hand and began to run with her out of the store.

As they came around the passenger side of the truck Katelyn saw the limp and bloodied form of the driver in the car with the door open and began to scream. Jack ran up and closed the car door. He pulled the door to the truck open and yelled for her to get in. She stood there frozen, screaming. He ran up and grabbed her and pulled her to the truck.

"Katelyn! Get in the truck now!"

She got into the truck never taking her eyes off the man in the Impala next to her. Jack slammed the door, ran to the other side, started the truck, and they left.

CHAPTER FIVE

Life had never thought twice about throwing Jack a curve or two. From growing up with an alcoholic father who could be abusive, to the divorce of his parents when he was barely a teenage boy, Jack always seemed to find his way. Shortly after he started working for the Sheriff's Office, his Mom had a heart attack and died at a young age; Jack found himself responsible for his sister the last couple of years she was in high school. He took it in stride and made sure she went to college.

Stress had become a normal environment for him between work and life. Though his time with Amy was mostly good, there was stress there, too. Katelyn was a gift because the couple was pretty sure they were unable to have children. And though both were grateful to have Katelyn, Amy wasn't exactly ready to give up the career for which she had worked so hard. They agreed that it was very important that a parent be home with Katelyn; they just couldn't agree on which parent it should be. So there was a constant tension in the background until Katelyn was old enough to go to school and Amy could go back to work.

Lieutenant Jack Foster had faced many stressful, and even life threatening, situations while working in "The Port". He had done a pretty good job of climbing the ranks. But climbing the ranks comes with its own stresses as well. Between simply losing friends, making enemies in the department and the responsibility, he often wondered if it was worth it. Additionally, Jack was part of the Corrections Emergency Response Team;

a tactical unit inside the facility utilized in high-risk situations. He had been charged with quelling a riot, and did so with minimal injuries to his team and minimal damage to the facility. He had been in his share of fights with inmates. Some worse than others, but Jack never had to take another man's life. Until now.

All the stresses Jack had faced in the past seemed to be seconds on a clock, just ticking away the instant he took that man's life.

He drove right past his house with a distant glare out the rain-splattered windshield. His mind was racing with so many thoughts. Regardless of how hard Katelyn tried, she could not stop crying. She too stared out the window without a blink.

They came to a stop at a flashing red light. The sky was covered in gray ominous clouds that raced along. As he watched them bring dark curtains of rain across the horizon, Katelyn frantically undid her seatbelt.

"I'm gonna be sick," she said as she flung the door open.

Jack rubbed her arching back as she heaved with a groan. 'What does she think of her father now? How would life be for her from this point forward?' he thought.

"Are you all right?" he asked, brushing the hair from the side of her face.

She responded with a nod. He looked down at the steering wheel and closed his eyes. 'I can't believe I just killed a cop.' crashed into his thoughts.

After the driver of the Impala stopped fighting, Jack reached around for his wallet. He had made some enemies, but none that he thought would actually want him dead. Who was this man that wanted to kill him? To kill Katelyn? Jack ripped the wallet out and flipped it open. "Manatee County Sheriff's Office" was the first thing Jack saw. "Deputy Mark White" was the next. Jack looked at the I.D. and then at the lifeless driver. Why?

"Kat, I have to get you out of here," Jack said talking to the steering wheel.

"Dad, you killed that man," she said almost in a whisper.

"I had no choice," he said in a somber tone.

Just then a horn sounded behind them. Jack's head snapped to man, looking irate, honked the horn again, a little bit longer this time. Jack waved and proceeded on.

"Dad, why aren't we there waiting for the police?"

"You need to go back to your Mom," he ignored her.

"He was trying to kill us, right? Why are we running away?"

"Where is your Mom right now?"

"Dad! Let's go back! I don't understand!" Katelyn turned toward him, yelling.

"Because he was a cop! I killed a cop!" Jack yelled back.

"I don't understand. What do you mean?"

Jack stopped at a four-way stop. "Neither do I. That was a cop. A sheriff's deputy that was going to…" 'Was that gonna be a hit?' flashed into Jack's mind. His mind was racing with more questions then ever before. And though he had solved murders and missing person's cases, none of them involved him personally. None of them were a matter of survival. This was by far the biggest challenge he had ever faced. He was always up for a challenge; whether mental or physical; but this one was both. He would need to be at his best; which meant he needed to find a safe place for Katelyn so he could focus.

They drove around a couple of blocks; four left turns to be sure that no one was following them. The rain and wind had kicked up quite a lot and the roads were deserted for the most part. Jack spied down the street to his house. 'Not a soul around, I hope.' he thought.

"Listen, Kat, it's obvious there's someone that wants to hurt me. I need to get you as far away from me as possible; someplace safe," Jack said looking up and down the street as he started to pull out.

"Don't you mean kill you? Not hurt you, but kill you?" Katelyn said as a gust of wind rocked the truck.

"Yeah, I guess that's what I mean."

"Dad, please call the police. You didn't do anything wrong," she pleaded with him.

"But that's just it, Kat. He was a cop. Something is not making sense and until I can figure it out, I'm not trusting anyone." Jack said as they pulled back into the driveway.

"But you have friends. You were a cop, too," Katelyn leaned over to get in his face.

But Jack was concentrating on the house. He tried to watch it through the falling rain on the windshield and the back and forth movement of the wipers. She sat back down in a huff.

"Kat, I haven't been with the department for awhile now. I'm not sure who to trust right now. Not as long as you are with me." Jack reached up and started rubbing his chin. "Do you remember how to drive this truck?"

"What about that detective I met yesterday?"

Jack pondered the idea. But there was no trusting anyone at this point. Not until he could get more answers, and especially, as long as Katelyn was with him. "That's a good idea. I'll give him a call as soon as I get you somewhere safe. Now about the truck, can you drive the truck?"

"Dad, I only have my learner's permit. Besides, why do I need to drive the truck?" Katelyn asked shaking her head no.

"I'm gonna go check around the house. I want you to slide over here. If I'm not out in two minutes, you leave," Jack said as he undid his seatbelt.

"Where am I supposed to go? I don't want you to go in there." Katelyn had begun to cry again.

"Honey, relax. I'm sure everything will be all right, but ya gotta have a plan, right? Two minutes, and if I'm not out, go home" he said holding her chin up with his thumb and index finger.

"But what if I get pulled over? You said it was the police, right?" she asked with a tear running down her check.

'Why didn't I think of that?' Jack thought as he looked toward the house.

"You're right. If someone is trying to get me, they are gonna be looking for this truck." His mind was searching for what to do next. "You'll have to come in with me. You must do everything I tell you to do. Do you understand?"

Katelyn nodded.

"All right, we're going around the back. I'm going to hold your wrist to keep you close to me." And with that, Jack turned off the truck.

Jack ran down the garage side of the house with Katelyn in tow. They slid between the stucco house and the trailered skiff. It had only been fifteen minutes since they fled the Kash-n-Karry parking lot, but the wind and rain had intensified ten-fold. Tree branches flapped radically while attempting to hold onto what leaves they had left. The garage side of the house, being the north side, was sort of a haven from the north, northeast winds spinning off of Lynn.

Jack felt confident that if there was someone in the house waiting for them, they didn't know Jack and Katelyn were there. Before they left for the store Jack was kind of impressed with himself for the cave-like atmosphere of the inside of the house. He made sure to cover every window completely and that task was made easy with the pre-cut makeshift wood hurricane panels. Jack, with Katelyn in one hand and his Harpy in the other, grabbed a quick look around the back of the house to the lanai. There he saw Bear huddled at the back door, crying. As Jack pulled his head from around the corner, he was angry with himself for forgetting the cat.

Katelyn looked at the disturbed expression on her dad's face. Jack was shaking his head looking down.

"What is it Dad?"

"I forgot the cat."

"Oh, my God!" Katelyn gasped.

She tried to run around the corner, but Jack snatched her back and grabbed hold of her shoulders.

"What are you doing?" he said in a forceful, but muted tone.

"I… I was checking on Bear." She could tell that her dad was very angry and stood starring at him, frightened, with her jaw hanging open.

"Bear is fine. I'm mad at myself for forgetting to bring him in." he said as he looked over her head and scanned the surrounding houses. "Listen to me. Don't do anything unless I tell you to," he said sternly.

Katelyn bobbed her head in agreement.

Jack knew that the plywood made for great cover for them, but it also made for great cover for anyone inside. They ran up to the lanai and Bear turned and started meowing right away. Jack shushed the cat, snatched him up, turned and handed him to Katelyn. Bear was wet and cold and began to purr right away in Katelyn's arms. She leaned in to kiss him and he turned up and started licking her nose. She smiled and giggled a little. That did not go unnoticed by Jack and he grinned in spite of himself. He stood outside the house by the door contemplating what to do next.

'Do something!' he commanded himself and took a deep breath. He grabbed Katelyn by the shoulders and sat her and Bear against the wall, next to the door. Jack handed Katelyn the knife.

"Listen honey, I don't know what else to do at this point. I've got to get inside the house. I want you to take the knife in case you need it."

"Dad, I don't know what to do with this!" her eyes were beginning to well up again.

"Kat, it's better that you have something to protect yourself; I can at least fight." Then it dawned on Jack that he had an old fillet knife in the boat. "Hold on," he said as his head snapped up and he looked around. Wind gusted and caused the screens on the lanai to bow. "Don't move."

Jack scampered back around the house and slid into the skiff. He pulled a tackle tray open and grabbed the slightly rusted fillet knife. As he held the knife, he looked at the gash in his palm. It was still bleeding, but not bad. He slid back over the gunnel and dashed back to Katelyn and Bear.

"All right, I got this," Jack said brandishing the knife before Katelyn. "You stay here. It's simple; keep the knife out of sight. As soon as someone is close enough to touch you, cut them with it. Can you do that?"

She looked at the blood-stained knife in her hand, closed her eyes and nodded. Jack leaned in and kissed her forehead, then he reached into his pocket and pulled the keys out. He held them in the palm of his hand, flipped through them with his thumb, and then inserted the house key ever so slowly into the door knob. He turned the key, unlocked the door, and then slid his hand over the knob. Jack turned the knob looking at Katelyn. Her eyes darted back and forth from his eyes to his hand on the knob. And without saying a word, he flung the door open. It swung around twice as hard as Jack threw it because it caught like a sail in the wind. There was the slam of the door, the sound of wind and rain in their ears and rain tapping on the aluminum roof above.

Jack poked his head in the doorway and then back. He saw nothing. He did it again. Nothing. Jack could barely hear the TV over the drumming rain.

"Did you leave the TV on?"

Katelyn looked down, then up to him and shrugged. Jack nodded and glanced back into the house. He took three deep breaths, let them out slow, and lunged into the house. The house was empty.

Katelyn sat rocking Bear in her arms when Jack yelled for her to come in. She let out her breath and let Bear go. The cat ran into the house and Katelyn fought the door shut. She looked around for her dad when she heard him in his bedroom.

Jack pulled the bi-fold doors to his closet and grabbed his gun locker off the top shelf. He laid his hand on the five button system, punched the code and the tray popped open. Jack removed a Heckler and Koch USP .40 S&W and two high capacity magazines. The gun was in an Uncle Mike's pancake holster. He ejected the magazine to be sure it was topped off, jammed it back in, put it back in the holster then tossed it onto the bed. Then he removed a Smith and Wesson M64 .38 special revolver with a four-inch barrel and a box of .38 +P ammunition.

With the guns sitting on the vanity, Jack stripped his clothes off into a pile in the bathroom. He hopped into the shower and turned the water on. It came out hard and cold at first, but warmed up and he stuck his head under the showerhead. As he looked down he could see the crimson-tinged water swirl down the drain. Jack sighed and closed his eyes.

Jack came out of the bedroom pulling over his head a Guy Harvey t-shirt depicting a Snook ambushing finger mullet in the mangroves. Katelyn stood next to the dinning table soaking wet. She was cradling Bear in her arms, rocking him back and forth. She pressed her forehead against his and the cat purred harder.

"Kat, put Bear down and change into something dry. Then grab your stuff, I'm taking you home."

Katelyn walked over and put the cat down on the couch. She pet him a little more and then made her way back to her room without saying a word.

Jack loaded the revolver and double-checked to make sure the USP was loaded; then slid it into the holster that was now strapped to the small of his back. He grabbed an old fanny pack out of the coat closet by the front door, stuck the revolver in it, and set it down on the dining room table.

Katelyn came out of the bedroom in dry clothes, but not carrying her things.

"Kat, where's your stuff?" Jack asked looking around.

"It's still in the room."

"I thought I told you to get it."

"Dad, I don't want to go home. I don't want to leave you."

"Katelyn, are you crazy? Do you understand what's going on here?" he said walking past her toward her room.

She turned toward him as he was about to walk into the room. "She's not home."

Jack stopped.

"Mom is not there."

Jack looked to her, puzzled. Then Jack looked past her. He saw Bear abruptly stop cleaning himself and look to the back door. Jack drew the gun from his holster and put it by his side. He held up his finger to his lips telling Katelyn to be quiet. She looked back over her shoulder and when she turned, around Jack was beside her. Jack looked at the fanny pack sitting on the dinning table then to the slowly turning door knob. The backdoor cracked open and a gust of wind pushed into the house. Jack knelt down and pulled Katelyn down with him.

CHAPTER SIX

Katelyn had gone the past couple of years dealing with the separation of her parents. Of course, in the beginning it was very difficult to accept since up to that point her life was with them together. Katelyn was not completely shocked by the divorce, either. She had recognized the frustration that her mother tried so hard to hide from her. She, too, had frustration and missed spending time with her father who had always managed to make time for her in the past.

The divorce forced her to grow up faster than she should have had to. Katelyn found herself having to be the strong one at times. Some days it was picking up extra chores around the house. Other times it was comforting her Mom as she wept or hiding her own tears as not to upset her Mom.

Now a couple years older and more accepting, Katelyn tried to make the best of the situation. In fact, to her, there really didn't seem to be much difference between now and right before the separation. Except now when she was with her father, his focus shone completely upon her. He didn't try to dash out with friends or drag her somewhere to ignore her. They would catch a movie every now and then, but most of the time it was just the two of them talking. He would engage her in conversation as if she was an equal. He would ask her opinion as if it meant something and then listen to what she had to say.

Her father and mother were always good at treating her with respect and not just as a child. She strived and achieved very well because her parents expected it, but more so because they truly believed she could and supported her so. That was one thing her parents always did well, put her first.

The divorce was not ugly, but it was not nice either. Katelyn's mother knew one thing for sure; no matter how hurt she felt by Jack's actions, or lack there of, he truly was a good father and loved his daughter dearly. She would not deny either of them that bond.

So, Katelyn's mother felt very comfortable sending her to spend the given time with her father. Even if there was a hurricane threatening the west central coast of Florida, Jack would never do anything intentionally to harm Katelyn and would surely take whatever action necessary to ensure her safety. Besides, it would no doubt turn into another great adventure. Katelyn would be frothing to tell her mother once she got home. This visit was definitely like no other before.

Bear jumped off the couch and scampered underneath it. Jack extended the USP just below his line of sight and pointed it down the hallway. Whoever was holding the backdoor couldn't any longer. Another large gust of wind caught the door and slammed it into the house. The wind pushed its way into the house. The curtains and blinds clamored back and forth as the wind swirled through the living room. The TV guide sitting on the coffee table flipped open, riffled through its pages, and then blew off the coffee table. Jack steadied his breathing.

A man wearing a ball cap and a raincoat entered the backdoor. He crouched as he took long steps into the dinning room. He held a Heckler and Koch MP-9D3 up in his line of sight. He made swift swinging motions with the sub-machine gun as he looked through the house. He slowly looked down the hallway as he swept wide against the wall across from it. Nothing in the hall. Then the first door on the right slammed shut.

He held his hand up as if motioning for a second man to come in. He made a gesture causing the second man to focus on the door that just slammed shut; then he moved into the hallway with his gun held in his line of sight. He turned and put his back against the wall opposite of the door.

Just as he was about to kick the door knob, Jack poked his head and shoulders out from his bedroom at the end of hall and fired a single shot center mass. The man groaned in pain and fell at the mouth of the hallway. As the man fell, Jack saw the second gunman rush up.

The second gunman squeezed the trigger of his submachine gun and it spewed lead into the hallway hitting the wall at the end and splintering Jack's doorway. Jack had tucked back into the room at the last second. The door frame slowly disintegrated and Jack was showered in wood chips and splinters. He rolled to get further into the room. The second gunman let go of the trigger and Jack heard the last of the brass casings jingling as they hit the floor in the hallway.

'He's right here!' Jack thought; lying on his back with his feet toward the doorway he held his gun up. Again the second gunman squeezed the trigger angling his shots into the room. Jack could see small explosions make their way around the room as the bullets pulverized everything they came in contact with. Everything seemed to be in slow motion. Then Jack saw the brass casings hit the floor outside his door. With that Jack fired two shots through the wall next to the door, one low, one high. The shooting stopped. And then a thud.

The second gunman fell into the opposite wall and then to the floor outside the door. Jack kept his gun pointed on him. Jack sat up and then got to his feet and crouched down with his knees nearly in his chest; always keeping the gun pointed at the man. He leaned forward and saw the large fresh wound in the second gunman's left cheek oozing blood. Jack reached over and pulled the submachine gun away and tossed it into his bedroom.

Motion at the end of the hall immediately drew Jack's attention. The first gunman was gasping for breath and attempting to get to his feet. Jack drew down on him.

"Drop your gun!" Jack commanded. "Drop it!"

The gunman slowly got to his feet keeping his focus on Jack. He staggered back a couple of steps and turned to get out of the house. Jack went down the hall after him. As Jack made it to the end of the hallway he ordered the gunman to stop and drop his weapon. The gunman looked back to Jack as he moved through the backdoor. He lifted his gun and fired at Jack. Jack fired in return.

Katelyn dropped down with her father's pull. He pointed his gun out the hallway and leaned into her and whispered "As quiet as you can, crawl into the office and get in the closet." never looking away from the hallway. He gave her a little nudge.

Jack's home office, where he ran his charter business, was the first door on the right in the hall. Katelyn crawled into the room. As she was halfway in she reached back with her foot and nudged the door to shut. Just as she was closing the closet door the door to the room slammed as the draft grabbed hold of it. She jumped.

The closet was dark. She felt around above her and pulled a heavy Pea coat down and over her head. Katelyn could hear the wind rushing against the house. She could hear the blinds whipping in the living room from the wind. Then she heard the loud bang of a gun. She buried her face into her hands and began to whimper. Then she heard rapid fire.

It started at the mouth of the hall and moved down the hallway, past the office and toward her father's room. It paused, then started again. Then nothing but the wind. Next she heard her father yelling. 'Thank you!' she thought and started pulling the coat from over her head. Her father yelled some more.

Just as she was pulling the bi-fold door to the closet open, rapid fire rang out again. The bullets cut through the wall of the office and found home through the clothing above her head and into the wall behind her. She yelped and slammed the closet door shut once more. Katelyn groped around for the coat and pulled it over her head once more. She waited for what seemed an eternity. Then she heard someone moving through the office. The old metal closet door squeaked. Katelyn began to cry and gripped the coat tight. Someone tugged at the coat.

"Please!" she begged through her tears.

The gunman lifted his submachine gun and began to spray hot lead into the house as he made his way out. Jack raised his gun and returned fire as he dropped to the floor. The gunman's bullets ripped through the wall behind Jack. Jack managed to send chunks of the dining table flying into the air as his bullets made contact with it. Jack lay on the floor with his gun pointed to the doorway.

He watched as gusts of wind shifted the rain almost horizontal. Leaves, branches, and other debris flew by causing Jack's eyes to dart back and forth as he focused on each item. He waited for the gunman to return, but he didn't. After what felt like a few minutes, Jack made his way to the backdoor and looked out. He was gone. Jack forced the backdoor shut once more and then went to the office where Katelyn was hiding.

Before he went in he looked down the hall at the second gunman. His body was still a motionless slump. Jack shook his head. Twice in one day he did something he hoped he would never have to do.

He opened the door to the office and looked in. Right away he saw the bullet holes through the closet door. Jack's heart sank. He walked over to the closet afraid to open the door. He slid the door open ever so slow. Then he heard her cry. He was overcome with relief.

"Kat, come on, we got to get out of here."

But his mind didn't give him long to go through it. Automatically his mind began to work the puzzle. What move to make next? He called to Katelyn and she sprung into his arms sobbing with relief. He took her hand and they walked out of the office. Katelyn looked down the hall and saw the second gunman's body. She looked down to the floor.

"Kat, you know I wouldn't if I didn't have to protect you or me. You know I wouldn't hurt a soul."

Katelyn nodded her head without looking up. Then she asked "Why? Why do they want to kill us, Dad?"

"I'm not sure yet, but I'm gonna find out."

Jack picked the fanny pack up off the splintered kitchen table. He walked up to Katelyn and put it around her waist.

"Kat, remember at the beginning of the summer when I took you to the shooting range?"

She looked into his eyes and nodded.

"The same gun we shot at the range is in this fanny pack. Do you think you could shoot it if you had to?" He said taking her face into his hands. He looked into her eyes and nodded.

Somberly, she answered yes.

CHAPTER SEVEN

Captain Tom Underwood had made a good life for himself out of the charter fishing business he started several years ago. Capt. Tom, as he was regarded, was very much a people-person. At about six foot, with sandy blonde hair, he was a good looking man at the midpoint of his life. Fishing wasn't something Capt. Tom did, it was something he was. Through and through he was a fisherman, and pretty damn good one at that. Giving his demeanor, looks, and ability, Capt. Tom's business flourished. He was a pretty good business man and made calculated moves to bolster his good name in the community, such as charity fishing tournaments for the Boys and Girls Clubs. He had the pleasure of appearing on the cover of a few magazines including "Florida Sportsman". One was considered to have made it pretty good if he or she made it on the cover of "Florida Sportsman". And so a framed copy of the cover hung in his office.

As good as Capt. Tom was on the water and with people in general, he was not as good in the several relationships he had through the years. He was very good at getting them started, but Capt. Tom tended to grow tired of his female companions. Not to mention his female companions could not compete with his mistress, the water. Capt. Tom's friends often joked that Brad Paisley's song "I'm Gonna Miss Her" was written based on Tom's love life. So he went through life as a perpetual bachelor. Between relationships Capt. Tom found himself spending a little time and some hard-earned cash at one of the local strip bars. There he found what would ultimately be his demise.

If there ever was sea nymph created by Poseidon to lure Capt. Tom to his death, her name was Dawn Peterson. She was a very attractive young woman who had all the right assets for the stripping industry. She was, after all, the top show for the club. It only took the first time Capt. Tom saw her dancing to knock the wind out of his sails.

He sat in his usual seat near the catwalk. The club DJ was yammering about some hot new dancer. Capt. Tom was not really paying much attention to what was being said. His mind drifted to the next day's business. He was running through the routine in his head of running out and catching bait at five in the morning, then running back to the ramp to pick up the charter. The music started. It had a sensual beat and he started to come back to the present. Then she strolled out onto the stage. Capt. Tom's attention was quickly drawn to her beauty, but her beauty was not what grabbed him.

Dawn moved on that stage like no one Tom had ever seen before. She graced the stage like a slow flickering flame on a pool of gasoline and Tom was a moth. Her hips, with Capt. Tom's eyes locked on them, swayed side to side. She lifted her arms over her head and slithered in the air. Her movements called to him. Beckoning him to come closer and closer to the flame. As she made her way around the stage with her slow gyrating motions, her eyes caught Capt. Tom's helpless gaze and she gave a slight smile. A smile Capt. Tom would later swear stopped his heart.

Capt. Tom had seen various acts over the years and he liked them fine, but none affected him like this one. He could feel himself becoming aroused just by watching her. That had never happened before. He was so taken by her that he left hefty tips hanging from her garter belt in hopes of gaining her attention. It worked.

It was not too long before Capt. Tom found Dawn in his bed. He tried to convince her to leave stripping, but she was convinced she made good money, and she did, thanks to the likes of him. He spent plenty of money on her and she repaid him in the way his lustful heart desired. But she continued to work at the club.

What Capt. Tom would learn later was he was not the only one Dawn shared her company with. And though most men might cut their losses, Capt. Tom couldn't let go of Dawn. Finally something had Capt. Tom hooked harder than fishing. And try as he might to reel Dawn in, nothing worked to the degree he wanted. In Capt. Tom's furious fight to obtain the love of Dawn, he failed to think of whose toes he might be stepping on.

CHAPTER EIGHT

Rick Daniels stepped through the torn screen porch and slid down the back of Jack Foster's house against the onslaught of wind and rain. He managed his way to his truck, grimacing in pain. He pulled the door open and tossed his submachine gun onto the passenger seat. Then he grabbed the steering wheel and pulled himself into the truck grunting all the way. He took shallow breaths because anything else was excruciating. He started up the truck, put it in gear, and backed away from the house, leaving his partner behind.

The truck shuddered as it was bombarded with wind and rain. Heading down the road he pulled out a cell phone, scrolled through the numbers and hit 'send'.

"Hello?" came a monotone voice over the phone.

"T.J., he got Mendoza," said the gunman.

"What the… Did you get him?"

No answer.

"Did you get him?" said the voice, slow and stern.

He took a few short breaths "No."

"No? No? How in the fuck did you not get him?" he now was screaming.

Daniels looked down at the steering wheel defeated "I don't know," he said almost in a whisper.

"What?" came blaring out of the phone.

A few more short quick breaths "I don't know!" he yelled.

"Get back here. We're all here now." And with that, Sergeant Terrence Jackson hung up the phone.

Daniels continued to breathe shallow because it hurt so much. He took his cell phone and chucked it against the passenger door. He closed his eyes and groaned in pain. Keeping one hand on the wheel he reached down into his shirt and felt for blood. No blood, but very tender.

Daniels was furious with himself. He and his partner, Carlos Mendoza, were sent to take care of a problem. Mendoza got killed and he got shot. And all by someone that they didn't believe had tactical combat training. On top of this, he was going to have to explain to Sergeant Terrence Jackson, T.J., how this happened. Daniels knew that he was in for it as T.J. had a vicious temper.

He stopped at a four-way stop. The wind rocked his truck and Daniels winced with pain. There was no other traffic out in these conditions. Leaves and other rubbish shot across the path of the truck. He continued.

He thought to himself that the only way to make things right with T.J. and the rest of the team was to finish the job he was sent to do. He looked over at the submachine gun sitting on the seat next to him. He slowed down to a crawl. Should he turn around and go finish it? Another gust rocked the truck and he winced with pain again. He decided he was in no condition to try. He would have to go face his team. He would have to go face T.J.

Sergeant Terrence Jackson was a good-looking man in his thirties who had a rock solid frame from being an avid weightlifter. Due to his size, he was very intimidating when he wanted to be; but he could also be very charming as well with his winning smile.

He was with the Sheriff's Department four years when he joined the Cobra Squad, an elite unit that was hard-hitting and intimidating; something with which Jackson was very comfortable. The unit was responsible for investigating and handling vice and gang-related criminal activity. Those who the Cobra Squad targeted wondered which side the unit was really on.

Not long with the unit, Jackson found himself the focus of an Internal

Affairs investigation for an excessive use of force situation. Jackson, for the most part, was even keeled, but when he snapped, he snapped all the way. Jackson had beaten a crack dealer bad enough to send him to the hospital for spitting in his face. The problem was the crack dealer was handcuffed at the time and ended up having to have his broken jaw wired shut.

The Cobra Squad was a very tight unit and Sergeant Weiss, the squad leader at the time, was not about to lose a good man because some crack dealer didn't know his place on the food chain. So Sergeant Weiss and the rest of the team counseled Jackson and then paid a visit to the crack dealer in the hospital. Oddly, the IA investigation stalled when the complainant and only witness decided that he had made the whole thing up. After that Jackson learned the truth about the unit. He learned that there was good money to be swept away when dealing with drug dealers or pimps. The Cobra Squad, tasked with putting an end to vice and gang activity, was so corrupted itself, that it created a need for its own existence. They made enough arrests not to draw suspicion, but not too many to hurt business. They made alliances with those who would just assume kill them; but could not beat the kind of protection the team could give from competitors, as well as the police.

Now a few years later Jackson found himself promoted to Sergeant and in charge of the Cobra Squad and nothing had changed; the squad was taking care of business as always; and part of business was survival. So when he learned from an insider that Jack Foster was snooping around the CID asking questions about Tom Underwood's death, he sent Mark White to collect Jack and take care of him in fear that the retired jailer and former cold case investigator might learn of their criminal activity. The same criminal activity that Jackson had made the mistake of letting his stripper girlfriend learn about.

Jackson learned of White's departure shortly after his demise through his department radio. Jackson knew he had to end this quickly so as not to draw any more attention to the squad. So he sent Daniels and Mendoza to finish the job. Now Jackson found the squad another member short thanks to the has-been jailer.

CHAPTER NINE

TTAA00 KNHC DDHHMM
BULLETIN
HURRICANE LYNN ADVISORY NUMBER 21
NWS TPC/NATIONAL HURRICANE CENTER MIAMI FL
9 AM CDT SUN AUG 20 2006

... DANGEROUS CATEGORY THREE HURRICANE LYNN CONTINUES
EAST-NORTHEASTWARD BUT EXPECTED TO TURN NORTHWARD...

A HURRICANE WARNING IS IN EFFECT FOR THE WEST CENTRAL GULF COAST FROM BRADENTON TO FT. MYERS FLORIDA. PREPARATIONS TO PROTECT LIFE AND PROPERTY SHOULD BE RUSHED TO COMPLETION.

FOR STORM INFORMATION SPECIFIC TO YOUR AREA...

INCLUDING POSSIBLE
INLAND WATCHES AND WARNINGS...PLEASE MONITOR
PRODUCTS ISSUED
BY YOUR LOCAL WEATHER OFFICE.

AT 4 AM CDT... 0900Z... THE CENTER OF HURRICANE
LYNN WAS LOCATED
NEAR LATITUDE 26.4 NORTH...LONGITUDE 84.0 WEST OR
ABOUT 275 MILES
SOUTH-SOUTHEAST OF THE MOUTH OF THE MISSISSIPPI
RIVER.

LYNN IS MOVING TOWARD THE EAST-NORTHEAST NEAR 10
MPH. A GRADUAL
TURN TOWARD THE NORTHWEST IS EXPECTED LATER TODAY.

MAXIMUM SUSTAINED WINDS ARE NEAR 120 MPH WITH HIGHER
GUSTS.
LYNN IS A CATEGORY THREE HURRICANE ON THE SAFFIR-
SIMPSON SCALE. SOME STRENGTHENING IS FORECAST DURING
THE NEXT 24 HOURS.

HURRICANE FORCE WINDS EXTEND OUTWARD UP TO 60 MILES
FROM THE
CENTER...AND TROPICAL STORM FORCE WINDS EXTEND
OUTWARD UP

TO 120 MILES.

ESTIMATED MINIMUM CENTRAL PRESSURE IS 962 MB...28.41
INCHES.

COASTAL STORM SURGE FLOODING OF 15 TO 20 FEET ABOVE
NORMAL TIDE
LEVELS...LOCALLY AS HIGH AS 25 FEET ALONG WITH
LARGE AND DANGEROUS
BATTERING WAVES...CAN BE EXPECTED NEAR AND TO THE
EAST OF WHERE THE
CENTER MAKES LANDFALL.

RAINFALL TOTALS OF 5 TO 10 INCHES...WITH ISOLATED MAXIMUM AMOUNTS OF 15 INCHES...ARE POSSIBLE ALONG THE PATH OF LYNN ACROSS THE GULF COAST AND THE SOUTHEASTERN UNITED STATES.

REPEATING THE 4 AM CDT POSITION...26.4 N...84.0 W. MOVEMENT
TOWARD...WEST-NORTHWEST NEAR 10 MPH. MAXIMUM SUSTAINED
WINDS...120 MPH. MINIMUM CENTRAL PRESSURE...962 MB.

AN INTERMEDIATE ADVISORY WILL BE ISSUED BY THE NATIONAL HURRICANE
CENTER AT 7 AM CDT FOLLOWED BY THE NEXT COMPLETE ADVISORY AT 10 AM CDT.

FORECASTER THOMPSON

Jack dragged the second gunman into his office as Katelyn sat on the couch petting Bear who was sitting next to her. Jack shut the office door and stood silent for a few seconds. He looked down at the gash in his hand. It was bleeding again. He turned around and went into the bathroom in the hallway and cleaned and redressed the wound.

Katelyn was blankly watching news coverage of the storm when the power went out and the house became devoid of light. She quickly snapped to and frantically looked in the direction of the windows and doors. She whispered "Dad?"

"Well," Jack said walking out of the bathroom "that's that."

"I can't see. Dad!" Katelyn said nervously.

Jack walked around into the kitchen and grabbed a large MagLite off the counter. He turned it on and pointed it toward the ceiling. It illuminated the house softly, but gave Jack a grim appearance as it shone up on his face.

"Come on, Kat, we've got to get going."

"Where are we going to go?" she asked as she rose from the couch.

"Well, first I'm going to find a safe place for you to hide. Then I'm going to figure out what the hell is happening so I can put an end to it," Jack said as he made his way to the backdoor. He motioned for her to come. She shook her head.

"Kat, come on. I don't have time for games."

"I want to stay with you."

"That's not going to happen."

"Please, Dad. Remember what you told me about those guys in Antarctica? They survived because they stuck together. We need to stick together."

Jack stood with his hands on his hips slowly shaking his head.

"Dad, I need you. Don't push me away again."

"Push you away? I'm trying to make sure I get to see you again." He ran his hand through his hair. "Baby, I can't protect myself if I'm too busy trying to protect you."

"Don't underestimate me," she said as she walked up to him.

Jack looked at her in the dim light. His heart was saddened as he no longer saw a little girl. Just another situation forcing Katelyn to grow up faster than she should have to. What amazed Jack was the fact that she always seemed capable and willing to step up. "You have to do everything I tell you."

Katelyn nodded.

"Come on, let's go."

"What about Bear?" she asked as she looked back to him still sitting on the couch.

"He'll be fine in the house. Ready?"

As the two made their way out, the wind ripped the door right out of Jack's hand and slammed it into the house; this time breaking the doorknob off. Jack, gun in hand, looked around, and then stepped out; Katelyn followed. She stumbled a few steps as the gusting wind shoved her around. Jack walked the door closed and then grabbed and hugged Katelyn.

He looked around. 'What to do?' he thought scanning the area. Then they heard a crash coming from an adjacent house.

"Come on," said Jack taking Katelyn in tow to investigate.

The wind had blown down a carport leaving the Jeep Wrangler it once protected exposed. The Jeep belonged to one of Jack's neighbors, a kind, but eccentric old man. Jack remembered that the old man once asked him where the best place was to put a hide-away key.

The two made their way over to the Jeep. Jack holstered his gun and retrieved the key from inside the rear bumper and told Katelyn to climb in.

The wind caused the canvas top and doors to flap furiously as Jack pushed the Jeep to go as fast as it could in these conditions. The slapping sound was deafening and Katelyn put her hands over her ears.

"Why are we taking this Jeep?" Katelyn yelled over the slapping canvas.

"No one's looking for a Jeep!" Jack yelled back.

Katelyn nodded in understanding.

Jack's mind was working on putting the pieces of the puzzle together. He didn't hear the slapping canvas. He didn't hear the rain pelting the Jeep. Jack focused on what he knew, what had occurred over the past couple of days. Of course, nothing in his life had changed for some time. That was until he discovered the body of his late friend, Capt. Tom.

It was painfully obvious to Jack that someone in the Sheriff's Office was afraid of him, afraid that he might become interested in finding out who had taken the life of Capt. Tom. Why would someone want to kill Tom? So that was what Jack set out to do; find out who killed Capt. Tom and why. Those answers would surely bring him closer to danger, but Jack believed in the old adage of keep one's friends close and one's enemies closer.

Jack's biggest concern was not for his own safety, but that of his daughter's. But Jack felt that he could protect her better then anyone at this point. He looked over at Katelyn. She was sitting with her elbows resting on her knees and her hands over her ears.

Jack decided that he needed to find out how well he really did know Capt. Tom. He hoped that Capt. Tom's victimology would lead Jack to the killer or possibly killers. Jack headed for Capt. Tom's house in hopes that it would serve two purposes; as shelter and a source of answers.

Jack and Katelyn pulled into the driveway of Capt. Tom's nice canal front home off of Pearl Avenue, east of US 41. The Spanish-style house had maybe half of the windows covered with hurricane shutters. Jack suspected that Capt. Tom had probably left them up from the last storm that threatened the area, about a month ago.

"Stay here," Jack said undoing his seatbelt.

He readied himself as he undid the latch for the door. The wind pushed against the door, but Jack was ready. As he slid out of the Jeep, the rain pelted any exposed skin with a sting. Jack held the door firmly in one hand and his Miami Dolphins ball cap to his head with the other. He pushed the door shut and Katelyn reached over and did the latch.

Jack made his way around to the back of the house. He saw Capt.

Tom's Hewes swaying on davits hanging over the canal. The boat had a holographic paintjob making the hull look like a giant redfish. Jack smirked and shook his head as he read the name, *Her Thorn* on its side. Capt. Tom came up with the name because he often referred to fishing as a thorn in the side of whichever woman he was dating.

Jack popped the screen door to the lanai open and walked up to one of the sliding glass doors. He was getting ready to pop it off its track when the door slid open. The wind caused the drawn blinds to clatter back and forth. Jack drew his gun and peered into the dark house between the shifting blinds.

A quick search of the house showed that someone had been there. Probably detectives looking for the same answers that Jack was. He wondered what they may have taken that he might have needed.

Not wanting to fight with the wind and the front door, Jack ran back around to the front of the house in the gusting wind and rain.

Katelyn saw him come jogging around the house waving her to come out. Jack got up to the passenger side of the Jeep just as Katelyn lost her grip on the door. Jack put his hands up just in time to stop the door from planting into his face. He looked around the door with a grimace.

"Sorry," Katelyn said with a shrug.

Jack responded with a nod and pushed the door shut. He grabbed Katelyn by the elbow since she had her arms folded across her chest; and they jogged into the house. Jack pushed the slider shut and Katelyn let out a breath of relief as she slid off the hood from her jacket. She looked around and instinctively reached down to turn on a lamp. To their surprise Capt. Tom's house still had power.

Jack went right to work looking throughout the house. He found himself in Capt. Tom's home office. On the walls were framed copies of various articles printed about Capt. Tom. And of course, his beloved cover of "Florida Sportsman". Jack thought to himself about how good Tom was on the water. Jack wasn't too bad himself, but lacked the desire for the fame that Capt. Tom had.

He picked the framed cover off the wall and a folded piece of paper fell from behind it.

CHAPTER TEN

Dawn Peterson had found refuge from the storm and from her deranged boyfriend at her aunt's house in Palmetto. The house was an eighty-year-old plantation style and had seen many a storm in its time. The lawn maintenance crew was kind enough to button up the old house for a small additional fee.

Dawn's aunt had no idea of Dawn's personal life. At least not her real life. She was under the disinformation that Dawn was attending classes at Manatee Community College while working part-time as a waitress somewhere. This was true in the beginning, but Dawn slowly found school was not for her. She heard from a friend, that she used to waitress with, about the money to be made in stripping.

Dawn never told her aunt about the stripping. Her aunt was the only family she had left in the state and she was afraid that her much older, conservative aunt would not think too highly of her current profession. Fact was, neither did Dawn. The thought of some of the people that ogled her every move on the stage caused her to shutter, but for the money she made in tips, she would deal with it.

Her father and mother had moved away a few years ago when her father's job transferred him to Chicago. She loved the sun and the beaches and was content on finishing her degree where she was, so she elected to stay. Now she found herself dreaming about what her life might have been like if she had moved to Chicago. It most certainly wouldn't have anything to do with murder.

Dawn sat at the kitchen table sipping a hot cup of green tea her aunt had made for her. She looked through the green stained water to the bottom of the cup. She sighed and felt incredibly guilty for the life of Tom Underwood. Though he was considerably older, she did enjoy his company.

As she thought about poor Tom, she began to clinch her teeth. She was furious with T.J. Then she closed her eyes and released the tension. She was furious with herself. Dawn knew that T.J. was very possessive. She knew that he had an extreme temper. Part of her attraction to Tom had nothing to do with Tom at all. It was the thrill of having the relationship and keeping it a secret from T.J. Dawn never fathomed that if T.J. found out, he would kill Tom.

Dawn looked up to the single light that hung above the table. She closed her eyes and wondered how she got into this mess. Life just happened to her. No aim, no goal; she just did whatever and lived in limbo. She wondered what her parents would think of her if they knew. Would they take her back? She wondered how long she could hide from T.J. and his insane friends.

Dawn set down the cup and placed her palms on top of the cool laminate table. She hoped that there was someway she could right her life and leave everything behind. In her head she wished there was a stop button she could press so she could change the vague tune of her indistinct life. She just wanted it all to go away and for everyone to just forget about her. She had no idea that her relationship with Tom was about to be discovered by another person. Someone, who on the contrary, would want her very much alive.

CHAPTER ELEVEN

Jack watched the paper flutter to the floor. He smiled and bent over and picked it up. He walked over to Capt. Tom's desk with the folded piece of paper in one hand and the framed cover in the other. He sat down in the chair, never taking his sight off the paper. He set the frame on the desk and held the folded piece of paper in both hands. The rain tapped into the picture window behind him. Jack hoped that he would find the pieces of the puzzle he needed wrapped in this piece of paper. He unfolded it; it was a letter.

Dearest Dawn,

I am truly worried about your safety. One because you continue to work at the club and two because of the things you told me about your boyfriend.

'What had Tom gotten into?' Jack thought. He continued reading:

I told you to come live with me. We could leave this place and I can take care of you. I can catch fish anywhere in this state and probably any other place for that matter.

Jack rolled his eyes.

I know you think it's better that you and I don't see each other anymore, but I can't stop thinking about you. You won't even take my calls anymore. You boyfriend sounds very dangerous, but I am a grown man and can take care of myself. Why would you want to be involved in that? I care so much for you! I beg you to stop dancing and you ignore me. I beg you to leave him and you ignore me. Please don't ignore me any more. Can't you see I only want what's best for you? You are so young and beautiful. You have so much to live for. Don't throw your life away with this scumbag cop. Just say the word and I will come to your aunt's and get you anytime. You don't have to keep hiding. Please call me!

Love always,
Tom

Dawn would never see the letter. Why did he hide it behind the picture? Who is the scumbag cop Tom referred to? More importantly, who is Dawn? Jack felt he was getting closer, but now had even more questions to answer.

Jack folded up the letter and put it in his pocket. He looked on the desk and flipped through some papers in a tray. Nothing. He looked in the drawers in the double pedestal desk. Nothing. He looked over to the computer monitor sitting on the return of the desk. He looked for the CPU, but it was gone. He looked back at the desk. There was an open spot that Jack figured belonged to a Rolodex or something of the sort.

"Damn detectives," he grumbled.

Just then Katelyn's head popped into the doorway. "Dad, I'm kinda hungry," she said, giving a shrug.

Jack smiled, "I'll be there in a second, honey."

Jack walked into the kitchen. Through the pass-through he saw Katelyn curled up on the couch. She was intently watching TV. He opened the refrigerator door and saw some fresh fillets in a Ziploc bag sitting on a shelf. Fresh grouper no doubt, caught slow trolling Sarasota bay just a couple of days ago.

Katelyn called to him, "Looks like the storm is going to hit right on us." She never took her eyes off the television.

"Oh, really?" Jack responded as he looked through the cabinets. He grabbed some batter mix and some oil.

"The weather guys are predicting that the eye might turn north and then catch a trough and then come right over Bradenton. The storm is not too far off shore either! Are we really safe here without the rest of the windows covered?"

Jack looked out the kitchen window. Though it was late morning, the sun was hidden behind the massive gray blanket and gave the appearance of dusk. As he set a cast-iron skillet on the stove top, he wondered if he should go out and secure the rest of the shutters.

Soon Katelyn could smell the fish frying in the pan. It was almost as if the smell had grabbed her by the nose and pulled her toward the kitchen. She took a seat on a stool at the pass-through and watched her dad cook the fillets.

"That smells great, Dad!"

Jack smiled. He thought of how different she was from her mother. Her mother really did not care for fish. Her mother. Jack wondered where she was and who she was with.

"So, where is Mom?"

Katelyn looked down to the counter top. "She is in Tennessee," she said never taking her eyes off the counter top.

"Tennessee? That must be nice! Who's she with?" Jack said with a hard fought smile.

"You're not going to burn that, right?"

"No. Kat, who's your Mom with?" now a little more serious sounding.

"Dad..."

Jack looked at her with his eyebrows raised waiting for her response.

"Dad, Mom met a nice guy at work." Katelyn's gaze was now on the ceiling.

"You think he's a nice guy?"

"Uh, yeah, I do," she said in a soft voice. She felt as if she was betraying her father by saying it, but she did feel that way.

"Fish is done, let's eat." And he turned off the stove.

Katelyn had mixed emotions about her mother's relationship. She had given up the dream that her mother and father would get back together. She knew that a new relationship was healthy and good for her mother, but she knew that inside, her father there was still a yearning for her mother. A yearning that kept him interested in her family. A yearning that made him call more often then he might have otherwise called. A yearning that she hoped gave her father his ultimate puzzle to solve. But what now if the yearning was to go away?

Katelyn's hunch about her father's feelings for her mother was right. Jack did think deep down inside that he and Amy would get back together. He had no idea that she had met someone. He had a few dates but nothing very meaningful. They just did not match up against Amy. Jack thought he would get his act together soon enough and be able to work his way back into her heart. He felt that she still had feelings for him or at least he hoped so. He had no idea how lonely he was going to feel after the divorce. Even through it there was quite a bit of interaction between the two of them. Granted, it was not all pleasant, but she did not totally write him off, either. She, of course, maintained contact mostly for the benefit of Katelyn. But if Jack really wanted to talk about something when he dropped Katelyn off, she would wait and listen. Jack was actually quite proud of her for going through with the divorce. She was right. Only he knew it too late. It was not until now that he realized that he may be too late again.

They sat adjacent to each other at the long dining table not speaking a word, eating the perfectly fried fish. Then the lights flickered. They both looked up and around.

"So how did Mom meet this guy? What's his name?"

She finished chewing "At work and his name is Rob." She reached over, grabbed her glass of water and took a drink. She watched him as she swallowed.

Jack took a bite. He put his elbows up on the table, folded his hands together and rested his chin on them while he chewed. He stared straight ahead. Katelyn put the glass down and grabbed her fork.

Just as she was getting ready to put a bite in her mouth he asked "Is your Mom happy?"

Katelyn hesitated to put the bite in her mouth. Then she took the bite off the fork.

Talking out the side of her mouth she said "Ya know, Dad, I think she is."

Jack nodded and took another bite.

"He treats her real good." she added.

"What about you?"

"Yeah, he treats me good too. It's not like I spend a lot of time with

Rob, but when I do, he's nice to me."

Jack had feelings of hurt and anger. The feelings of hurt he had no one to blame but himself. The feelings of anger came from the idea of a stranger in the house with his daughter.

"Do you spend time alone with him?" Jack asked then popped another bite in his mouth.

"Dad," Katelyn looked at him sideways. "He's not a pervert or anything, and no, I don't spend time alone with him."

"Well, as long as he's good to you both," he said with a tone of one can never be too protective.

They sat eating quietly once more.

Katelyn took a deep breath "Dad? Do you miss Mom?"

Jack turned and looked at Katelyn. He was a little shocked by the question. He took his hand and held the side of her face. "Yeah, honey, I do," he said in a somber voice.

Katelyn reached up and held his warm hand against her face and closed her eyes. Jack took his other hand and wiped a tear from his eye.

CHAPTER TWELVE

Lynn had done what meteorologists feared most. She ate up the warm water of the Gulf and strengthened to a category four. The eye wall was thirty miles off the coast off southern Longboat Key. Lynn changed from a lumbering storm out in the middle of the Gulf into a charging nightmare ready to unleash.

She was now moving at a clip of 14 knots. Her outer bands were dropping plenty of rain and even spun off a tornado that ripped through Myakka State Park. It would only be a couple of hours before she made landfall and people were still scrambling to shelters. Those few that thought they would tough it out were now doubting that decision since the news of the category four increase.

Lynn seemed to be doing everything right to be everything wrong. She was a very well-formed storm. Satellite pictures showed a very defined, almost perfect, circle eye. The images from above showed the entire center of Florida engulfed by the massive swirling cloud form known as Lynn.

Flooding became a major issue for the Emergency Operations Center(EOC) of Manatee and Sarasota counties. The city of Sarasota, which flooded on a typical day of rain, feared the worst. Marina Jacks was only a couple miles away from downtown Sarasota. No doubt the streets would be flooded and probably many of the businesses as well. All of the barrier islands were under mandatory evacuation. Bradenton was not without its own need for fear. Several areas had been known to flood there as well. One being US 41, the major thoroughfare north and south through Bradenton. Planners were working frantically to figure out how emergency vehicles would be able to get to victims.

Sergeant Jackson could feel his blood pressure rise. Thoughts and images swirled in his head like the wind and rain swirled around the outside of his apartment. Jackson could not fathom that Jack Foster was still alive and that two of his squad members were dead.

On top of this, his slack-jawed girlfriend was still managing to hide from him. He snickered at the thought of that. He never really gave her much credit for being smart, but she was smart enough to be afraid of him. He would be sure to take care of her like he took care of the stupid fisherman she ran her mouth to. It would only be a matter of time before she let him know where she was.

Since killing the redneck fisherman, Jackson bugged Dawn's phone, but that led to nothing. Keeping tabs on her cell phone yielded pretty much the same. Somehow she learned of the fisherman's demise and had gone underground. Jackson was pretty sure he knew everything that was underground. That too bothered Jackson. Had she been keeping tabs on him?

Jackson walked out of his bedroom and into the living room where three members of the Cobra Squad sat.

"T.J., what's up with Daniels and Mendoza? Did they get it done?" asked Bill Evans. Evans had been on the team as long as Jackson. He was the oldest member on the team. He sat on the edge of a recliner leaning forward. He was very anxious about the news.

Jackson just glared at him.

"What? What is it?" Evans asked, looking to the other team members for support.

"Yeah, what is it?" asked a mountain of a man with jet black hair that was slicked back. Joseph Iorrio, like Jackson, was an avid weightlifter. In fact, he was Jackson's workout partner. He was taller and considerably bigger then Jackson. Most likely due to his off again, on again use of steroids. He sat on the couch with the television remote control in his hand.

Iorrio had been on the team the longest. He had no desires to be the leader. He found it much easier to have Jackson's ear while in the gym. He would suggest whatever he felt would benefit the team, or more likely, himself, when no one was around. He was very good at making Jackson think it was his idea.

The third and newest member of the team sat on the opposite end of the couch from Iorrio. He was the same young man that tried to stop Jack and talk to him on his way to the grocery store. He flipped through a "Muscle Fitness" magazine, rolling his eyes from time to time. He himself was of a thin build and he thought of Iorrio and Jackson as muscle-bound idiots.

His name was Daniel Stone. He was the youngest member of the Cobra Squad ever. He was twenty-four-years-old and very intelligent. Unlike Iorrio he was quite ambitious. He looked forward to the day that he would be in charge of the squad. He was also the most devious member of the team.

Stone never looked up from the magazine; even after Jackson heaved his cell phone across the living room shattering it into pieces as it made contact with the refrigerator. The other two sat with there mouths hanging open.

"Mendoza is dead. Daniels is on his way back," Jackson said looking to the floor, clenching both fists.

"How did that happen?" Evans asked. He seemed to be becoming more frantic with each passing minute. "Daniels got him though, right?"

Jackson shook his head.

"What the fuck?" Iorrio yelled throwing his hands in the air. "Who the hell is this guy? He's like, fuck'n forty-something and he's kicking our asses!"

Evans looked to Iorrio nodding his head in agreement.

Stone saw this out of the corner of his eye and shook his head. Evans was forty. Then Stone chimed in "Papa bear protecting his cub, I guess."

"What the fuck is that supposed to mean?" Iorrio said, now jumping to his feet. His massive arms still raised in the air.

Stone looked up to Iorrio. "His daughter."

Jackson looked at Stone with a puzzled look.

Stone saw the look and explained further "His daughter is with him."

"How come you didn't tell us that earlier?" Jackson demanded.

"What difference does it make? You kill him. You kill the daughter. Done," Stone said raising the magazine and turning his focus on it again.

"That's bullshit!" Evans exclaimed, jumping to his feet as well.

"Go fuck yourself!" Stone yelled as he threw down the magazine and leaped up.

"Enough! Everyone calm down! Stone is right; if she's with him she'd have to go too." Jackson yelled trying to gain control once more.

Stone smiled, sat back down, and picked up the magazine again.

"Once Daniels gets back, we'll regroup and take care of this once and for all." Jackson said motioning for everyone to sit down.

Iorrio turned and walked away "I need something to drink." He tossed the remote next to Stone.

"I'm not so sure I can kill a little girl." Evans said as he sat back down.

"Don't worry about it. I'll take care of it." Stone said as he winked at him over the magazine.

Jackson shook his head and walked into the kitchen after Iorrio. Just as he was about to say something, there was a bang at the door. They all looked to the door.

"Be quiet!" Jackson whispered as he quickly walked over to the door. He looked through the peep hole.

"It's Daniels." He said and opened the door.

Daniels was wincing and biting his lower lip. He was in a great deal of pain from fighting the wind to stay upright. The wind caught Jackson off guard and he almost lost his hold on the door. Wind and rain blew in and Jackson motioned Daniels inside.

CHAPTER THIRTEEN

Jack was placing the dishes in the sink when he saw the swaying skiff hanging on the davits. Jack felt compelled to do something. He knew the boat would get destroyed hanging out there. He felt as if he needed to as a sign of respect for Capt. Tom. Jack knew how much fishing meant to Capt. Tom and that boat was his pride and joy. You could not convince him there was another boat besides Hewes.

Jack went back out in the wind and rain. Katelyn sat in the house and watched him through the sliders. Once again she admired her father's calm and collectiveness, but she was beginning to wonder if he was not a tad bit crazy. Why would he go out there to try and save someone else's boat? She thought it was a really nice boat, but after all, poor Capt. Tom was dead. It was not as if he would be using it anymore.

Jack stood near the seawall wearing his rain jacket. He had the hood pulled up over his ball cap and cinched around his face. With his hands in the pockets of the jacket, Jack contemplated what to do. His body would rock side to side as the rushing wind ran into him. 'Gotta sink it.' he thought.

Jack decided he would pull the plug and lower the boat into the water deep enough to fill and weigh it down. Jack worked his plan out in his head a couple times to be sure it would work.

There really was not much in the way of rain; it was more of a drizzle. But the wind was steadily blowing and the gusts were extremely strong, lasting up to ten seconds. As Jack worked his plan, a powerful gust blew into him. He had to steady himself as it almost pushed him off the sea wall. It caused the boat to swing and sway and it banged into the davits. As he stood there, a stream of water spewed out the side of the hull. *It must be the Auto Bilge.* Jack decided he needed to stop thinking and start doing.

He made his way over to the boat on the lift. He paused to see if another gust would come, then he grabbed hold of the rub rail and pulled himself up and into the boat. Another gust blasted the boat banging it into the davits again. Jack cringed at the thought of the hull chipping away and quickly went to work.

He raised the hydraulic jack plate to its maximum height. Then he tilted the motor all the way up. While the motor was tilting up, Jack opened the console hatch, not sure where the battery was. There he found a medium sized black binder zippered shut. Jack took it, stuffed it under his jacket and slipped it in the waistband between the small of his back and his gun. Then he slid on the rear deck on his stomach and reached down the transom and pulled the plug. Jack found the battery and pulled it out.

The boat swaying, Jack knelt on the port gunnel and tossed the battery onto the backyard. The shift in weight caused the boat to sway hard and Jack almost fell out.

Katelyn, still watching, jumped to her feet when he almost fell out. She put her hand over her beating heart once she realized he was all right.

Jack lowered the davits. The boat hit the choppy water and he stopped. He waited a minute and lowered them a few more inches. Then again and again. Eventually the water was just a few inches lower then the deck. It pained Jack to see the boat like this. He knew the damage the saltwater would cause, but he figured it was better then her being picked up and tossed into a house.

He turned, grabbed the battery, and headed back to the house where Katelyn met him at the door and pulled the slider open for him.

"Thanks." he said as he set the battery on the floor.

"What's with the battery?" Katelyn asked shaking her head.

"Auto bilge. Didn't want it pump'n the water out while I'm trying to sink it."

"Oh," she said raising her eyebrows and rolling her eyes.

"Besides, we might need it for something."

She shrugged her shoulders.

"I'm gonna try and get some more of those shutters up. If this thing is as nasty as they say, we're in for a hell of a ride."

As Jack turned to go back outside he felt the binder in the small of his back. He stopped, reached back and pulled it out.

"But first, what do we have here?" he said brandishing the binder to Katelyn.

CHAPTER FOURTEEN

There was a reason that Amy Foster let Katelyn visit her father other than it was his turn. Amy had met someone. Someone who gave her the attention she missed at the end of her marriage to Jack. Someone who wanted to take her and Katelyn to Tennessee for a nice getaway. Katelyn, of course, would rather be with her father. It was not that Katelyn did not like Rob, but she wasn't about to give up her time with her dad. And rather than argue and ruin any chance of a good time, Amy let her go to her father's.

Amy Foster had enjoyed the road trip with Rob. It was a great opportunity for her to really talk with him. He was personable and had a pretty good sense of humor. But she could not help wonder what was happening back in the Sunshine State. She had left her teenage daughter with her ex-husband and an impending storm. Jack was more then capable, but the last news they heard as they were leaving Florida via I-75, was that Lynn was going to be a nasty one. Jack did not have an invincibility complex, but she thought he had a lack of due fear sometimes. She was sure that they would be long gone to some other part of the state if Bradenton was to take a direct hit.

For a good reason, her motherly instinct doubted what she kept telling herself 'I'm sure they are just fine.' She had told Rob that she was going to call and check on them a couple times on the way up, but he insisted that she try to relax and to focus on the two of them. After all it was the first big outing for Amy and Rob. Rob had plenty of music on hand so they were not distracted by any news reports on the radio. Amy was a good sport about it. Rob was being very sweet and he did make the trip enjoyable, so she went along with it.

She went along with it all the way there. But once they got settled in the cabin, Amy made sure to surf the channels on the television until she found a weather update on Lynn. And when she did, she was not happy. When she tried to get a hold of Katelyn and Jack but could not, she became quite distressed. Rob did his best to try and calm her, but it was to no avail. She demanded that they return to the weather-torn state immediately.

The ride back was quite different from the ride up. There wasn't much talking. There was no music. Amy switched from channel to channel until she found one giving more details to the havoc Lynn was wreaking. Rob apologized several times. He was under the perception that Jack was a competent father. Amy really did not blame Rob. She blamed herself and, at this point, there was no time for small talk or apologies. She was on a mission. A mission to get home and make sure her baby was truly safe.

When Amy learned that Lynn's path was most definitely going over Bradenton, she began to panic. It did not matter how fast Rob could drive, there was no way they were going to make it to Bradenton fast enough. Try as she might, her calls to Jack went unanswered. The land lines were dead and his cell phone, which sat on the kitchen counter of Jack's house, rang and rang, then went to voice mail until the battery died.

Rob continued to be as supportive as possible and did his best to keep Amy calm. Rob suggested that maybe Amy could get a hold of someone willing to go check on Jack and Katelyn. Amy attempted a few friends; all of which were out of town for the storm or hell bent on staying in their homes.

But Amy did finally get a volunteer to go and check on Jack and Katelyn. And when Jack's fellow charter captain and friend, Brian Richards, arrived at Jack's place, he thought for sure there would be nothing wrong. Of course, he was sadly mistaken.

Though Jack's truck was still at the house, no one responded to Brian's banging on the front door. Now fearing something bad had happened, he made his way through the onslaught of wind and rain around to the back of the house. There he saw the small aluminum screen porch had collapsed blocking the back door. He climbed over the rubble to reach the door missing its knob, but unlocked. Brian lifted the metal mess in order to open the door. The wind obliged him by catching the panels and heaving them further into the backyard. He looked down at his hands expecting to see blood from having the jagged aluminum ripped from his grasp, but there was none.

Once he managed to pry open the door, the wind pulled it away from him and slammed it into the house. Brian stood in the doorway and yelled for Jack and Katelyn, but the only response was a raspy meow from Bear as he peeked his head out from under the couch. The gray light from the storm illuminated the dark house enough for Brian to notice what appeared to be bullet holes in the walls. His calls for Jack and Katelyn became more frantic the more he saw. When he cautiously walked into the hallway he could see the glinting of the shell casings scattered down the hall. His stocky figure froze in fear of what he might find.

Though the wind swirled through the house Bear stayed next to Brian, rubbing his head against his calf, giving a deep raspy meow every so often.

Brian ignored the cat's continued attempts for attention. He reached over and clicked the hall light switch up and down, but of course there was still no power. He yelled again for Jack and Katelyn. No response. He turned and saw the large MagLite on the kitchen table, walked over grabbed it, and clicked it on. Again, he headed down the hallway ever so slowly. He saw Jack's bedroom door open. He paused by the splintered doorframe, closed his eyes, took a deep breath and proceeded through. No one. Then he went across to Katelyn's room; no one.

Brian was feeling a little more relaxed at the lack of discovering what he feared he would. Then he went to Jack's office; and there, of course, he found the slain body of Mendoza. The gruesome discovery was quite shocking and consoling in the sense that it was neither Jack nor Katelyn.

He found himself sitting on the couch trying to calm his stomach; the body of Mendoza made him feel queasy. The backdoor was still open and the wind still swirled through the house pushing a spray of rain soaking the splintered dining table. Bear was once again at him for attention. Brian scratched him behind the ear.

"Where's your Daddy and what's he gotten himself into?" he asked the cat.

Bear responded with purring.

Brian got up and walked over to the phone hanging in the kitchen. It was dead. He saw Jack's cell phone on the counter, then reached into his pocket and pulled out a tiny silver cell phone and flipped it open. He was hesitant to call anyone. He thought to himself 'Why hadn't Jack called the police? Were he and Katelyn kidnapped?' Then he thought about what he would tell Amy. What could he tell her? He didn't know what was going on.

He entered a number and hit send. He put the small phone up to his ear. He pressed it hard into his ear with his index finger so that he could hear better with the wind blowing. The phone rang and rang and rang.

"911, what is your emergency?" came the voice on the other end.

Brian took a deep breath "Uh, yes, there's been a shooting," he said with uncertainty.

"Has anyone been hurt?" the operator asked.

He looked to the office "Uh, yeah, someone is dead." He closed his eyes. *What in the world am I going to tell Amy?*

CHAPTER FIFTEEN

Jack slid his jacket off, trading the binder from hand to hand as he pulled his arms out of the jacket and dropped it on the floor in front of the slider. He walked over to the kitchen table with Katelyn following close behind. He pulled out a chair and sat down. He set the binder down in front of him.

"Well, what is it, Dad?" Katelyn was anxious.

"I'm pretty sure it's his business planner."

Jack undid the zipper and, sure enough, it was a business planner. Jack's heart began to thump a little harder. He knew in his gut that he had found something. He just did not realize yet what it was.

The front of the planner was three pages of business cards. Some from other Captains, some from various bait and tackle shops. Jack chuckled because he knew that Capt. Tom probably took them as a courtesy. The only place Capt. Tom bought tackle from was a place up in Tampa called Monsters and Minnows. Jack had gone up a few times with Capt. Tom and had to admit; good deals and good people. Jack pinched the tab labeled 'Numbers and Addresses' and pulled the planner open. He carefully perused each name.

Katelyn sat adjacent to her dad as she did during their meal. With her elbows on the table and her chin resting in her palms, she watched him. She watched each expression he made. She studied him. She wanted to know if she could see the moment he found whatever it was he was looking for. Would she be able to pick up the facial expression that said 'Ah ha!'?

The book had quite a few names, numbers, and addresses. Jack tried to be patient, but as he turned each page, doubt grew a little in his mind. Then he came across a name that sparked his interest: Dawn Howard. Jack flipped the page, studied the back quickly and then tore the page out. He set the page on the table above the planner.

Katelyn saw her dad's eyebrow rise. A little smirk came across her face and she watched him tear the page out. She leaned in to look at it and then she reached over and turned the page so that it faced her. Jack looked up to see what she was doing, and then he went right back to flipping through the planner. She scanned the names and then turned the page back the way her dad had set it.

Jack found another one: Dawn Peterson. Just as before, he flipped the page, scanned, then tore it out, placing it next to the first one.

Katelyn did as she did before then she asked "Dawn? Is Dawn the name you are looking for?"

Jack reached into his back pocket, pulled out a folded piece of paper and handed it to her. With eyebrows raised, Katelyn unfolded it and read the letter to Dawn, then set it down on the table next to the torn-out address pages.

When Jack was done looking through the names, he looked up to the two pages. He sat and studied them. He started rubbing his chin. Katelyn sat very quiet and still. She was afraid that if she moved she might throw off her dad's train of thought.

Jack looked at her "I could use something to drink, how 'bout you?"

Katelyn nodded and got up from her seat, anxious to help. She walked over to the refrigerator. Jack looked back at the pages 'Which one?' he thought. Then Jack went ahead and started aimlessly flipping through the pages of the calendar.

"He has tea, Dr. Pepper, Coronas, or bottled water." Katelyn called over her shoulder, looking into the refrigerator.

Jack looked over to her still turning the pages "Dr. Pepper sounds good."

Katelyn smiled. She guessed it would either be the Dr. Pepper or the tea. Her whole life, she never saw her father drink alcohol. She once asked her dad why he never did and he replied that it, "Clouds the mind and the mind is the most important thing I got." She hoped more then ever that his mind was not clouded.

Jack looked down to the planner to see days crossed though with a line and the name Dawn written on the line.

"Grrr," Jack sounded. "Which one is she?"

"Why don't you just call them?" Katelyn asked extending a Dr. Pepper to her father.

Jack looked at her and nodded in appreciation as he took the drink.

"What if the phone lines are dead?" he asked as he popped the can open.

"What if they're not? If they are, you can figure it out then," she said taking a sip from the water bottle.

Jack looked at her and smiled "Would you hand me the phone please."

"Certainly," Katelyn said with a grin of which the Cheshire cat would have been proud.

She leaned back in the chair in order to reach the phone sitting on the breakfast bar. Just as she reached the phone, the chair started to fall backwards. She tried to correct herself, but it was too late. Then Jack reached over and grabbed her knee. It was very fast and surprised Katelyn. He stopped her from falling over and pulled her back until the feet of the chair plopped onto the floor.

"Thanks!" she said a little startled.

Jack shook his head "Come on now, we've made it this far."

She handed him the phone and he looked at the first page.

"Here goes," he said with a shrug.

He turned the cordless phone on; dial tone. He dialed the number. A series of beeps.

"I'm sorry, but the number you are trying to reach is no longer connected. Please hang up and try again," came a recorded female voice through the phone.

As soon as Jack heard the beeps his eyes shifted and he looked at Katelyn sideways. Jack hung up the phone. "Well, there's one down."

Jack looked at the next number and dialed. This time the phone rang. Jack raised his eyebrows and Katelyn started grinning again.

CHAPTER SIXTEEN

Daniels was no stranger to injuries. He suffered various broken bones from his youth as a motocross racer. He had been stabbed in the forearm and had been cold-cocked across the jaw, but those were just from one night of bar fights. Being on the Cobra Squad, Daniels had not received much in the way of injuries; he was too busy giving them out. Of all the fights and close calls, he had never experienced anything like being shot. The impact that he took on the side-plate of his ballistic vest knocked the wind out of him instantly. He folded on the spot. The pain was excruciating. Even as he made his retreat from the home of Jack Foster, Daniels had no idea how lucky he was until he was examined by Evans.

Evans, who had started his public service career as an EMT, had Daniels sitting on a kitchen chair and was removing his jacket, shirt, and then his vest. One inch higher and, no doubt, the bullet would have ripped through Daniels' torso. Instead the vest did its job and saved his life; only leaving him with a severe contusion and a few broken ribs.

"I'll bet you got a broken rib or two and you're gonna have one hell of a bruise, but you'll live. You shouldn't do much 'cause you don't want to aggravate it," Evans said standing over Daniels, laying a sympathetic hand on his shoulder.

"Thanks, but I got to finish my assignment," replied Daniels, taking a deep slow breath before speaking.

Just then Jackson walked up to them.

"So what's the deal? You gonna be OK?" asked Jackson sounding somewhat concerned.

Daniels nodded.

"All right then. We need to get organized," said Jackson looking around to the other squad members.

"You should have taken me instead of Mendoza," Stone said to Daniels walking into the kitchen.

Daniels did not respond. He felt around on the side of his ribcage, wincing whenever his fingers would run over the already black and blue mark.

Jackson was gathering everyone together when Iorrio's cell phone rang. Iorrio flipped the phone open and looked at the caller I.D. He quickly looked to Jackson with a serious gaze.

"Dep. Iorrio," he answered.

"Yes, Iorrio, this is Detective Roberts. I'm afraid I have some very bad news. It appears that Mark White was killed earlier today. I'm very sorry."

"Oh, my God!" Iorrio sounding shocked.

Jackson looked at him and shrugged his shoulders. Iorrio held his finger up signaling everyone to wait.

"We're not sure, but it looks like someone attacked him in a parking lot."

"That's horrible! Do you guys have any leads?"

"Well, we do have fingerprints and there might be some blood samples. We hope we'll get a hit on the prints soon." replied the detective.

"Well, please let us know if there is anything we can do to help you."

"I just wanted to let you guys know since he was a member of your squad. I did try to get a hold of Sgt. Jackson, but his phone doesn't seem to be working."

"Ah, yeah, I think he dropped it in a puddle or something. He's with me so I'll let him know."

"Very good. Again, I'm very sorry."

"So am I," Iorrio said as he hung up the phone. "CID, they're working on White's murder."

"But they don't know who did it?" asked Jackson.

"Not yet."

Evans chimed in "Why didn't you tell him?"

"How is it we know?" Stone asked Evans. Stone really did wonder what Evans was doing in this squad.

"Exactly," Jackson said nodding at Stone. "Now we got to get him before they do. I don't know how much he knows or if he still has any friends in this department, but I'm not going to let them walk him into an interview room."

"We just gotta find out where he's at," added Iorrio.

Now all of them gathered around the small circular kitchen table in the apartment. Daniels nursing his ribs, Evans resting his elbows on the table and his chin in his hands. His left knee was rapidly pumping up and down with nervous energy. Iorrio was sipping a cold beer. Stone sat back in his chair with his arms crossed. Jackson laid out the plan.

"All right, we'll break-up into teams. Evans and Stone, Me and Iorrio."

"What about me?" Daniels said offended. You just gonna leave me here?"

Jackson reached over and poked Daniels' ribs.

"Ahh! What the fuck are you doing?!" screamed Daniels.

"That's why you'll stay here," Jackson barked back. He pointed at Evans and Stone "Now, you two, head back to his place and see if you can figure out where he may be hiding. We'll head over to the fisherman's house and see if he decided to go snooping around."

Then the phone rang. They all looked to it hanging on the kitchen wall. It rang again. And again, and again. Then the machine picked up.

"Hi, I'm not here right now, but leave me a message and I'll get back to ya," said a young female voice.

"Hi, this is Jack Foster; I'm a friend of Tom Underwood. I'm looking for Dawn Johnson. Please call me back at his place as soon as possible."

Jackson turned back to the group "change of plans."

Jack hung up the phone. He had no idea that he just kicked a hornet's nest. Katelyn sat at the table still sipping her water.

"Now what, Dad?"

"I'm not sure. I still need to get out there and try and get some of those shutters up. We're gonna be getting it pretty hard any minute now. Hopefully we'll be able to just hang tight until this thing blows over," Jack said as he took his seat at the table.

"Well, then why are you sitting down?" Katelyn asked puzzled.

"I guess you're right." Jack downed the last of his Dr. Pepper and headed to the door. He grabbed his jacket and slipped it on. He looked out the slider. The wind had really begun to pick up, moving sheets of rain across the backyard. Jack could see little whitecaps cresting in the canal. He took a deep breath and headed out the door.

Jack was tired. It wasn't that he was out of shape. He made it part of his daily routine to do some sit-ups, push-ups, and pull-ups. On top of the few times a week he ran, Jack didn't have a trolling motor on his boat, so he would use the push pole. On a typical outing he would probably pole the boat around for a couple of miles. No, Jack wasn't out of shape.

He made mental exercise a daily activity as well. The puzzles he did weren't done solely out of loneliness. He truly loved the mental challenge they provided. Crosswords, jig-saws, Sudoku, and, on occasion, solve a crime; he did them all. It was his typical lack of sleep and the constant mental and physical challenges that were beginning to wear on him. But he knew that there was no time to rest now. Now was the time he needed to muster everything he had to finish this puzzle. Now he needed to be perfect to protect Katelyn.

Jack stayed close to the house. He worked on the side of the house out of the wind. Of course there were only two small windows to cover. Jack wondered how he would cover the large picture window of Capt. Tom's office. He walked around the side of the house and got blasted by the wind. It took Jack a few steps backwards to regain his balance. As he walked into the wind it ripped the hood off of his head and almost took his cap with it. Jack reached up and slapped his hand to his head in order to catch the hat. He grimaced with pain from the gouge on the palm of his hand that he just used to save the cap. He moved his hand down to the bill of the cap and pulled it down snugly. He looked at the bandage on his hand. It started to seep a small amount of red fluid. Jack shook his head and continued on battling the wind.

Jack was struggling to put the shutter over the picture window when the wind ripped it from his grasp. The shutter went tumbling down the back of the house and Jack took off after it. The shutter whipped around the protected side of the house and laid flat on the lawn between Capt. Tom's and his neighbor. Jack ran over to it and stepped on it hoping that it would not go airborne again. He bent over and dug his hands underneath the shutter while he continued to stand on it.

"Come on you piece of shit!" he murmured to himself.

He stepped off and picked it up. He walked it over to the side of the house. There he took a minute to catch his breath and ready for the upcoming battle against Mother Nature. Jack rounded the corner and planted the shutter against the back of the house. Leaning into the shutter with both hands and all his might, Jack walked along the back of the house sliding the shutter along the wall.

He got back to the picture window and had the shutter up and was just about to attach it when there came a loud rapping against the window. It startled Jack and he released the shutter and went for his gun. The shutter was held in place by the wind for a couple of seconds and then it leaned back. The gusting wind grabbed hold of it and sent it flying.

Jack ducked the projectile shutter with his gun in hand. He saw Katelyn at the window frantically motioning for him to come inside. Jack looked at her confused and pissed off. She took the business planner and slammed it against the window and began waving him inside again.

A crash sounded at the neighbor's house. Jack dropped to a knee and rotated with his gun drawn to where the crash sounded from. The airborne shutter had found an obstacle, the neighbor's pool cage. The large metal shutter had traveled a good 30 yards in the air before ripping through the screened two-story pool cage. It managed to take out two of the supports before making its landing in the kidney shaped pool. The wind now finding the weakened structure took the rest of the cage down laying metal and screen over the pool.

Jack cringed. He felt bad for the neighbor. Still on one knee and gun in line of sight he turned his head up to the window. Katelyn was now jumping up and down waving for him to come in. Jack got to his feet using the side of the house to help aid him against the battering wind. *This better be good!* It was.

Jack was greeted at the slider by a very excited Katelyn. He could barely get his jacket off.

"Dad, come on! Come on!" Katelyn said grabbing his forearm and pulling him back to the dinning table.

"Kat, what is it?" he said shaking his arm out of the sleeve.

"You should have looked through the rest of that planner! There's more stuff in the back. I think it's important! There's another phone number with "Dawn's Cell" written above it!"

Jack's eyebrows were raised; as he made it to the table he saw that Katelyn had laid out some papers. A closer look revealed they were satellite photos. Jack recognized them as photos from TerraServer, which took photos of the earth via satellites. Katelyn had laid them in an order from the farthest view to the closest, the length of the table. The first photo page Jack recognized instantly as the Manatee River. Every one after was merely a close up of the same spot. Jack paused at each one. Closer and closer the photos zoomed until the last one which showed houses along the northern bank of the river near the Green Bridge. One of the houses was circled.

As Jack walked along looking at each photo, Katelyn walked behind him. She anxiously glanced back and forth from the photos to her father's face. As Jack bent over and studied the last one, Katelyn reached around and turned it over to reveal the phone number she told him about written on the back.

Jack turned his head to face her. He was smiling very big. "You've done real good kiddo!" he said with a wink. He reached out and pulled her in to him and gave her a hug. She closed her eyes and squeezed him tight. Jack couldn't help but be impressed with his little girl.

He was just so very proud at how smart she was. She had always impressed her dad with her intellect. Her poise and maturity through the divorce had simply amazed him. Now, in this stressful time, she had once again made him marvel at her abilities. He kissed her forehead. He felt rejuvenated by her.

"Oh!" she said as she pulled away from him and turned to get the phone. As she reached it the house went dark. "What the…?"

"Power finally went out. I'm surprised it lasted as long as it did considering the winds." he said surveying the darkened house.

She shrugged her shoulders and brought him the phone. He tried to turn it on, but nothing. He looked at it confused for a second. Then it dawned on him, cordless phone, doesn't work without power.

She looked at him as he put the phone down on the table and start looking around. "What is it?"

"Cordless, won't work without out power. Got to be a corded phone here somewhere," he said as he walked into the living room.

Nothing in there. He walked into the office, nothing. He walked into Capt. Tom's bedroom; another cordless. Jack was beginning to become frustrated. "How in the world don't ya have a corded phone? Damn power goes out all the time in this frig'n state!" he griped as he came out of the room.

"Got it!" He heard Katelyn call from across the house.

In a guest bedroom on an end table next to a fold-out couch sat what appeared to be a bass sitting on a rock. Of course, closer examination revealed that it was a corded phone. The phone struck Jack odd since Capt. Tom did not care for freshwater fishing. He figured it must have been a gift from someone who did not know much about Capt. Tom or fishing, but someone whom Tom cared for so he displayed the phone even though the corny thing did not match his likings.

Jack picked the bass up hoping to hear a dial tone and he did. He quickly dialed the cell number and waited for a response.

CHAPTER SEVENTEEN

ZCZC MIATCPAT2 ALL
TTAA00 KNHC DDHHMM
BULLETIN
HURRICANE LYNN INTERMEDIATE ADVISORY NUMBER 25A
NWS TPC/NATIONAL HURRICANE CENTER MIAMI FL
NOON CDT SUN AUG 20 2006

...POTENTIALLY CATASTROPHIC CATEGORY FOUR HURRICANE
LYNN
        CONTINUES TO APPROACH THE WEST COAST OF
FLORIDA...

A HURRICANE WARNING IS IN EFFECT FOR THE TAMPABAY
AREA SOUTH TO VENICE.
PREPARATIONS TO PROTECT LIFE AND PROPERTY SHOULD BE
RUSHED TO
COMPLETION.

FOR STORM INFORMATION SPECIFIC TO YOUR AREA... INCLUDING POSSIBLE
INLAND WATCHES AND WARNINGS...PLEASE MONITOR PRODUCTS ISSUED
BY YOUR LOCAL WEATHER OFFICE.

AT NOON CDT...THE CENTER OF HURRICANE LYNN WAS LOCATED NEAR LATITUDE 27.0 NORTH...LONGITUDE 82.8 WEST.

LYNN IS MOVING TOWARD THE NORTH-NORTHEAST NEAR 14 MPH...AND A
TURN TO THE EAST IS EXPECTED.
MAXIMUM SUSTAINED WINDS REMAIN NEAR 135 MPH WITH HIGHER GUSTS.
FOUR IS A CATEGORY FOUR HURRICANE ON THE SAFFIR-SIMPSON SCALE.
SOME FLUCTUATIONS IN STRENGTH ARE LIKELY PRIOR TO LANDFALL...AND
LYNN IS EXPECTED TO MAKE LANDFALL AT EITHER CATEGORY FOUR OR THREE INTENSITY. WINDS AFFECTING THE UPPER FLOORS OF HIGH-RISE
BUILDINGS WILL BE SIGNIFICANTLY STRONGER THAN THOSE NEAR GROUND
LEVEL.

LYNN REMAINS A VERY LARGE HURRICANE. HURRICANE FORCE WINDS EXTEND OUTWARD UP TO 105 MILES FROM THE CENTER...AND TROPICAL STORM FORCE
WINDS EXTEND OUTWARD UP TO 230 MILES. A WIND GUST TO 98 MPH WAS
RECENTLY REPORTED FROM NAPLES.

THE ESTIMATED MINIMUM CENTRAL PRESSURE IS 952 MB...28.11 INCHES.
AN AIR FORCE RESERVE UNIT RECONNAISSANCE AIRCRAFT IS CURRENTLY
INVESTIGATING LYNN.

COASTAL STORM SURGE FLOODING OF 18 TO 22 FEET ABOVE

```
NORMAL TIDE
LEVELS...LOCALLY AS HIGH AS 28 FEET...ALONG WITH
LARGE AND DANGEROUS BATTERING WAVES...CAN BE
EXPECTED NEAR AND TO THE SOUTH OF WHERE THE CENTER
MAKES LANDFALL.


REPEATING THE NOON CDT POSITION...27.0 N...82.8 W.
MOVEMENT
TOWARD...NORTH-NORTHEAST NEAR 14 MPH.   MAXIMUM
SUSTAINED
WINDS...135 MPH.   MINIMUM CENTRAL PRESSURE...952
MB.


AN INTERMEDIATE ADVISORY WILL BE ISSUED BY THE
NATIONAL
HURRICANE CENTER AT 1 PM CDT FOLLOWED BY THE NEXT
COMPLETE ADVISORY AT 4 PM CDT.


FORECASTER THOMPSON
```

The room was aglow with candles set atop the fireplace mantle. The power had gone out about half an hour ago and Dawn had made her way to the living room by following her aunt's voice and a slight glow from the match she had struck to light some candles. Now she sat curled up on the couch listening to the wind blast against and around the old house. Constantly running through emotions of hate, sorrow, and fear had exhausted her. She began to drift asleep.

She saw herself walking along the white soft sands of Siesta Key beach. Not another soul around. The sky was bright blue and clear. She looked toward the bright burning orb above and felt the warmth on her face. She looked at her arms and admired her golden skin. She paused to look at her hourglass figure in the white bikini when her cell phone began to ring. She turned her hand over to see the phone and answered it. It was her aunt calling.

"Dawn."

"Hello, Aunt Gloria."

"Dawn."

"Yes, Aunt Gloria, I'm here."

"Dawn."

She woke to find her aunt gently shaking her shoulder calling her name.

"Dawn, your phone was ringing. Here, honey," said her aunt handing her the phone.

"Uh, thanks." Dawn took the phone a little confused.

She saw that her aunt had started a small fire in the fireplace. She looked down to the phone, opened it and pulled up the last caller. The name was Tom Underwood. Now she was thoroughly confused. She sat up and stared at the phone. Then the phone beeped and she jumped, startled. "1 New Voice Message" appeared on the screen of the phone. Dawn slowly dialed her code and brought the phone to her ear. She hoped that she would hear Tom's voice; that this whole thing was nothing but a dream. A very bad dream. But she didn't and it was not. What she did hear was a Jack Foster pleading for her to call him. He said he was a friend of Tom's. Jack Foster. The name was vaguely familiar. Then she heard Tom's voice in her head "Capt. Jack". He had made mention of him at dinner or something.

Dawn sat in the middle of the couch holding the phone in both her hands. She was biting the corner of her lower lip staring at the chemical flame dance on top of the man-made log. The number he left was Tom's home number. Why was he there? What if this was just a trick of T.J.'s in order to find her? Dawn stood up and paced back and forth in front of the couch. She was tapping the phone against her forehead in time with each step she took.

"If you keep doing that you're going to bruise that pretty little head of yours."

Dawn looked up to see her aunt standing in the doorway holding another hot cup of tea.

"Thank you, Aunt Gloria," she said taking the steaming cup. "How did you make hot tea?" she asked baffled.

"Gas, honey. We have a gas range," her aunt replied with a soft, loving smile.

Dawn's Aunt Gloria was her mother's considerably older sister. Gloria was in her mid-seventies and was a very lovable widow. Dawn often found it sweet and sad how she often referred to things as if she was still married. Dawn's Uncle had died eight years ago. She remembered him as a tall, gentle man who loved Aunt Gloria very much. She remembered how affectionate he was toward Aunt Gloria at family gatherings. He was also very kind to her and, though he was elderly, he always seemed to muster the strength to play with a very young Dawn.

At his passing she felt confused. She often thought of him more of a grandfather. Her mother's father had passed away long before her birth, so she never knew him. Her uncle was close in age to her grandfather from her dad's side, so she just considered him in the same light.

Throughout Dawn's life, her relationships with men were often confusing. Her father was 40 when she was born. She was the last of four children. She, like her mother, was considerably younger then her siblings. Her birth came as a surprise to her father, but not to her mother. Her father was distant and cold to Dawn. Probably the reason she always craved interaction with older men like Tom and even T.J. was because she did not really receive it growing up with her father. Another reason could be that an age gap was a consistent model in her life. Her mother was ten years younger then her father. Her Aunt Gloria was much younger then her late uncle.

Dawn's aunt sat down on a glider and put her feet up on the matching gliding ottoman. She picked up a set of knitting needles in the middle of making a scarf or something out of a pocket on the side of the glider and went straight to work. She started humming a tune that Dawn did not recognize. Her aunt was extremely calm; almost too calm.

Dawn stood for a moment examining her. Dawn watched her move back and forth on the glider knitting away. It gave Dawn an eerie feeling which caused her spine to tingle. She shook it off and walked back into the kitchen, leaving her aunt alone in the flickering flame-lit room.

In the kitchen a hurricane lamp was burning on the table. Dawn looked at her cell phone again. She dialed Tom Underwood's number and hit send. The phone rang twice before she heard Jack Foster's voice on the other end.

"Hello?"

She didn't say anything.

"Hello, who is this?" asked Jack.

Still, Dawn felt almost frozen in a mixture of fear and confusion and said nothing.

"Dawn, is this you?"

She took a deep breath "Yes."

Jack could hardly believe that things seemed to be going his way after the start of the day. He felt as if he was finally getting somewhere and that this horrible experience would be behind him soon enough. Jack felt as if he was coming out of the slight haze he had in his head. He did not feel mentally worn out anymore. He was getting his second wind.

Actually getting a hold of Dawn Peterson, given everything that was going on around them, seemed to be an extreme stroke of luck. Now the question would be does Dawn Peterson hold the answers he so needed in order to try and gain back his life.

It amazed Jack how fast things were going. Just a couple of hours ago he was getting ready to ride out this storm. Now he felt as if he was part of it. So many things had happened in Jack's life in such a short period of time. But then again life was like that. Things seemed to be on autopilot for the longest time and then the engines would cut. Unlike his divorce and other instances in Jack's life, this one seemed to be unfolding at warp speed. His life wasn't the only one racing out of control.

"Dawn, I'm Jack Foster. Maybe Capt. Tom has mentioned me?"

Hesitation "Yes, uh, Tom has mentioned you."

"Are you aware of what has happened to Capt. Tom? I mean, Tom?"

"Yes," Dawn replied. It came like a whisper.

"Dawn, can you tell me anything about what happened?" Jack asked. His heart was starting to beat a little faster. He so desperately wanted to know.

"How do I know you are who you say you are?" she asked sounding defensive.

"Uh, I don't know. How can I prove it to you?"

"I don't know," She said. It sounded as though she was drifting away. Dawn was beginning to tear up. She was feeling guilty again. She wondered why she ever got involved with Tom. She liked him enough, but she surely did not love him. Now she was trying to figure out who his friends were. How well did she really know the man she felt responsible for killing. "I have to go," Dawn said with a sniffle and she hung up the phone.

Jack was shocked. He pulled the receiver away from his ear and stared at it. He quickly grabbed the photo page with her number on it and canted it in the light to see it.

"What happened?" Katelyn asked with a frantic look in her eyes.

"She hung up," Jack answered as he was redialing the phone.

"What? Why? Why did she do that?"

"I don't know."

The phone was ringing again.

"The storm is getting worse," Dawn answered.

"Dawn, listen to me."

She hung up again.

"Holy shit!" Jack yelled.

He pulled the plastic bass from his ear again and redialed the number. It began ringing again.

"You know it's my fault," She answered this time.

"What? No, listen to me. Dawn I need your help." Jack was desperate to keep her on the line. Jack's tone deepened and became more soothing "Tom cared about you very much. He wouldn't blame you for this."

Katelyn recognized the tone right away. It was the way her father sounded whenever he tried to console her.

Dawn began to cry.

"Dawn, please listen to me. I know you did not hurt Tom. I know you know who did. They tried to kill me and my daughter this morning."

"Oh, my God," she gasped. "Are you all right?!"

"Yes, yes, we're fine. These people won't stop until they get us though. I need you to help me stop them." Jack said pleading, but still warm.

"How can I help you? I'm nothing but a whore," Dawn said. She was sitting at the kitchen table. She was resting her elbows on the table. She held her forehead in one hand and the phone to her ear in the other.

"No! Stop that! You are not!" Jack was trying to stay relaxed, but he was becoming frustrated. "I know Tom would not want anything to do with a girl like that."

He heard crying on the other end of the phone.

Jack took a deep breath. "Dawn, where are you?"

"I... don't want to... tell you," she got out between sobs.

Jack was rubbing his forehead. "Listen, Dawn, somehow you got caught up in something you didn't want to. You had no idea that things would happen like they did. Let me help you. Together we can take care of the guys who did this. Together we can make sure they pay for what they did to Tom."

"There's too many of them. They're cops, don't you understand?" now she was yelling.

Jack was not sure if he should tell her that there were two less then when they started.

"Dawn, I can protect you. I…"

"What's the name of his boat?" she blurted out, interrupting him.

"What?" he asked caught off guard.

"Tom's boat. What's the name of Tom's boat?" now more insistent.

"The "Her Thorn"," Jack was not sure what that proved. Anybody at the house could have answered that question. Maybe she was not very bright, he thought.

"And why did he name it that?"

Jack grinned. "Because his boat was always a thorn in the side of the women in his life." He answered very confident. Jack liked her style. A captain names his boat usually with something of a personal meaning. Who else but a good friend would know that?

"Please help me!" she begged as she began to cry again.

"Tell me where you are."

CHAPTER EIGHTEEN

"Natural ability to lead" read the scouting reports on Southeast High School senior, Terrance Jackson. He was like a man amongst boys on the football field, playing middle linebacker. Physically he was a specimen, mentally he was quick, and his temper ruled his heart, giving him the tenacity defensive coordinators dreamed about.

Talks of T.J. going to college were a daily event for the young man. His grades weren't great, but were good enough for the University of Florida, Florida State University, and North Carolina State to come snooping around. Yes, for all intents and purposes it seemed as though T.J. would be living the American dream. But that all came to an end two games shy of finishing his senior season.

The game was pretty much under wraps for Southeast as they were beating Bayshore by two touchdowns midway through the forth quarter. Hoping to bolster his impressive stats even more, T.J. refused to leave the game. It was a run up the middle by Bayshore and T.J. was in position to make another textbook tackle when one of the defensive linemen rolled into his right knee.

The crowd let out a gasp and rose to their feet as the pop of T.J.'s knee could be heard over the game. The knee dislocated, ligaments and tendons tore, he was taken off the field and loaded into the back of the ambulance waiting nearby. T.J. looked out onto the crowd to see faces covered in terror. He knew as the doors closed on the ambulance so did the doors close on his football career.

Try as he might, he could not get back to the level he played at and colleges and universities quickly lost interest in him. But one person found a great deal of interest in T.J. and took him under his wing. Deputy Weiss was the school resource officer and convinced him that he could have a great future in law enforcement.

And when Deputy Terrence Jackson and Sergeant Weiss reunited in the Cobra Squad, it was teacher and student once again. Only this time Weiss taught T.J. how to get the things he wanted in life through corruption. Between Weiss's guidance and T.J.'s natural ability to lead, it was no surprise when Sergeant Jackson became the Cobra Squad leader. Now it was time for Jackson to use those skills the scouts thought so highly of to find Jack Foster.

The remaining five members of the Cobra Squad were gathered around the small kitchen table. Now having the whereabouts of Jack Foster, Jackson was figuring a new plan.

"All right, now we know where he is. We'll head on over there and take care of this problem once and for all. Then we can get back to business as usual."

"What about your stripper girlfriend?" Stone asked with a sly smile.

Jackson's eyes shifted to focus on Stone. "Don't you worry about her. I'll take care of that bitch."

Stone put his hands up in front of him. "Don't get mad at me. She's still out there, and as long as she is, there's a chance she could talk to someone else. Don't get me wrong, I'll off her whole fuck'n family if I have to, but I'd rather nip it in the bud."

"What the fuck did I just say? I'll take care of her!" Jackson slammed his fist into the table.

Stone kept his hands up, shook his head and leaned back in the chair.

Iorrio put a hand on Jackson's forearm. "No, Stone is right on this one."

100

Jackson turned and looked at Iorrio in disbelief.

"Listen, we've got to take care of her, too. The sooner the better. You've got no idea who she's talked to. We need to get to her before he does." Iorrio motioned over to the answering machine.

Jackson started staring at the middle of the table. "We don't know where she's at. But we do know where he's at. If we get to him before he gets a hold of her then that's that."

"You can't think of where she'd be hiding?" asked Iorrio.

Jackson's head snapped around to give Iorrio a burning glare.

"All right, all right." He knew when to back off.

Evans sat at the table, his leg still pumping like a piston, his arms folded across his body. He would nervously turn and look to whoever was speaking at the time, but said nothing.

Daniels sat very still and said nothing as well. The expression on his face shifted from pain to pouting every so often.

"Let's get the gear and go get this guy. We owe him big time. Between White and Mendoza, we ought to make this guy suffer," Jackson said getting pumped up.

"We should take care of the daughter in front of him," Stone piped in.

The others just looked at Stone for a second or two. Daniels wondered why they put this sicko on the squad to begin with. It would figure that he was laid up with a few broken ribs and this kid was able to bring his sick ideas to the table.

"What? You don't think that would get him?" Stone asked, not seeing anything wrong with his suggestion.

"I'm not doing it," Evans finally spoke up. "I can't kill a kid. She ain't got anything to do with this," now shaking his head.

"What do you mean she's got nothing to do with this? She's with her old man who wasted White and Mendoza! Do you think she's gonna let us off her old man and say nothing?!" Stone was yelling at Evans.

Evans leg stopped pumping. "Fuck you, you piece of shit! I oughta take you by the neck and kick the shit out of you! You're the fucking newbie on this team! Why don't you shut your fucking mouth and just do what you're told!" Evans stood up abruptly, and kicked the chair out from underneath Stone causing him to fall to the ground.

Stone looked up at Evans who was now standing over him with his fists clenched. He then looked at the faces of the others. Iorrio was standing up, Jackson stayed seated, frustrated, with his face in his hands, and Daniels just started laughing despite the pain. That was when Stone decided he would kill Evans. Not here, not now, but someday when the opportunity was there.

"Evans, calm down, man!" Iorrio ordered.

Evans looked at Iorrio who was pointing at him. He slid his chair back over by the table and sat down not saying a word.

"Get off the floor kid and watch your mouth. We work together here. There's no reason to get like that." Iorrio lectured as he sat back down.

Stone picked the chair off the floor and sat back down.

"Are you all done fucking around?" Jackson asked muffled through his hands cupped over his face.

No one said anything. Then the answering machine started clicking. They all turned and looked at it puzzled. Then it played its message again.

"What's it doing?" Daniels asked

"Holy shit! She's checking her messages!" Stone yelled jumping up from his seat.

Jackson and Iorrio jumped from their seats as well and raced to the machine since they were closest to it.

"...I'm looking for Dawn" was the last words the machine uttered as Iorrio's fist came crashing down like a sledge hammer onto it. He then ripped it away from the wall.

"What do you think that means?" Evans asked, now reverting back to his nervous behavior.

"It means she knows Foster is looking for her." Jackson responded.

Evans shrugged his shoulders and shook his head not understanding what difference that made.

Jackson took a deep breath. "That means we have to find her before they find each other."

Darkness.

"What the ..." uttered Daniels.

"Shit! The power is out!" Stone cursed.

No one moved in the pitch-black apartment.

"Damn it! There's a flashlight on the end table. Evans, can you get it?" asked Jackson.

Evans slowly got up and felt for the couch behind him. He walked along it till he came to the edge. He found the flashlight and turned it on. The room was now dimly lit by the single flashlight. Stone got up and headed for his gear bag. On the way he bumped Daniels chair.

Daniels grit his teeth with a moan. "Watch what the fuck you're doing!"

"Sorry, it's dark," Stone said unsympathetically. He rummaged through his bag and came up with his tactical flashlight and clicked it on. Jackson and Iorrio went and retrieved their flashlights as well.

The wind started hammering the apartment. It roared as if a jet was taking off in the parking lot. Lynn's eye wall was pushing into Bradenton. The rain had increased ten-fold. There was really nothing to slow the winds of the category four hurricane as she crossed Sarasota Bay. The men, rustling through the darkened apartment, had no idea that they were trapped; at least they were if they wanted any chance of surviving the onslaught. It was not until they tried to leave that they realized how strong the storm had become.

"Holy shit!" grumbled Iorrio as it took everything he and Jackson had to close the apartment door.

"Well, I guess we're not going anywhere for awhile." Evans commented, plopping down onto the couch.

Jackson started inhaling deep breaths through his nose trying to relax. He was becoming quite frustrated; partly because of all that had happened and partly because his plans were not unfolding to his liking. He knew that the other members would view this as a sign of weakness. Especially Stone. It was obvious that the kid thought he was the shit, but he did not have the experience or the support to take control of the team from Jackson.

"We'll go after the storm passes," Jackson said sounding a little defeated.

"Why wait that long?" asked Stone.

Everyone looked to him for further explanation.

"After the first wall passes we should go while the eye passes over."

"That's insane," Jackson said shaking his head.

"Hold on T.J. Go on Stone," Iorrio said looking to Stone.

Jackson looked at Iorrio in shock again. Iorrio had always backed him. This was the second time today that he overrode Jackson to go with what this kid was saying.

"No one, I mean no one, will be going out during the eye," Stone continued. "The storm is pretty big and not moving really fast. The fisherman's place isn't that far from here. We could get over there, take care of the old man and his daughter and ride out the last wall at the fisherman's place."

"Hmm, not too bad an idea." Iorrio said rubbing his chin in thought. "What do you think T.J.?"

"I think it's insane. I ain't driving in no damn hurricane!"

103

"But it's perfect, you see? That's what everyone else will be thinking." Stone pleaded with Jackson. "You know how they tell everyone to stay in their homes because the next wave is still coming. Well? Everyone will be hunkered down waiting for the next wall to come through, including the old guy and his kid. I'm telling ya, we could make it over there and finish this before the next wall hits."

Jackson stood with his large dark arms crossed in front of his wide chest shaking his head.

"T.J., I think we should do it." Iorrio said walking up to him. "What if this guy hauls ass as soon as the storm calms down a little?"

"Who the fuck is in charge of this team?" Jackson asked loudly through clenched teeth. His jaw muscles flexed as he ground his teeth in anger.

Iorrio walked over and cautiously placed a hand on Jackson's shoulder. "You're in charge of the team, but we are a team. *We* need to make decisions."

Jackson looked down at Iorrio's large hand and followed his arm up to his cocked head. In his mind he was sizing Iorrio up. Iorrio was much larger than him, but he knew he could take him if he had to.

"I hate to admit it, but I think the kid is right too." said Daniels, cautiously shifting on the couch.

"Well? Evans?" Jackson asked in frustration.

Evans looked around at the faces of the other members. He looked at Iorrio who gave him a slight nod. "I guess it gives us our best chance."

Jackson threw his hands in the air. "Fine." And he turned and walked into the kitchen. Iorrio motioned for everyone to stay put and followed Jackson into the kitchen.

"Come on brother, you're leading this bad boy. Get in there and give assignments. So we went with the kid's idea, so what. It's only a small portion of what we need to do."

Jackson had his back to Iorrio. He was facing the counter leaning against it with his palms.

"T.J., come on, it's game time," Iorrio said again over his shoulder.

"All right. Let's get this thing done." And with that Jackson turned around and walked into the flashlight-lit living room. "Listen up, this is how it's gonna go down."

CHAPTER NINETEEN

In the middle of Jack's conversation with Dawn the phone went dead. All Jack really got was that she was staying at her aunt's house; the house on the river. Lynn's squalling winds had knocked out all power and almost all telecommunications. Capt. Tom's house fell right in the grid with having neither. Jack and Katelyn sat huddled in Capt. Tom's bedroom. The room was one of the rooms that had all the windows covered by the metal shutters.

Jack had gone looking through the house for anything that he thought they may need and found an old transistor radio. Jack hooked up a 9-volt battery he found in one of the kitchen draws and the little radio worked. He had also found a couple of flashlights, a deck of cards and, of course, a hurricane lamp.

Through the little radio they learned more of the ever-present Lynn. That's when Jack decided it was time to hunker down in the bedroom. The two sat at the foot of the bed, both with their legs folded. Jack sat with his hand in front of him watching Katelyn sift through her cards. She would pull one out and put it back in the order she preferred.

"It's your go," she said not looking up from her cards.

Jack drew a card from the top of the deck, looked at it, looked at his hand, and threw it down on the pile. Katelyn glanced down at the card and picked it up. She pulled a card out of her hand and threw it down on the pile.

Jack looked at his only child. He looked at her long brown hair as it lay around her shoulders. Katelyn had such a beautiful face and the flame from the lamp danced around it reminding Jack of camping in the Keys with her as a child. Her vibrant blue eyes always reminded Jack of the water. Jack felt the mixed emotions of pride and fear.

Jack was very proud of how his daughter had grown. She was such a delight to be around. Katelyn always had a way of fitting in, in any situation and never shied from being around Jack's friends. It seemed as though she was more comfortable with adults than her own peer group. She did not have the normal desires to go hanging out at the mall or going to the movies with her school friends. Instead she found it fascinating to spend time with adults. To learn from their experiences; always wanting to hear the stories they had to tell.

Not only had Katelyn grown psychologically, but she had grown physically, as well. This is what scared Jack the most. His experiences through work left him struggling to let go of her. She was well on her way to being a beautiful young lady. Jack saw her beauty as a double-edged sword. As easy as beauty can help one make it through life, it can also act like blood in the water for predators. Jack feared that Katelyn's looks would make her more of a target for the sick and twisted he dealt with his whole career. His work with the cold case unit only solidified his fears. There he got to truly study the evils that men do.

The case that cost him his marriage was one such case; an attractive young mother and her five-year-old daughter brutally murdered. The monster had watched her for some time, becoming more and more infatuated with her. His sick and twisted desires rose to boiling point the night he killed them. His overwhelming lust turned to rage when she spurned his advances. His desires for sex turned to rape; turned to murder when she tried to fight him off.

The darling little girl woke to find him brutally stabbing her Mommy. No witnesses, so he turned the knife on her.

"Come on, it's your turn again." Katelyn called to him.

Jack snapped back to the game, his heart pounding. "Uh, right." Jack looked at the card lying on the pile and picked it up with a grin. "That ought to do it. Thank you very much," he said with a wink and a smile and laid his hand down.

"I knew I shouldn't have thrown that one away," she said, her eyes darting back and forth from her hand to the pile.

A rumble off the back of the house made them both jump. They both sat and stared at the door. Jack put a finger up to his lips. Katelyn nodded. He slowly got to his knees and drew his gun. He motioned for Katelyn to go around the side of the bed. Jack then got to his feet, but stayed low. He went over to the door and listened. He could hear nothing but the roaring wind and the crackle of the little radio.

Jack reached up and turned the doorknob ever so slowly. He put the gun up into his line of sight. He pulled the door and it swung open at a nice even pace. From Jack's angle, he could see out the sliders on to the back porch. He looked with amazement as the wind had crippled the screen cage that surrounded Capt. Tom's pool. Now the wind had hold of it and was dragging it along the ground like a grave robber dragging along a corpse.

Jack was always fascinated with Mother Nature, but looking out those glass doors made him nervous. The wind and rain was rushing past the house like an avalanche. Then a metal deck chair came spinning into the picture and crashed through the slider shattering it. Jack jerked his head back as glass and rain came bursting into the house. The vertical blinds on the sliders flapped hysterically as the storm forced its way in. Jack quickly shut the door.

"What the hell was it?" Katelyn asked peering over the bed.

"The wind blew the pool cage down and a chair flew into the sliders. This is really bad." Jack said as he quickly looked around the room. He jogged over and began pushing a large dresser in front of the bedroom door. Katelyn came over and helped him as he struggled to move the large wooden dresser.

Just as the two had got the dresser in front of the door they heard more glass crashing. Cool damp air flowed under the bedroom door.

"What's going on?" Katelyn asked.

Jack could see the fear in Katelyn's eyes. "The hurricane is moving over the house, but we'll be OK," Jack said as he reached over and put a comforting hand on her shoulder. "Let's turn this thing so it's pinned between the door and the bed."

The dresser just fit. Then the sound of things banging into the wall was heard.

Katelyn crawled up on the bed "Dad, I'm really scared."

Jack got on the bed and gave her a hug. The two sat on the bed as crashes and bangs happened on the other side of the door. He rocked her back and forth and she began to cry.

"Shh, shh, shh. It's gonna be all right, sweetie."

Katelyn squeezed him tighter. Jack leaned a cheek on top of her head and stroked her hair.

'I won't ever let anything happen to you.' Jack thought as he squeezed her back. Katelyn was nearly as tall as him, but as they rocked together she was his little girl once again.

CHAPTER TWENTY

Captain Tom Underwood had become more attached to Ms. Dawn Peterson than any other female he had been in a relationship with. There was the obvious physical attraction to the young blonde siren. Her young tight skin curved at all the right places. Her wavy locks framed her round blue eyes, soft cheek bones, and full lips. But there was something else he felt for her that he did not feel for the others. It may have been the fact that Dawn made him feel young again. It may have been the fact that she was blasé about their relationship, which made Tom more intent in making her want him. It could have been that Tom had actually fallen in love with her.

Whatever it was, Tom was blinded by it. He had begun to slack off in his business that had so consumed him before. Any blank day in Tom's business planner he set aside in the off chance Dawn would want to do something with him. There were several days in which Tom could have, and probably should have, been on the water. But Tom didn't want to take a chance of not being available when Dawn wanted him. Tom had actually begun to shun the only woman that never let him down, the sea. So it was quite ironic that the last breath Tom took was nothing but saltwater.

Tom had decided that he could not be without Dawn. That he was what she needed and vice versa. So when he finally got up the gumption to go and confront Sergeant Terrence Jackson, he figured there was no better way for him to prove to Dawn how much she meant to him. And how much he was willing to risk for her.

Tom's biggest mistake was not thinking things through fully. For one, he did not heed the warnings that Dawn gave him. She tried time and time again to crack Tom's thick skull and get the idea that these people were very dangerous. Dangerous enough to kill him. Another mistake Tom made was thinking he was smarter than they were desperate.

When Tom contacted Jackson to meet him and discuss a business proposal, he thought that a nice seafood dinner and the threat of going public with the Cobra Squad's criminal enterprise would surely get Jackson's attention. What Tom did not know was Jackson was well aware of him. Jackson was already working on a plan to do away with the possible leak.

Quite frankly Jackson had no intention of killing Tom. The scenario Jackson saw in his head was more along the lines of a setup and black mail. But when Tom so forcibly put it to Jackson that he would no longer have anything to do with Dawn Peterson or he would report his actions to the sheriff and the press, Jackson's temper flared and quickly shifted the gears in his head. Tom Underwood would have to die.

Jackson actually did a very good job of acting concerned with the possibility of Tom's threat. Inside he was plotting the charter captain's death. He quickly decided that this would be Tom's last meal. Jackson excused himself to go to the bathroom where he called Daniels and quickly explained the situation. He told Daniels to come to the parking lot of the Anna Maria Oyster Bar and wait for him.

Once Jackson returned from the bathroom, he gave off the impression that he was defeated. Tom finished his meal quietly, but with a grin of victory. The more Jackson watched him, the more disgusted he became with him. And with every bite Tom took, Jackson became surer of Tom's end.

When the meal was over, Jackson walked with Tom into the darkened parking lot.

"You really must love that girl," Jackson asked, walking with his hands in his pockets scanning the cars for Daniels' truck.

"I really do," Tom answered in a boyish way.

Jackson rolled his eyes at the thought of anybody truly loving Dawn.

He considered her more of a possession. She was pretty and Jackson wore her on his arm like a piece of jewelry. Not many of the people Jackson associated with knew Dawn was a stripper and those who did, did not dare bring it up to Jackson. But that was what she was and Jackson did not think she would amount to much more.

"Well, I'm really glad we could come to an understanding," Tom said as he put out his hand.

Jackson looked at Tom's outreached hand for a couple of seconds and then took it and flashed Tom his winning smile. Tom was a bit mesmerized with how perfect Jackson's smile was. Jackson gripped his hand quite firmly. In fact, too firm for Tom's liking. And when he tried to pull his hand back, Jackson did not let go. That is when the look of concern washed over Tom's face.

"Is this the guy?" Daniels' asked from behind Tom.

Tom turned quick with a jerk as Jackson released his grip. He saw Daniels walking up to him. As Daniels did, he lifted his shirt revealing his gun and with the other hand put a finger to his lips warning Tom to be quiet. Tom's jaw dropped. It was then that Tom realized he had not fully thought this through.

Jackson put his arm around Tom's shoulders and squeezed him tightly, "This is one of my partners, Tom."

Tom turned his head and looked at Jackson who was now smiling at Daniels. He became frozen in fear and when Jackson tried to direct him toward Daniels' truck, Tom stumbled and almost fell. Jackson squeezed his arm even tighter around Tom, stopping him from falling to the ground. The extent of Jackson's strength was then recognized by Tom so he did not think to run. Fear kept him from screaming. For sure they were just trying to scare him. It was definitely working.

When they got to the truck, Daniel's opened the back door of the quad-cab truck and motioned Tom to get in. He turned and looked back toward the entrance to the restaurant to see people coming and going, but none of them looked his way. Tom got into the truck without a word or resistance.

"You like boats, right?" Jackson asked as he turned from the passenger seat to look at Tom who was staring out the window; no answer.

"Daniels here has a real nice one. We're gonna go for a little ride."

Tom turned to look at Jackson. His face was expressionless. Daniels gave a snicker as he looked at Tom in the rearview mirror. And that was when Tom realized this was way more then a scare.

Tom started taking in slow deep breaths trying to calm his pounding heart. "Listen, you don't have to do this. I have plenty of money. We can work something out." he began pleading.

"How much money?" Jackson asked. He really did not care, but he figured he would string Tom along to the last minute.

"I… I… don't know. But I'm sure I can work out a deal," Tom now hoping that he had changed Jackson's mind.

Jackson did not respond and just turned around in his seat.

"Please!" Tom begged leaning forward and putting his hand on Jackson's shoulder.

"Get your hand off of me," Jackson said in a very cold tone staring forward.

"You don't have to do this!" Tom's hand still on Jackson's shoulder.

"I said, get your hand off my shoulder," this time slow and deliberate.

Daniels whipped out his gun and stuck it to Tom's head "He said get off, asshole!"

Tom shot back into the seat. His face was ugly with fear as he looked down the barrel of the gun. He began to tremble.

They arrived at the 59th street ramp. The trucks lights revealed another man holding a 24-foot Mako walk-around in the ramp. No one else was around. As the men got out of the truck a breeze rustled by. Tom stopped and looked to the deep purple sky.

"Come on, let's go," Daniels ordered as he grabbed Tom by the elbow.

Tom jerked his arm away in defiance, but started walking as he saw Jackson coming over to them.

Iorrio stood at the ramp with a foot on the starboard side of the boat. "Are we ready to go?" he asked.

Jackson looked to Tom "Probably not, but we'll go anyway."

The men loaded into the boat. Tom, Jackson, and Iorrio climbed into the small cabin while Daniels fired up the engine. No one spoke a word.

Oddly enough, as the men were making there way out of the channel into the Manatee River, they passed Brian Richards who was returning from hitting the lighted docks for Snook. Brian gave a friendly wave and Daniels returned it with a devious grin. Richards shrugged his shoulders and continued in.

Daniels killed the engine and dropped the anchor about three miles out of the mouth of the river. The boat canted slightly back and forth in the mild chop. There they ordered Tom to the stern of the boat at gun point. Daniels held a small revolver in his line of sight and cocked the hammer. He turned his head and looked back at Jackson who gave a nod.

Tom catching the nod put his hands up in front of him, but it made no difference to the full metal jacket rounds that exited Daniels' gun and entered Tom's chest cavity. Daniels double tapped, putting the two shots four inches apart in his frame. Tom stumbled backwards and flipped over the transom, hitting his head on the outboard. His body went immediately into shock causing him to pass out. As he lay in the water face down, he took his last breath filling his lungs with the salty brine. His body convulsed as it sank down into the ebony soup.

The three men stepped to the back of the boat and watched Tom's body fade away.

"Well, that's that," Daniels said and tossed the revolver into the water.

It was a dead low tide that Tom fell into and as the waters rose, the currents swept his body into Terra Ceia Bay. When the gasses began to develop in Tom's rotting corpse, he floated to the top and finally came to rest in the very mangroves where he had made his living.

This was actually the first time that the Cobra Squad had committed murder. Through the unit's term of corruption, it was responsible for deaths, but none committed by any member of the Cobra Squad. There were many beatings resulting in hospital stays and some maiming, but no deaths. Time to time, the unit leaked information that resulted in someone's death. And of those deaths, there were times when the information was false; but no member of the unit had actually pulled the trigger.

After Tom's fatal boat ride, the three members went to the dead man's house to make sure there was nothing that the fisherman may have left lying around that may indicate them as the ones responsible for his murder. There was nothing. Tom had really gone off the cuff when the idea of confronting Jackson developed in his love-sick head. This made discovering Tom's killer a matter of luck or for someone to talk. Unbelievably, Tom's soul had both going for it.

All members of the Cobra Squad seemed to agree with the termination of the fisherman. All but Evans. Evans' distaste for crack heads, gang bangers, and whores was well known amongst the team members, as well as some of his personal acquaintances. Evans did not mind in the least robbing these people or kicking them when they were down. After all, they were either scum of the earth or so stupid they did not have a right to anything. That is what everyone on the team thought. But the killing of Tom Underwood left a bad taste in Evans' mouth.

In one sense, Evans could relate to the middle-aged fisherman. He himself was single and lonely. He had caught himself ogling the beautiful blonde girlfriend of Jackson's. But what made Evans really not like the idea at all was the fact that Tom Underwood was not a crack head, or a gang banger, or a whore. Tom Underwood was a tax paying, working citizen. Those were not the people that the team took advantage of, let alone kill. Evans found himself wondering what separated them from the others.

CHAPTER TWENTY ONE

Deputy Matt Darby sat barricaded in his home with his wife and two sons. He sat alone in his little den flipping his attention from his department radio to the LCD weather station that sounded off with a series of beeps as updates became available. The weather station was gift from his wife that she bought at one of the gadget stores in the Brandon Mall. He had pretty much shunned his wife and kids since the storm had begun. Darby was pretty much the asshole everyone thought he was, even to his own family.

Scattered around him in his small room were charts and graphs. Maps of the North Atlantic Basin, with waves of red, orange, and yellow, hung on the walls. Stacks of reports produced by the Tropical Prediction Center/National Hurricane Center were piled on the desk.

Darby had boarded up his house a few days before the storm actually hit. He told everyone that they were going to get hammered by the storm. And he was actually right. But for Darby that wasn't enough. No one had come out and said "Yep, you were right!" Again Darby failed to get the recognition he wanted. In actuality people were saying that very thing, but they weren't going to say it to Darby. No one really wanted to talk to him.

115

As he sat there pissed off at the world, his wife and young sons sat in the living room playing Shoots and Ladders. Another opportunity to be a husband and father wasted by Darby. No one really could understand why his wife stayed with him. She was sweet and pleasant, but she also had very low self-esteem. She continued to put up with Darby because she didn't think she could do better or deserved better.

So, when her husband came bounding into the living room and said he had to go out, she really wasn't completely surprised.

"In the middle of the storm?" she asked confused.

"Police work. I keep telling you, I'm on call," he lied.

"Uh, well, be careful then."

He left without saying a word.

Why did Darby leave in such haste, in such a bad storm; a storm that he had been tracking from the very beginning? Because, as he sat there in his little den, someone spoke to him. That someone was the dispatcher over his department radio. He didn't actually call out to Darby, but the message that was relayed was music to his ears. The call came out that there was a Signal 7 at the home of Jack Foster. Because of the sustained winds being over 45 miles per hour, no department vehicles were to be on the roads, so no one could respond. No one but Darby, who looked at this opportunity as a chance to finally get the glory he so desperately desired. It was also a chance at being responsible for burying Jack Foster.

He always knew Jack was nothing but trouble. What were the odds that Jack found a dead guy that he knew yesterday and now had a dead guy in his house and not be responsible? Darby thought that Foster had finally flipped his lid and started killing people. Maybe things were getting too slow in the cold case section so Jack decided to start a few cases of his own. That had to be it. And now was Darby's chance to solve a couple murder cases of his own and put that smart ass Foster away. Darby was still mad about feeling like a fool for losing his lunch from the smell of the rotting flesh of Foster's so-called friend.

As Darby loaded himself in his Dodge Ram 2500, the winds were ripping at 55 miles per hour. The big black truck rocked side to side as Darby pulled out of the driveway. Darby's ego told him that the wind couldn't hurt his big truck, so he continued on his way to Jack Foster's house. Darby's belief that he knew what Hurricane Lynn was all about enhanced his bulletproof mindset so he didn't think twice about heading further into the storm.

Brian Richards sat impatiently in Jack's home. He was advised by the 911 operator to stay at the house until a deputy got there. What had been twenty minutes felt like an hour of waiting. He elected not to call Amy back in hopes that good news might come his way. Brian continued petting the attention-starved Bear. He had found a Dr. Pepper in the fridge and a Little Debbie Swiss cake in the cupboard and was snacking on them when loud banging came at the front door.

"Sheriff's Office, open up!" Darby commanded.

Bear jumped down and scurried under the couch. Jason put his drink down on the coffee table, got up and walked over to the door. He looked through the peep hole and saw Darby trying to stay upright in the wind. He unlocked the door and pushed, but the door didn't want to budge. Brian put his shoulder into it and it started to come open. Darby reached his hands around the door and pulled. As the door opened the rain rushed in, showering Brian. Between the two of them, Darby was able to slip in the door. Once in, the wind slammed the door shut.

"Where's the Signal 7?" Darby asked looking around the darkened house.

Brian looked at the dripping wet Darby a little confused, "Where's the what? Who are you?" he said as he wiped his face.

Darby, a couple of inches taller than Brian, looked down at him "I'm Deputy Darby and I asked you where the body is." Darby was becoming frustrated.

"All right, no need to be a dick about it. It's not like I killed him," Brian said as he pointed toward the hallway.

Darby just looked at him with distain. "What's your name?" he asked through clenched teeth.

Brain said his name ever so slow, pausing between his first and last name.

Darby made a mental note of the name. He would be sure to deal with him later, but for now he had to catch Jack Foster. He gave Brian a slow nod and proceeded down the hall.

"You've gone too far. It's the first one on the right," said Brian as grabbed his drink and plopped back down on the couch.

The flickering flame of candles behind him, Darby stood in the hallway looking at the glinting shell casings scattered throughout. He pulled a little flashlight out of his pocket, turned it on and shone it down the hall. He saw the splintered doorframe leading into Jack's room. This was not what he expected. His mouth hung slightly open and he squinted as he inspected the carnage that took place. He turned and headed to the office door.

The door knob turned with a squeak. Darby saw the lifeless form of Mendoza lying on the floor, face up in the dark room. Darby was confused; he saw the submachine gun next to him. Slowly he came to the realization that the dead man was a cop by the way he was dressed and the choice of firearm. He stood over Mendoza's body shining the light on his face. There was a deep crater about the size of a nickel just below his left cheekbone. The two trails of blood coming out of his nose tied into the one that was coming out of the crater. Both of Mendoza's eyes were set in blue-black flesh and the right one looked like a glass fireball from all the capillaries bursting; both gazed at the ceiling. Mendoza looked vaguely familiar, but he couldn't place him.

Darby was not keen on dead people; one reason he never wanted to work homicide. He could feel his stomach turning the longer he was in the room with Mendoza's body. But by now Darby was fully intrigued as to why there was a dead cop in Jack's home. It was obvious that there was a shoot out, but why would there be a raid on Jack, and why would they leave one behind? Darby had to know who the dead man was. He crouched down and pulled on Mendoza's waist toward him, turning the body onto its side. He tried to ignore the soft spot on the backside of Mendoza's head that was matted in blood clots and gray matter. Darby reached over and felt around for a wallet in the back pocket. Nothing. Now he turned Mendoza's body onto the other side and could see the bulge of a wallet.

As Darby pulled the wallet out of the pocket, Mendoza let out a breath, wheezing and gurgling. Startled, Darby fell back dropping Mendoza onto his back once more. Darby sat for a second waiting to see if Mendoza would move, but he did not. Slowly, Darby got onto his hands and knees and crawled over to Mendoza. He leaned over him and looked into his constant blank gaze. Darby blew into Mendoza's face. Nothing.

"Death rattle," Darby said in a whisper as chills ran up his spine and over his shoulders. Darby had heard the term from other officers who had dealt with dead people. From Darby's shifting of Mendoza's body, the last breath Mendoza took crept from his lungs and into the room.

Darby stood up and held his flashlight in his teeth as he opened the wallet to learn the identity of the dead man and confirmed his theory that Mendoza was a cop. Darby squinted in thought as he tried to recall what section Mendoza worked in, but nothing came to mind. Darby's mind began to race as now; he wasn't so sure what he had gotten himself into. Then his eyes shot wide open as he remembered hearing about a deputy being killed earlier.

"So what's the deal?"

Darby jumped and dropped the wallet at the sound of Brian's voice. "Holy shit!" Darby barked.

"Relax; I just want to know what I'm supposed to do? The storm is getting worse and I, for one, did not think I'd be spending the day held up with a dead guy." Brian said as he motioned toward Mendoza's body with his chin.

Darby bent over and picked up the wallet. "Well, I guess we don't have much choice in the matter, do we?" he said as he brushed past Brian in the door way.

Brian stood in the doorway with his head hung down. He could not believe what bad luck he was having. He was trying to be a nice guy and some how he wound up tangled in this mess. He reached over and pulled the door shut, not looking at Mendoza's body.

Darby was pacing in the living room. He had not the slightest idea what to do. He wondered if he should notify Dispatch that the Signal 7 was a cop. But then, what was he doing at the scene. He had to figure this out and he had to do it fast. Darby figured the only way he was going to figure this out was to figure out where Jack was.

"Hey, Richards, right?"

Brian nodded.

"Why are you here?"

"Jack's ex-wife called and asked if I'd come check on him and his daughter."

Darby looked at him concerned "Daughter? What are you talking about?"

"Jack's daughter, Katelyn, is staying with him for a couple of weeks."

"Holy shit!" Darby said as he started pacing again. "How old is she?"

Brian looked at him confused "I don't know, fourteen, fifteen?"

"You're a friend of Foster, right?"

He nodded again, now looking at Darby sideways.

"Listen, I think he and his daughter might be in trouble and I need you to help me find them," Darby said sitting down on the couch.

Brian took in a deep breath "What do I have to do?" he asked wearily.

CHAPTER TWENTY TWO

```
ZCZC MIATCPAT2 ALL
TTAA00 KNHC DDHHMM
BULLETIN
HURRICANE LYNN INTERMEDIATE ADVISORY NUMBER 25B
NWS TPC/NATIONAL HURRICANE CENTER MIAMI FL
1 PM CDT SUN AUG 20 2006


...POTENTIALLY CATASTROPHIC HURRICANE LYNN BEGINNING
TO TURN
        EASTWARD   INLAND   ON   WEST   CENTRAL   FLORIDA
COAST...

AT 1 PM CDT...0700Z...THE CENTER OF HURRICANE LYNN
WAS
LOCATED NEAR LATITUDE 27.3 NORTH...LONGITUDE 82.9
WEST.
```

LYNN IS NOW MOVING TOWARD THE NORTH NEAR 14 MPH.
THIS MOTION IS FORECAST TO CONTINUE TODAY WITH A
GRADUAL INCREASE IN FORWARD
SPEED. A TURN TOWARD THE NORTH-NORTHEAST IS EXPECTED
LATER TONIGHT AND ON MONDAY. ON THE FORECAST TRACK
THE CENTER OF THE HURRICANE WILL BE VERY NEAR THE
EAST COAST OF FLORIDA LATER THIS EVENING.
HOWEVER...CONDITIONS ARE GRADUALLY DETERIORATING
ALONG CENTRAL AND NORTHER PORTIONS OF FLORIDA...AND
WILL CONTINUE TO WORSEN THROUGHOUT THE DAY.

MAXIMUM SUSTAINED WINDS ARE NEAR 135 MPH WITH HIGHER
GUSTS.
LYNN IS NOW A CATEGORY FOUR HURRICANE ON THE
SAFFIR-SIMPSON SCALE. SOME FLUCTUATIONS IN STRENGTH
ARE LIKELY AS LYNN CONTINUES TO TRAVEL ACROSS THE
STATE.

LYNN REMAINS A VERY LARGE HURRICANE. HURRICANE
FORCE WINDS EXTEND OUTWARD UP TO 105 MILES FROM
THE CENTER...AND TROPICAL STORM FORCE WINDS EXTEND
OUTWARD UP TO 230 MILES. DURING THE PAST HOUR...A
WIND GUST TO 83 MPH WAS REPORTED FROM A UNIVERSITY OF
SOUTHERN MISSISSIPPI BUOY LOCATED JUST EAST OF THE
CHANDELEUR ISLANDS...A GUST TO 75 MPH WAS REPORTED
AT GRAND ISLE LOUISIANA...AND A WIND GUST TO 60 MPH
WAS REPORTED IN NEW ORLEANS.

THE MINIMUM CENTRAL PRESSURE RECENTLY REPORTED BY
AN AIR FORCE
RESERVE UNIT RECONNAISSANCE AIRCRAFT WAS 952
MB...28.11 INCHES.

COASTAL STORM SURGE FLOODING OF 18 TO 22 FEET ABOVE
NORMAL TIDE
LEVELS...LOCALLY AS HIGH AS 28 FEET...ALONG WITH
LARGE AND DANGEROUS BATTERING WAVES...CAN BE
EXPECTED NEAR AND TO THE EAST OF WHERE THE CENTER
MAKES LANDFALL.

REPEATING THE 1 PM CDT POSITION...27.3 N...82.9 W. MOVEMENT
TOWARD...NORTH NEAR 14 MPH. MAXIMUM SUSTAINED
WINDS...135 MPH. MINIMUM CENTRAL PRESSURE...952
MB.

THE NEXT ADVISORY WILL BE ISSUED BY THE NATIONAL
HURRICANE CENTER
AT 4 PM CDT.

FORECASTER THOMPSON

Lynn's eye wall was now passing over Bradenton. Like those storms before her, she laid down anything she could. The destruction was unbelievable. It was as though Lynn was a child throwing a major fit. She would kick over trees and power lines. She threw debris into homes, boats, and cars. She would peel off a roof and throw it at a neighbor's home.

And Lynn showed no prejudices. She attacked everything and everyone the same, even taking out half of Oneco Elementary, a designated shelter. Not a soul left in Manatee County was not scared and praying that Lynn would leave them alone. It did not appear those prayers would be answered anytime soon.

Jack and Katelyn remained huddled together on the bed for what seemed like an eternity. The sound. The sound of the wind was almost deafening. It was a constant roar in the background. The bedroom door rattled in its frame as the wind tried to rush past it. Jack was amazed that the dresser seemed to be holding it in place. Every so often you could hear a crash or a loud bang as things were hurled against the house.

Jack was amazed that the room was actually holding up to the onslaught of the storm when water started to stream down from the ceiling. Together they watched as the drywall of the ceiling in the corner of the room began to sag as water pooled on it. Huddled next to Katelyn, he hoped and prayed with every fiber of his being that nothing would happen to her. In his head he found himself bargaining with God. 'Take me, not her, if you have to!' he pleaded. Then the ceiling ruptured causing water and insulation to dump onto the floor with a splash.

Katelyn continued her clench on her dad. She had wrapped her arms around his body and was locked on. She remained quiet, for the most part, only releasing a whimper at the sound of a crash or a boom. Though, at this point, while this was the most terrifying event of her young life, she truly believed that her dad would not let anything happen to her. He had always protected her and comforted her in her times of need. And no doubt he would do it now.

"Are you all right?" Jack attempted to yell over the wind.

Katelyn, whose head was pressed against Jack's chest, looked up to her father and gave a slight nod. Jack leaned in again and kissed her head and looked over to the hurricane lamp sitting on the large dresser. Its flame danced wildly, but still remained lit. The house had been breeched by the winds and rain and the bedroom door clattered in its frame as the wind swished by it. Jack expected it to come flying off the hinges at any moment. Still the door held, being braced by dresser, which was braced by the bed, which was braced by the wall.

He found himself wondering, and hoping, that Dawn Peterson was all right. Even with all the destruction that was going on around them, Jack was still working on the puzzle in his head. After talking to Dawn, Jack now had an idea for the motive to kill Capt. Tom, but he was not sure why they were coming after him. Maybe they suspected that Tom had told him something. Either way, they were out to get him and Jack was going to see to it that he figured this out before they had another chance. His best bet was Dawn.

Their short conversation was enough to convince Jack that he was heading in the right direction. Now knowing that it was the Cobra Squad, Jack hoped that he still had friends in the sheriff's office; namely David Roberts. He figured that if he could get Dawn to Roberts, then the tide would turn in his favor. Now it was a matter of riding out this God-forsaken storm and then getting out of there and over to Dawn's.

Dawn looked at the dead cell phone for a few seconds. She was not quite sure she had done the right thing. She was not sure whom she could trust, but she was at a breaking point; it was now or never. Either T.J. was going to get her or she was going to get away. Doing nothing just gave her time to over think everything and grow to trust even less.

But now there was something to distract Dawn's thoughts. Lynn's eye wall had begun to knock on dear Aunt Gloria's house. The old house creaked as if its walls were going to topple over at any moment.

She followed the candlelight glow back into the living room. Her aunt was still humming and knitting as she rocked back and forth. Dawn stood in front of the couch as if she was going to sit down, but slowly looked around the room as if expecting it to collapse on top of her. There was a slight haze of smoke. Dawn looked at the fireplace, puzzled as the flames hissed at her.

Dawn looked around frantically, and then ran into the kitchen. She came back with the kettle from the stove and doused what was left of the man-made log and quickly closed the flume. Doing so stopped the wind and ran from forcing their way down the chimney.

"Sit down, dear," Her aunt said in a pleasant tone.

Dawn looked at her with her face scrunched up with confusion. "Are you sure we are safe here," she asked as she took a seat, still surveying the room.

"Oh, this old house has been through so much. You know, if these walls could talk?" Aunt Gloria said with her eyebrows raised.

Dawn looked at her with curiosity "Well, what would they say Aunt Gloria?"

"I'm sure they would tell the stories of all the close calls. You know, the storms, the earthquakes, the volcanoes," she responded focusing on the knitting needles.

"What? Aunt Gloria, did you say earthquakes and volcanoes?"

"Oh, yes, dear. There was the earthquake that knocked all my good china out of the cabinets. And then Mount Saint Helens erupted not too far from here," she said still focusing on the knitting.

Dawn was bewildered. She leaned forward to get a better look at her aunt. Through her squinted eyes she saw that her aunt was gone; her mind was elsewhere. Dawn rested her elbows on her knees, cupped her face in her hands and quietly began to cry. She felt so alone.

"Don't worry, honey, Albert will be here soon."

Dawn pulled her hands down from her face "Uncle Albert?" she asked after a sniffle.

"Yes, of course, who else? I'm making this scarf for him." She paused and gave a big smile. "I've been waiting for him for a long time now," she said as she went back to knitting.

"What does that mean?" Dawn asked in almost a whisper. Her gaze changed from shock to fear. Uncle Albert, now dead for eight years, was coming to visit or was it that they were going to visit him?

Aunt Gloria looked to the candles sitting on the mantle "I've missed him so, my dear," now her voice quivering.

Dawn wiped away her tears and looked into her aunt's eyes. She could see the reflection of the cavorting candle flame in her eyes welling up with tears. A tear ran over her eyelid and ran down her wrinkled and weathered check.

Dawn got up and walked over to her, knelt down beside her and took hold of her hands. She looked up to her "Aunt Gloria, I need you," a tear now running down Dawn's face.

"I know honey, but I need to be with Albert again," she responded, never looking away from the tiny flames.

Dawn's head dropped and then there was a thunderous crash down the hall that caused the house to tremble. Dawn jerked her head around and looked down the almost pitch-black hall. "What the hell was that?"

"I wouldn't worry about it, probably just the wind." And with that Aunt Gloria pulled her hands back and started knitting again.

Dawn got up and walked over to the mantle and picked up a large candle. She looked over her shoulder at her aunt and headed down the hall. Her aunt continued knitting and humming as if nothing had happened.

As she made it down the hall and to the door at the end of it, she heard cracking. She slowly opened the door to discover one of the massive oaks surrounding the old house had toppled over and landed on the roof. The weight of the grand oak had caused the exposed beams in the ceiling to snap and the roof was coming down. Water streamed down from the folded ceiling and soaked into the mattress of the bed in the middle of the room.

Dawn stood staring, not sure what, if anything, to do. Blankly she closed the door and stood in the hallway. Her mind began to race. Pictures in her mind of all the recent events that had taken place in her life left her thinking the end was surely near. Everything was crumbling down around her. She had no one left here. Her only hope was a man she had never met before. And that was if Jack Foster could survive the storm as well, let alone survive T.J. and his gang.

She leaned against the wall and slid down until she was sitting with her knees in her chest. She blew out the candle, wrapped her arms around her knees, and began to cry.

CHAPTER TWENTY THREE

The weather forecasters were doing a very good job of tracking Lynn's movement and relaying conditions, as well as the probable effects the hurricane might produce. Where they got it wrong was predicting storm surge.

As Lynn traveled north along the gulf coast her churning winds actually pulled seawater away from the coast. This coupled with a low tide made the water height minimal when Lynn finally turned inward and made landfall. To the dismay of the fanatical surfers who waited with a hunger to shred killer waves, the actual storm surge was nothing more than rough surf of six to eight feet.

As the Cobra Squad prepared for the tactical hunt they were about to begin, Lynn's eye moved over Bradenton and, like Stone predicted, the rain and wind ceased. Jackson pulled a flash-bang out of his duffle bag. He eyeballed the cylinder as the pin dangled from it. The device was something he managed to pick off during a cross-training day with the SWAT team.

Jackson never used it since: one, he was not authorized nor trained to, and two, an investigation into such use might lead to someone snooping into the Cobra Squad's other activities. But this occasion was one in which everyone would be focusing on the hurricane.

He stuffed it in the cargo pocket on his pants and ordered everyone to finish up. The men gathered their gear and moved to the front door without saying a word.

Iorrio was first at the door and looked back to Jackson who was standing behind him. Jackson gave a nod and Iorrio opened the door. Daniels sat at the kitchen table with his back to the door. He was playing solitaire and acted as if he was all alone.

The men exited the second-story town home and stood on the landing in amazement. The pine trees that stood in all the landscape islands had been snapped and toppled over, some landing on parked vehicles. One van was on its side. One of the end units of the complex roof was peeled off and lying in the parking lot. Luckily for the Cobra Squad, their vehicles remained mostly unharmed though Iorrio's 1997 30th Anniversary Edition Camaro SS had a nice dent in its hood from a branch.

"Ah, fuck! Look at my car!" Iorrio yelled.

"Take a look around, you're lucky that's all that happened to it," said Evans.

"We're waste'n time. Let's go!" Jackson ordered as he made his way down the stairs. "Me and Iorrio in one vehicle and you two in another."

Stone, the last one coming down the stairs, stared at the back of Evans head, "I'll drive."

Evans looked back at Stone over his shoulder and shrugged, "Whatever."

Iorrio instinctively went to his car. He shook his head as he examined the dent and other scratches and dings. He unlocked the doors with his keyless entry, opened his door and tossed his bag in the back. Jackson, on the passenger side did the same thing.

Stone walked over to Daniels truck and unlocked it.

"What are you doing? That's Daniels' truck!"

Stone looked over at Evans "Well, he ain't use'n it and we might need a truck to haul stuff away."

"Does he know you're use'n it?" Evans asked standing in front of the truck.

"Like I said, he ain't use'n it and we may need it."

Jackson rolled the window down "Let's go, ladies! You're waste'n more time and I ain't gonna get caught in this fuck'n storm!"

Evans looked to Jackson and was about to say something when Jackson told him to just get in.

Contrary to Stone's beliefs, the Cobra Squad would not be the only ones trying to take advantage of the subdued weather inside the hurricane's eye. Jack was on the same page and figured it was the best time to go to Dawn Peterson's aunt's house.

Jack and Katelyn moved the dresser out of the way to discover that the house was a wreck. Wind and rain had come through the shattered sliding glass doors. Furniture was knocked over and moved around. The carpet squished with water under their steps.

With the black business planner in hand and Katelyn behind, Jack opened the front door. Once out, Jack could not believe his eyes. Oak trees lay on their sides with roots in the air. Every pine tree was snapped like a toothpick. In the distance they could see the gray wall of wind, rain, and destruction churning in the background. Jack turned toward the Jeep only to discover it was on its side and pushed up against the house. A good portion of the tiles were missing from Capt. Tom's roof

"Shit," Jack whispered to himself.

"What do we do, Dad?"

Jack surveyed the neighborhood. No other vehicles to be found. He lowered his head, closed his eyes and began to think.

"Dad?" Katelyn asked as she moved around in front of him. "Dad?"

Jack put his hand up motioning her to wait. Then he looked up at her. "The boat!" And with that he took off running to the back of the house.

Katelyn took off after him "Dad, what are you talking about?"

Jack ran over to the davits and looked upon the submerged boat. The poling platform, the cowling, and the console were all that stuck out of the water. Jack walked over and hit the controls to lift the boat. Nothing.

"I need power," he mumbled looking around.

"Dad, how are going to use a boat that's underwater?" Katelyn asked, chasing her father around.

"Kat, we need power to lift the boat. We got to do it fast," Jack said as he ran back into the house through the broken slider. He ran over to and in the garage. It was very dark. He ran out and into the bedroom where he retrieved a flashlight and went back into the garage. Jack was praying he would find a generator and he did. He looked around, grabbed an extension cord and headed back toward the boat. Once out there he discovered the generator had no gas.

"Kat, take this flashlight and go find some gas in the garage. Hurry!"

Katelyn ran into the house. Jack pulled out his knife and tore through the cable coming out of the control box. Then he cut the plug end off the extension cord and began to splice the two together.

"Dad, all I found was an empty gas can," she yelled from the slider.

"Are you sure that's all there is?"

Katelyn held the empty five-gallon can up and nodded her head.

"All right," Jack called back to her.

Jack finished with the splice and plugged the extension cord into the generator. He stood up and took the empty gas can from Katelyn. 'What the hell was he going to do with this?' Jack thought and shook his head. Then he looked up and around the back of the house. There he spotted a garden hose strung out along the house still attached to the spigot. He took off running for the hose.

The Camaro was speeding down US 41 ahead of the pick-up truck when it came to a submerged portion of the road. Iorrio slowed down and cautiously entered the water.

Stone, who had been chasing Iorrio and Jackson, finally caught up. He was extremely mad. He felt as if Iorrio and Jackson were racing him and Evans to the old fisherman's house. As he approached the Camaro, he went around, honked the horn and flipped Iorrio and Jackson the bird. He then proceeded down the road leaving a wake.

"What the hell was that?" Evans asked.

"Relax. I'm just giving them a taste of their own medicine. Besides we'll get there and take care of this."

"I don't think T.J wants us going in until we're all together."

"He didn't think that way when he sent Daniels and Mendoza."

"And look what happened."

Stone gripped the steering wheel tighter. He could not stand the thought of Evans being right or at least Evans thinking he was right. But he was not going to push the issue. He would just wait till they got there and then go from there.

Jack ripped through the hose with ease and then again. With the length of hose in hand and the gas can in the other, Jack was sprinting around the house to the turned-over Jeep. In continuous motion Jack dropped the hose and can, planted his hands on the Jeep and pulled himself up onto it. He grabbed and spun the gas cap off.

"Hand me the hose," he ordered Katelyn, just then catching up to him.

Katelyn, trying to control her breathing handed over the hose, which Jack stuffed down into the gas tank.

"Watch out, sweetie." And with that Jack leaped from the Jeep, grabbed the other end of the hose, placed in his mouth and inhaled.

The hose wriggled around as the gas came up and then down. Jack pulled away and spit gas from his mouth, and jammed the flowing hose into the can. Gasoline got into the gash on Jack's hand and burned. He squeezed his fist as if he was squeezing out the gas and the pain.

Iorrio's Camaro was slow moving through the flooded street and he and Jackson wondered if the car would make it. But it did and they were on their way. Jackson was furious with Stone. If anything, he should have stopped and they all could have loaded up in the truck. Jackson feared they would get caught in the hurricane.

Once on higher ground, Iorrio opened the fine-tuned Chevy small-block and they took off with a roar. It would only be a matter of minutes before the two caught up to Stone and Evans barring any other bumps, or in this case, dips, in the road.

The can now full, Jack and Katelyn raced back to the generator. Jack dumped gas into it until it came flowing back at him. With three strong pulls, the generator kicked up and started rumbling. Jack ran over to the control box and attempted to raise the boat once more.

The winches began to wind with a laborious moan, but the boat did not rise fast enough. Her decks were just now breaking the surface. Jack stopped the winches, turned and ran back into the house.

He found himself in the garage once more scurrying around. He found an old five-gallon bucket and sprinted back to Katelyn and the boat.

"Here, honey, I need you to take this, hop down into the boat and start throw'n the water out."

Katelyn took hold of the bucket and looked down at the submerged boat. She did not want to climb into the boat, but she knew she had to. Her dad would not ask her otherwise.

"How do I get down there? Do you want me to just jump into the water?" she asked as she stood on the edge of the seawall.

Jack looked. It was only a couple of feet down, but he did not want

Katelyn jumping and falling or slipping. He went and sat on the seawall's edge. "Come, Kat," he instructed as he pat the concrete next to him. She came and sat down next to him.

"You got a hold of that bucket?"

She responded with a nod. And with that Jack turn and slipped his hands under her arms, lifted her weight, turned back around, and set her feet on the gunnel; all in one swift motion. Jack got back to his feet and up to the controls.

Katelyn stood on the gunnel and looked toward her dad in awe. Her mind flashed back to when she was four or five and her dad would pick her up under the arms and throw her up into the air. That was the last time she could remember her dad doing that. She could not believe that he still could, though really he could not. Jack had it in him to hold her weight, but his little girl had grown too big for him to toss in the air.

"Kat, the water! Start shovel'n that water out!" he yelled as he ran back into the house to get the battery.

The big truck had proven to be the right choice of transportation. Stone and Evans were making very good time. And given that Capt. Tom's house was only twenty minutes away, they would have no problem getting there since there were no traffic lights and no traffic to speak of.

"You ready to do this?" Stone asked as he focused on the road.

"I told you, Jackson said that we go at this all together."

"I know what Jackson said, but we might not have any choice. If they're stuck, then we can't wait for them. We'll have to do it. We can't get caught in the storm," Stone replied as he looked at the gray off in the distance.

Evans pondered what Stone had said for a few seconds. "If we have to, then we have to. Otherwise, we wait for T.J. and Joe."

It had only been a couple of minutes, and Katelyn was exhausted, but she continued to dunk the bucket and dump the water over. It was working. The boat lifted out of the water slowly, but steadily and now the only water that remained was in the hull.

Jack stopped the winches, ran over, picked up the boat battery and set it on the seawall. He slid onto the boat, turned and grabbed the battery. He quickly hooked up the battery and the bilge pump kicked on. Water poured out the side of the boat and Jack climbed back onto the seawall. He turned and put a hand out to Katelyn to help her up and out. Then he went straight to the controls and started hoisting the boat once again until the transom drain was exposed.

For the first time in a long time Jackson had a bad feeling about the mission he was embarking upon. He was not sure if it was the storm that scared him or the fact that he knew so little about the target he was after. Jack Foster had proven to be more than they thought he was. He studied Iorrio's face to see if he felt at all concerned with what they were doing. All Jackson saw was frustration on Iorrio's face from speeding to every puddle and slowing down to go through them.

Iorrio was growing more furious with Stone every time he had to slow to a crawl to get through the flooded streets. Not to mention how that little punk had disrespected him.

The boat was out of the water, but still draining. Jack looked at his watch and figured the whole thing took them somewhere between ten and fifteen minutes. He was not sure how much water was still left in her hull and he was not sure if putting the plug in and running with whatever water there was left in the hull or waiting would give them more time.

Luckily the water coming out of the bilge started sputtering. Jack looked to the back of the boat and saw that the water was slowing down to a trickle. Jack spun around and started looking on the floors for the drain plug franticly.

"What are you looking for?" Katelyn asked.

"The plug! Where the hell is the plug?" Jack asked scurrying around.

"Here! Here! I have it! I didn't want to lose it," Katelyn said as she pulled the plug out of her pocket.

Jack reached up, snatched it from her hand, slid on his stomach across the back deck, and stuck the plug in.

"Come on get in!"

As Katelyn got into the boat, Jack got out. He hit the controls to lower the boat back into the water. As the boat was descending Jack hopped back onto the boat once again.

As Stone and Evans came upon the house, Stone saw Jack getting into the boat.

"Holy shit! There they are!" Stone yelled pointing to the back of the house.

"Fuck!" Evans exclaimed looking in the mirror for Jackson and Iorrio. Nothing.

"Get ready." Stone announced.

And with that, Stone jerked the wheel and aimed the truck toward Jack and Katelyn. The truck hit the curb and the front end went airborne, rocking Stone and Evans in the cab. The front came down and bounced, and then the back hit and up it came. Stone fought to maintain control of the careening truck.

The ground was soft and soaked. When the truck finally connected all four tires it began to spin as Stone continued to press on the accelerator. Grass and mud flew everywhere. Stone tried to correct the truck, but over-corrected and sent the truck sliding sideways until it came to an abrupt halt as it slammed into the side of Capt. Tom's house.

Stone slammed into the driver door and was dazed for a second or two. He fumbled to release his seatbelt.

"Go! Go get them!" he yelled at Evans as he searched for the release.

As the boat settled back into the water Jack was priming the motor and did not see the truck coming. The roar of the generator drowned out the sound of the out-of-control truck. As Jack sat up, he saw the truck slam into the side of the house.

"Get this thing started!" he yelled to Katelyn as he pulled his gun from the small of his back.

Katelyn looked over her dad's shoulder and saw the front of the truck beside the house. She slid over and started cranking and choking the motor.

Evans instinctively popped his seatbelt and slid out of the truck. He drew his gun and scooted down along the truck. When he peaked around the front-end he saw Jack with his gun up on sight. Evans jerked his head back. *Where the fuck are T.J. and Joe?*

Evans backed up to the passenger door and then moved out to the side of the truck trying to get a better angle on his target. The generator started sputtering and then died. Evans could hear the boat motor cranking. He took a deep breath, crept out a little further and started yelling.

Jack tried to use the seawall as cover as best he could and he tried to keep himself in-between Katelyn and the gunman. He kept switching his aim from the front of the truck to underneath the truck. 'Come on, you piece of shit, start!' he thought. Then he saw the gunman just to the outside of the truck.

"Sheriff's Office! Drop your gun! Drop your gun!" Evans yelled as he held Jack in his line of sight.

The motor shimmied as Katelyn continued to crank on the motor.

Evans slowly went down to one knee "Drop your gun! Don't make me shoot you!"

Jack held steady on Evans not saying a word. Then the motor started.

CHAPTER TWENTY FOUR

Brian Richards had done some crazy things in his life. There was the time that, on a dare, he hit on a girl in a bar who was sitting with her boyfriend. The boyfriend, who was easily twice his size, bruised more than his ego. One week later at the bar, the same girl came over and gave Brian her phone number. Or there was the time that he was fishing from the Skyway Fishing pier when a friend came by in a boat. Brian took a 15-foot plunge into the rushing water to get onboard. That day he caught his biggest Snook to date. Yes, he had done some pretty crazy things, but always seemed to land on his feet. This time he didn't feel so sure. Going out in the middle of this storm was just a little too crazy even for him.

Deputy Matt Darby had convinced Richards that they needed to act and act fast before something bad happened to Jack and his daughter. Truth was, Darby originally did not really care what happened to Jack. But now there was more to it. For one, there was now a girl involved and for two, Darby smelled crooked cops. This was his chance to prove to everyone that he was a top cop. Darby was trying to figure out what the next move was as he drove to nowhere specific.

Brian surveyed the passing sights in awe. He could not believe his eyes. Homes were left with their roofs peeled off like sardine cans. Trees toppled over and trash was everywhere. Brian could not help but think that there was still more of this to come, since the other side of the storm was still stampeding this way. 'What the hell am I doing out in the middle of this?' he wondered.

"So tell me again why we are not under water?" Brian asked staring out the passenger window.

"You remember Hurricane Charley that struck Charlotte Harbor in 2004? There wasn't much in the way of storm surge then, either. The reason was the path that Charley took. It came in and ran along the state before turning in and smacking the coast."

Out of Darby's peripheral vision he could see Brian looking at him confused. "Tropical cyclones north of the equator churn counterclockwise."

"Tropical cyclones?" Brian asked shaking his head.

"A hurricane is a tropical cyclone. Listen, as Charley ran north along the coast, the winds pulled the water away from shore. So when Charley abruptly turned into the state, the water was pulled away.

"Now, when Katrina slammed into southern Louisiana, her last leg was pretty much straight up the Gulf of Mexico. But this time, as Katrina traveled north, the counter-clockwise winds pulled water from the Gulf and pushed it ahead of the storm. All that water was just corralled in front of Katrina and when her right front quadrant passed over the west and central coasts of Mississippi, there was a storm surge of twenty-seven feet."

Brian's eyebrows rose "I thought you were a cop?"

"I am; hurricanes are a hobby."

"One heck of a hobby ya got there," Brian said nodding his head.

"I gotta get a hold of the department," Darby mumbled after trying his cell phone with no success.

"Why don't you call in on your radio? It's still working."

Darby looked down to the radio as it crackled with emergency codes being bantered back and forth.

Brian looked over at Darby confused, "Hello. Pick it up and call in."

Darby snapped his attention to Brian with a scowl on his face, "Who do you think is in charge here? That's right, me!"

Darby leaned over and picked up the radio. He tapped the antenna on his chin as he stared out the window.

Brian let out a sigh, pulled his cap off and ran his hands over his scalp.

Darby keyed the radio, it beeped. "I.D. number 897 to dispatch." he said.

A pause over the air.

"Go ahead 897," came a male voice over the radio.

"Can I get an operator on channel B7?"

"10-26."

Darby waited a couple of seconds then switched his radio frequency. "897 to dispatch."

"This is Jeff; go ahead Deputy Darby."

"Hey, I need to know what unit Deputy Pedro Mendoza is in."

"Do you have his I.D. number?"

Darby grabbed the wallet sitting on the center console and flipped it open, "Uhh... let... me... see what... I got." Darby pulled out a bunch of cards and fumbled through them as he pinched the radio between his knees and continued to drive. "Uh, no, it doesn't appear that I do," Darby finished.

"All right, I'll have to do some checking. It might take a couple of minutes. We are pretty busy handling calls dealing with the storm. Will you remain on this channel?"

Darby keyed the radio once more "No I'll be back on A1 again."

"Of course, I'll get you over there when I find out."

Darby switched the channel back and the rambling of emergency codes continued over the radio.

Brian looked over at Darby "Was that dead guy in Jack's house a cop?"

Darby took in a deep breath. He kept his focus on the road.

"Hey, was that guy a cop?" he demanded as he shifted in his seat.

"Yes," Darby replied, deadpan, and still focused on the road.

Brian ripped the cap from his head "Holy shit! Holy shit! What the hell is going on here?"

"I'm not exactly sure."

"Well, what the fuck? Do you think Jack killed that cop?" Brian asked turning in the seat to face him.

Darby didn't answer.

"Do you think that cop was trying to kill them?"

Darby was about to respond when he heard his I.D. number called over the radio. "Go for 897."

"897, switch to channel B7."

Darby twisted a knob on the radio. "897 to dispatch."

"Deputy Darby, Deputy Mendoza is assigned to the Cobra Unit."

Darby grimaced "10-26."

Brian squinted his eyes and shook his head "What is that supposed to mean?"

Darby whipped off to the side of the road and began rubbing his temples. Then he held his hands out and slowly raised his head. Darby's eyes were wide as he stared straight ahead. The synapses in Darby's head had just connected the murder of Deputy White earlier and the slain body of Mendoza. He was pretty sure that White was assigned to the Cobra Unit as well. But why was the unit after Jack?

"Well, what are we doing?" Brian barked.

Darby waved his hand at him telling him to be quiet; then he snatched up his radio and switched to the main frequency. "897; Dispatch," he said stepping all over the other traffic.

"Go ahead 897," came back the same operator, a hint of frustration in his tone.

Darby, not missing a beat, "Go to B7."

"10-4."

Darby quickly changed channels "Jeff, you there?"

"Uh, yeah," said the operator, a bit shocked Darby remembered his name.

"Who's in charge of the Cobra Unit?"

"Standby."

Brian looked out to the looming conditions "So what is it…"

Darby threw his hand up again "Come on, come on," he mumbled.

"Dep. Darby?"

"Go ahead."

"That would be Sergeant Terrance Jackson."

"Do you have an address for him?"

Darby scratched down the address, started the truck, and looked around to get his bearing. As the squealing truck took off Brian gripped the door and the dashboard.

"Here's the deal, I think the Cobra Unit may have kidnapped Foster and his kid."

"Why?"

"I don't know, but I think they tried to get them and Foster got one or two before they took them."

Brian braced for impact as Darby rammed the standing water covering the streets "What do ya mean 'or two'?" I only saw one dead guy.

"It's complicated," Darby said as he unlatched the glove box. Do

138

you know how to use one of these?"

Brian looked at the handgun Darby was holding in front of him. His heart started beating harder and he swallowed hard as he tried to choke down his nerves.

"Well?" Darby yelled.

"Do you really think it's gonna be necessary for me to use that?"

"Do you wanna save Jack or not?" Darby said as he shook the gun in front of him.

Slowly, Brian reached up and took the revolver from his grasp. The gun felt heavy to him.

"It's simple; just point and squeeze the trigger."

"I know how to shoot. I just don't like the idea of being in a shoot-out with cops."

Darby's head bobbed slightly in agreement. If ever there was a time that Darby's hermit-like existence in the department came back to haunt him, it was now. There wasn't a fellow deputy Darby felt he could contact to help him take on the Cobra Unit.

CHAPTER TWENTY FIVE

Everything seemed as if it was moving in slow-motion for Evans. His mind was rapidly trying to process everything happening around him.

He knelt on the rain soaked ground. His knee was cold from the water soaked into his pants. Out of his peripheral vision he could see Stone popping the seatbelt loose. Evans continued to yell commands at Jack, but it all sounded muffled to him as though someone else was yelling. Quickly he focused on Jack, then on the head of the person behind Jack.

He saw the cloud of two-stroke puff out of the engine as it started up. His mind, flipping through options, paused on shooting the operator of the boat. Could he get the shot? Yes, he could. He bore down on his target.

Evans' adjustment from Jack to Katelyn was so slight Jack could not notice.

As Evans' mind flipped from shoot, don't shoot, Katelyn turned and looked back over her dad's shoulder at him. In tenths of a second, Evans saw her young face. He saw a tear rolling down her check. The sun peering down the cylinder caught and gave a glistening to the tear.

Evans' mind raced again. He could hear his own voice "I can't kill a kid. She ain't got anything to do with this," it played back for him.

Evans lowered the gun and Jack yelled for Katelyn to go. She throttled up raising the bow. Instinctively she trimmed the boat out and put it on a plane in the channel. Jack continued to aim toward the truck. Then he saw the gunman fall over.

Stone having finally released his seatbelt slid out the truck. He saw and heard Evans yelling orders. As his feet were hitting the ground he heard the outboard motor fire up. He looked to Evans and saw him lower his gun.

Stone peeked over the hood of the truck and saw the bow of the boat lift and pull away. Stone looked back at Evans, raised his gun and shot him in the head. Evans' body slumped over then fell. Stone quickly turned and brought his gun over the hood of the truck and fired at the fleeing boat.

Jack saw the gunman fall over then saw another fire from over the hood of the truck. Jack returned fire shooting out a headlight and landing two more shots in the windshield beside Stone's head. Stone ducked quickly, his heart pounding in his chest. He could hear the outboard moving off into the distance.

Stone ground his teeth and felt the side of his head. There was a large bump from where his head smacked the window. He looked upon Evans' still body with a wry smile. Then he heard Iorrio's car coming down the road. Stone got back on his feet and headed to the road.

Jackson and Iorrio came rumbling down the road. As they approached the house they saw Stone on the side of the road waving his gun in the air. Then they saw the truck up against the side of the house. As the car came to a stop, Jackson saw Evans' body lying on the ground.

"What the fuck happened? Where are they?" Jackson yelled as he undid his seatbelt.

Stone leaned into the window "He was behind the house; they were getting on the boat. He pretty much ambushed us. He got Evans."

"Holy shit!" Iorrio yelled, slamming his fist into the steering wheel.

Jackson opened the door and got out "So they got away? Where the fuck are they going?" He looked over Stone's shoulder at Evans' body and shook his head.

Iorrio stood up and looked over the roof of the car "So now what?"

"I figure we got two options: head into the house and try to ride the rest of the storm out, or get in there, figure out where the hell they're going, and get there," Stone said as he looked upon the battered home. "Either way we got to get in that house. If we find something right away then we'll go; if not, we got to ride this thing out."

Jackson walked over to Evans' crumpled body, the bullet hole on the side of his head. "So much for your brilliant fucking plan! Jackson turned and barked at Stone.

"It was a great plan! How was I supposed to know that he would be heading out in the storm?" Stone yelled back at Jackson.

"You fucking idiot! Evans is dead, because you couldn't wait for us!" Jackson said now marching up to Stone.

Stone gripped the gun still in his hand. He wondered if he could kill Jackson and turn and get Iorrio before he got him.

"Come on, come on!" Iorrio yelled as he came around the car. "Even if we got here at the same time you don't know that Evans wouldn't have gotten it. The kid said it was an ambush."

Jackson stopped just shy of Stone. His hands balled into fists made the strands of muscles in his arms flex. He was grinding his perfect white teeth. Jackson, toe-to-toe with Stone, looked into his eyes. He was right on the edge of smashing Stone, but what he saw or did not see caught him by surprise. No fear. Stone showed no fear in the face of Jackson's furious figure. His gaze strolled down Stone's arm and saw the clinched sidearm. He snapped his focus back on Stone's face only to see a wry smile coming across his face.

"Enough! We're not getting anything done by having a face-off out here." said Iorrio, looking around to see if any of the surrounding houses were occupied by gawkers. "Let's get in the house and find out where the hell they're going!"

Stone looked up and around at the swirling gray, "We better get moving." He watched for any movement from Jackson through his peripheral vision.

"Fine," Jackson huffed through his clenched teeth as he turned and headed to pick up Evans' body.

Stone looked down at the ground, shook his head with a smile and holstered his gun. Iorrio walked over and helped Jackson lift the body of another dead Cobra Squad member.

They carried Evans' body into the house and rested him on the floor of Capt. Tom's living room. Stone followed them in and immediately began searching the ramshackle house for some clue of Jack and Katelyn's destination.

The skiff's outboard thundered as it made its way out of the channel and into Sarasota Bay. Jack tapped Katelyn on the leg, motioned for her to slide over, and then took over control of the bouncing boat.

Jack trimmed the boat out even finer and the slight porpoising effect faded away. The powerful outboard pushed the skiff with ease. Jack had fished from Capt. Tom's boat in the past and often rolled his eyes when Capt. Tom bragged about the massive power jetting off the transom. But now Jack was extremely happy with Capt. Tom's need for speed.

Speeding across to the bay they could see more of the destruction done by Lynn's first wall. Bay-front homes lay in carnage. The vast majority of trees that lined the coasts were laid low by the grueling winds that they stood before.

The conditions of Sarasota Bay resembled a child's shaken snow globe and the surface was littered with all kinds of debris, including a door that Jack had to use evasive maneuvering to avoid. The water itself looked more like pea soup from the bottom being churned, compared to the pristine salt-flats that were there before. Jack could not help but wonder what long-term effects the storm would have on his beloved pastime, not to mention his way of life.

The devastation made it difficult for Jack to navigate by sight. Most of the visual markers in his mind were left mangled and unrecognizable; especially at the speed they were traveling.

So when "Long Bar", a massive sandbar that practically ran the width of the bay came right up on them, to say Jack was caught a little off guard, was an understatement.

The sandbar hid under the murky waters like a predator waiting on passing prey. And as the skiff came by it reached out and grabbed hold of the 200 horses bolted to the transom. The churning propeller that so easily cut through the pea soup found it much more difficult the cut through the sandy bottom. The boat jerked and sputtered as it skipped across the lip of the sandbar. The outboard kicked up with a deafening whining pitch, a bang, and died.

Jack, without hesitation, slid off the side of the boat and into the water. "Raise the motor!" he yelled. Sloshing through the water, he shuffled his feet, around to the back of the boat. He braced himself against the polling platform and pushed. The boat gave way a little and slowly crept across the sandy bottom. The skiff probably drafted fourteen inches and the water was probably the same depth.

Katelyn turned to watch her father fighting against the skiff. Behind him she could see the spinning gray mass of Lynn's eye wall. Her heart pounded. Anxiety started to slither through her veins. Quickly she leapt to her feet. "Dad, what can I do?"

His legs pumping like pistons, Jack looked like a lineman working against a tackling dummy. He looked up and around. "Go stand… on the very tip… of the bow," he uttered between breaths.

Katelyn stepped on the gunnel and walked down to the bow. There she planted her heels together on the very tip of the bow. Her hundred and fifteen pounds were barely enough to see-saw the skiff an inch, but it was enough of a clearance to allow the skiff to float instead of drag.

Jack was running with all his might and soon the skiff traveled the twenty yards of shallow water. As the skiff started to drift on her on, Jack pulled himself up with the platform and planted a knee on the deck. "Kat, let's roll!"

She jogged back along the gunnel and plopped down beside him. He lowered the motor and fired it up once more. Steadily and firmly he pushed the throttle. Jack focused on the water, but could not help see Lynn moving before them. He hoped and prayed that the storm would not get between them and the Manatee River. He was pretty sure if they could beat the storm to the river, they would make it to Dawn Peterson.

CHAPTER TWENTY SIX

As Darby pulled into the parking lot of the apartment complex, he scanned for any signs of activity. There were a few people who were peeking from barely-opened doors at the destruction in the parking lot, as well as at the surrounding apartments. Having found Jackson's apartment, he parked a few spots down from it.

The seconds ticked on like minutes. Finally Brian blurted out, "So what are we doing? I mean are we doing this or not?"

Darby took a deep breath and let it out slowly. "Look, I'm gonna go up there. You stay here. If something happens to me, drive straight to the sheriff's office." Darby's gaze fixed on Terrence Jackson's door the whole time.

Brian nodded and, with that, Darby popped open the door and strolled over to the staircase leading to the apartment. Darby stood there with a hand on each rail and a foot on the first step looking at the door.

Darby was focused on the task at hand. He seemed to be oblivious to the increasing wind and rain. In his mind he ran through the three possible scenarios he thought could unfold:

First was, Darby goes up, knocks on the door, and no one is there; second was, he goes up knocks on the door and finds Jackson and his crew, but no Foster or his kid -- he was too late to save them; and last was, he goes and finds them getting ready to off Foster and the kid.

Scenarios one and two, Darby walks away. Scenario three he might walk away or he might not. He reached up and rubbed his chest; no vest. In his haste to be the hero, he never thought things could unfold like this.

For the first time in his life, Darby thought about his wife and kids before he did something. What would they do if he was to get killed? He wondered if they would actually miss him. Faced with the life or death situation, Darby began to see himself for what he really was. A friend to no one, not even his own family. Everything he did was out of selfishness. Darby gritted his teeth and shook his head; 'not this time', he thought as he started up the stairs two at a time. He drew out his Glock and held it down by his side. Another deep breath. His hand balled into a fist, he hammered it against the door three times; nothing. He did it again, this time calling for Jackson; no response again.

Adrenalin coursed through his body causing him to shake. He turned and stood in front of the door and grasped his gun in both hands. Darby drew back his foot and kicked the door with all his might.

Daniels, who was hell bent on not answering the door, almost fell out of his chair as the front door flew open closely followed by Darby who had his gun up in his line of sight. A quick sweep and Darby focused on Daniels.

"Get on the ground! Get on the ground!" Darby screamed as he ran up on Daniels.

Daniels eyes were huge as Darby's gun was inches away from his face. He held one hand on his ribs and put the other up trying to shield his face.

"I said get on the ground!" Darby yelled again.

"I can't! I can't! My ribs are broken!"

Darby took one hand off his gun and grabbed the hand Daniels' was using as a shield, spun him out of the chair and onto the ground.

"Holy shit, you fucking asshole! Ahhh! I told you my ribs are broke!" Daniels screamed in pain as he flopped on the floor.

With one arm pinned behind Daniels' back, Darby holstered his weapon and grabbed a pair of handcuffs from an ankle holster. He cinched one around his wrist and ordered Daniels to put the other behind his back.

Daniels complied with a grimace as he put his hand behind his back. Tears were welling up in his eyes from the pain.

With the click of the handcuffs, Darby drew his gun again and stood up.

Brian sat with his mouth hanging open as he saw Darby kick in the door and rush in. Quickly he slid over into the driver seat, never taking his eyes off the front door.

"Oh, man! Oh, man!" he whispered as his leg pumped nervously.

He was slowly inching closer to the ignition when he saw Darby in the doorway waving for him to come up. Brian snatched the revolver off the passenger seat and sprinted to the apartment. There he found Darby sitting Daniels up in his chair at the kitchen table. Playing cards were strewn about.

"So where are they?" Brian asked as he frantically looked around.

"Not here and neither is the rest of the gang. Where are they?" Darby asked turning his attention to Daniels.

Daniels sat there stiff as a tear rolled down his check "I don't know what you're talking about," he said through clenched teeth.

Brian squinted as he looked at Daniels. Something was familiar about him, but he wasn't sure what.

"Listen, asshole, I don't have time to fuck with you, so tell me where Foster and the kid are at."

"Go fuck yourself," Daniels said with a grin.

As Jason walked over it clicked. "I remember now. I saw you a couple of nights ago head'n out of 59th."

Darby looked to Brian, "You know him?"

"No, I just remember come'n in a couple nights back. He was headed out in a walk-around. I gave him the old friendly wave and he just gave me that shitty grin."

Daniels face was scrunched up as he looked at Brian. Then his eyes widened as he realized that Brian must have seen them taking Tom Underwood out for his final ride.

Darby caught the change of expression "What the fuck are you all up to?"

"Look, I'm a cop and you two are going to be in a world of shit."

"Yeah, so am I, asshole. Now tell me where the fuck they took Foster and the kid." Darby said, now inches away from his face.

"If you're a cop, then you know that you bust'n in here is illegal."

"So's killing innocent people," Darby said as he poked Daniels in the ribs.

"What the fuck are you doing?" Daniels growled; spit falling out of his mouth.

"Tell me where they are," Darby ordered again jabbing his fingers into his ribs.

Daniels' scream ended abruptly as it hurt too much to continue. His breathing quickened with short breaths, but Daniels still did not answer.

"That's fine, it's only going to get worse for you," Darby said as he made a fist and drew back.

Daniels jaw muscles flexed as he clinched his teeth "All right, all right! They're at Tom Underwood's house."

Brian was looking out the front door at the looming storm. "Captain Tom Underwood?" he asked with a snap of his head.

Darby stood up straight and looked to Brian as if the name meant something.

Brian caught the look, "Tom was murdered a couple of days ago."

Darby slowly turned and looked down at Daniels "You guys are the ones who killed Foster's friend."

Daniels sat there with his head hung focusing on making the pain stop and ignored Darby.

"How do we get to Underwood's house?" Darby yelled at Daniels.

"I know how to get there," Brian chimed in.

Darby turned back towards Daniels and kicked his chair over backwards. Daniels' eyes were huge as he braced for impact. Once the chair landed with a thud, Daniels moaned.

"Don't go anywhere," Darby said as he grabbed Brian's arm and headed out of the apartment.

CHAPTER TWENTY SEVEN

As Jack and Katelyn motored the skiff out of the channel and into the bay, three of the remaining four members of the Cobra Squad made their way into the ramshackle home of the former Capt. Tom. Each scrambled about the house looking for something; what, they weren't exactly sure of. They now found themselves in the same predicament that Jack and Katelyn were in earlier.

Iorrio was kicking around the kitchen when he spied a black book lying next to the generator in the backyard. He quickly came around the counter and darted out the shattered opening in the sliders. Shards of glass cracked and popped under the weight of his heavy steps. Iorrio snatched the binder off the wet ground and headed back into the house.

"Guys, check this out!" Iorrio yelled calling over Jackson and Stone from scavenging.

The two came up to Iorrio who was just opening Capt. Tom's business planner. As he unfolded the binder the first thing they saw was one of a stack of aerial photos. The top one had a house circled on it.

Jackson held it up to get a better look at the picture. As he did, light from outside allowed writing on the back to show through. Jackson turned it over to see a familiar name and phone number. "This is where they're going," he said.

"Where the hell is it?" Stone asked flipping through the rest of the photos.

"Palmetto," Iorrio said looking over Jackson's shoulder at the photo.

"Exactly!" Jackson said with a nod.

"How do you know that?" Stone asked tossing the photos and the planner on top of the kitchen counter.

"This is the Green Bridge, which leads into Palmetto," Jackson said pointing to the photo. "We've used these before for raids. That way we know what's around the target house."

"Well, let's get the fuck outta here!" Stone said heading toward the front door.

Jackson folded the photo and put it in his pocket. "Can we use that truck? We'll never make it there in the Camaro."

Stone shrugged "I don't know, but we can find out."

"You want me to leave my car?" Iorrio asked as he grabbed Jackson's elbow.

"Get your head outta your ass, Joe! There's no way your car can get us there with the streets flooded. We'll probably be lucky to make it before the fucking storm as is," Jackson scolded as he followed Stone out.

Iorrio stood with his fists clenched. He could feel the blood throbbing in his temples. He grinded his teeth back and forth as he watched Jackson head out the door. It was all his fault; Jackson and his fucking whore. Why did he care about her? He could have almost any girl. Sure she was pretty, but there were lots of pretty girls. They would not be out in this storm, risking his prized car, and probably ending his career if were not for Jackson and this stupid girl.

Thunder rolled off in the distance. Iorrio took a deep breath and looked toward the ceiling. But that was neither here nor there. It was time to put an end to this whole ordeal. Iorrio started to the door when Jackson called to him, then he started jogging.

Outside Iorrio found that Stone had managed to get the truck off the side of the house and on the road. He smirked when he saw the damage to the truck. *Daniels is gonna have his ass when he sees that.* He jogged around to the other side of the truck, pulled the door open and hopped in.

"You ready?" Jackson asked, looking at Iorrio over his shoulder. He held up his fist toward Iorrio.

Iorrio smiled. "Let's get this done," he said as he tapped Jackson's fist with his own.

"That's what I wanted to hear," said Jackson.

Stone rolled his eyes as he threw the truck into drive and mashed the gas peddle. With the wheels squealing the men took off down the road in a race against man as well as nature.

Jack and Katelyn were speeding along when it dawned on Jack that he needed to get ready to figure out where exactly it was they were going. With the skiff still at full throttle, he started glancing around for Capt. Tom's business planner.

He leaned into Katelyn. "Where is the black book?" he asked over the roar of the engine.

She looked to him confused at first, then raised her eyebrows and shook her head. Jack sat up and focused straight ahead. Katelyn looked at him. She could see the muscles in his jaw flexing as Jack clenched his teeth.

As the two flew out of Anna Maria Sound and into Tampa Bay, they could see the water was becoming rougher as the winds were picking up. The Skyway Bridge, which was usually a reliable marker, was engulfed in the gray mass of wind and rain and unable to be seen. The skiff handled the chop very well. Jack knew that this would be the roughest part of the water since there was no land between them and the Gulf of Mexico to help with the battering winds or break up the chop.

The three-foot swells were tight enough for Jack to keep the hammer down on the boat to skip across the top of the water. Soon they were in the mouth of the Manatee River, which was considerably calmer; from three-foot chop to two-foot chop.

Now it was up to Jack to probe his memory and come up with the location of the house on the river. He knew it was near the Green Bridge, so he kept the boat wide open till they got close.

Time was of the essence. Wind and rain were steadily picking up as Lynn's watchful eye continued upon her path over them. Soon the second wall of destruction would be bearing down on them.

Jack never closed his eyes. He scrutinized the houses along the north shoreline of the river. His mind cross-referenced everything he saw with the image of the aerial photo in his head. What made it so difficult was the devastation that lined the banks of the river.

As they got closer to the bridge, Jack eased up on the motor and they continued to idle down the river. As the boat raised and lowered in the chop, the exhaust of motor would make a blubbering sound as it sank into the water. Quickly Jack pieced together the parts of the picture that remained. Houses, trees, and sheds were all parts of the puzzle. His mind put the trees back up again next to the homes. He looked at roof lines to find which ones matched the image in his head. Then he saw it, the old house. It had a large oak toppled over on top of part of it. It was one house in from the river.

Jack counted off houses from the bridge until he came to the old house. He was sure this was it. In his head he saw the top of the large oak standing tall next to the roof of the old home as it appeared on the photo.

He looked around for a place to land the boat, but there was nothing but large coral rocks lining the shore as a seawall. A couple hundred yards down from where Jack had hoped to land the boat was a long dock. He looked up to the gray sky. Conditions were worsening by the minute as the back wall of Lynn's eye closed in on them. Jack had to make a decision: land the boat on the sharp rocks and ascend them, or hit the dock and race back to the house.

Jack's initial decision was to chance the rocks, but as he closed in on them the crashing waves made the bow bob up and down. He knew he could time the lift of the bow and just crash on top of the jagged coral, sealing the fate of the boat for sure. At this stage of the game, that was of little concern to him. More importantly to Jack was the fact that the transom still hanging in the water would cause the boat to pitch up and down making their assault on the shore line awfully difficult.

Jack quickly reversed the motor and backed away from the riprap causing swells to crash into and over the transom. Katelyn looked around confused by her father's actions. She jumped up as to not get soaked from the foaming saltwater rolling over the back of the boat.

"What are you doing? Where are we going?" Katelyn asked as she walked around to the front of the console.

Jack spun the wheel and popped the boat forward again. "Water is too rough to try and climb those sharp rocks. We'd get all cut up. I'm gonna shoot over to that dock and we'll have to run back to the house. Hold on." And with that Jack jammed the throttle, sending the boat rocketing across the tossing chop.

CHAPTER TWENTY EIGHT

Nothing it seemed was going to slow down Darby now. The euphoria of survival had him charging forward. That coupled with the feeling he was about to solve his first big case. The fact that it was not an assigned case was irrelevant. He knew if he could save Jack and the girl that everyone would think he was a hero. His whole life he waited for this moment.

Brian could sense the energy from Darby. He too was excited with the idea of finding and saving Jack and Katelyn. The ease of storming the cop's apartment had left him a little fooled about how dangerous the whole thing was. Things only seemed to be getting easier and, as long as they continued down that path, what could go wrong?

"When we get to Pearl you want to take a left," Brian said. He lifted his cap and ran his hand over his stubbly-shaved head then pulled the cap snug.

Darby responded with head bobbing when something down the road caught his attention. He squinted and leaned forward and saw a vehicle pull off a road ahead. As they came to a small bridge, the vehicle was driving over it. Darby noticed the vehicle was damaged and didn't think much of it

153

since almost everything they encountered had some sort of damage. As the two trucks passed, what did catch Darby's eye were the two bullet holes in the windshield.

"Oh, shit, I think that was them!" Darby said as his head jerked from the mirror to the road.

Brian's eyes were wide and he held his hands in the air "Were Jack and Katelyn with them?"

"I couldn't tell, but I don't think so."

"What does that mean? What do we do?"

Darby ground his teeth and squeezed the steering wheel. "How close is this place?"

"It's right down the road there," Brian said as he pointed.

Darby jammed down the accelerator as they came off the little bridge and turned the wheel. The truck leaned heavily and Brian braced himself.

"All right which one is it?"

"A couple down on the left," Brian's tone had turned solemn.

Darby jammed the breaks and the truck skidded to a stop inches away from the Camaro parked out front.

Brian's seatbelt dug into him as it locked. Before he could get his hands off the dashboard Darby was unbuckled, sliding out the truck and off in a jog toward the house. Brian looked around not sure what to do. He undid his seatbelt and ran out of the truck.

Darby held his gun in front as he rounded the tossed Jeep to the front door. His gun held up, Darby yelled, "Foster! Foster are you in here?" as he made his way into the destroyed house. There he saw a body on the floor with a curtain laid over it. "Oh, shit," he whispered as he lowered his gun.

"Jack! Katelyn!" Brian yelled as he appeared at the front door.

Darby was knelt down by the body "Wait there; don't come in!" he yelled as he held a hand up to Brian.

He froze as he saw the form on the floor.

Darby slowly lifted the curtain to see Evans. He scrunched his face up at the sight of Evans' mangled head then dropped the curtain and leaped up. "It's not him," Darby said as he began franticly looking around. He took off down the hallway yelling for Jack and Katelyn.

Brian closed his eyes and let out the breath he had been holding; his temples throbbed as his heart beat furiously. He opened his eyes and took in a deep breath. "Jack! Katelyn!" he yelled as he ran into the master bedroom.

"Nothing over here!" Darby yelled as he reentered the living room.

"Nothing in here either," Brain said as he emerged from the

bedroom.

"Damn it, they gotta be in that truck!" Darby said as he took off running toward the door.

The rain was coming down as the two ran for the truck. There was a strobe of lightening instantly followed by the sharp crack and boom of thunder making them both duck as they ran. They jumped in and before Brian could get buckled, the truck was started and in reverse. Darby jammed the brakes and turned the wheel causing the truck to spin around 180. As it came to a stop, Darby dropped into drive and jammed the gas. Brian did all he could do to hang on and buckled up as they sped down the road.

It struck Jackson odd that another truck was out running around in the storm, but his focus quickly changed to Stone's driving. He continuously rammed the large truck into the water flooding the street sending large waves over the hood and into the windshield. He would flip the wipers on high speed sloshing the sheet of water off the windshield and keep pushing on.

Jackson put his hand up in an attempt to stop the water from spurting on him from the bullet holes. Stone was quite aware that the weather was getting worse once more. Knowing that they had to go over the Green Bridge, even Stone, in his crazed mind, did not want to chance the grueling winds of Lynn up on a bridge.

Jackson kept on him about slowing down and being more careful, but Stone did not listen. With each passing minute, Stone's stability faded away. He was becoming consumed on finishing the task at hand: killing Jack and Katelyn.

There was always something about Stone that people could never put there finger on. He was definitely intelligent enough and possessed plenty of physical skills. But he had an odd, dark sense of humor. Being in his mid-twenties, many of his older peers just chalked it up to a maturity thing.

Daniel Stone was a spindly pre-teen that was tormented by overprotective parents and teenage bullies. His escape was through an extremely overactive imagination. Not uncommon for a boy his age, but it was the things he would imagine that were quite disturbing. He saw himself receiving retribution through the torture and murder of those who tormented him.

With age he managed to choke down his sadistic fantasies. He looked at law enforcement as a way of exacting justice from those who had wronged him. Plain and simple, Stone became a cop not to help people, but to be in control. Power. A badge and a gun would surely prevent others from victimizing him. And in fact, it transformed him from the role of victim to predator.

Stone always seemed to get things done. He made plenty of arrests and though there may have been questions on how those arrests took place, he still managed to find himself being asked to join the Cobra Squad. The rumors surrounding Stone's questionable uses of force or how evidence was actually found was exactly what Jackson and the others wanted to hear. Mark White had on occasion worked details with Stone and soon became his confidant. With the information he had gathered from those details, White was more than enthusiastic about vouching for Stone. But what White, now lying on an examiner's cold steel table, didn't know was just how sick Stone really was.

Sending molten brass into the skull of Evans had given Stone the thrill he had secretly dreamed of. Stone always wondered what it would be like to kill a person and, when he pulled the trigger on Evans, adrenaline coursed through his veins giving him a rush. Stone had awakened a starving headsman that lived inside of him. And with each bark from Jackson, he wondered if he could pin his death on the fisherman and his daughter as well.

As Stone's mind wondered down a sadistic path of murder, Iorrio was contemplating packing up and leaving. He had done pretty well as far as packing away his share of the Cobra Squads' racketeering funds.

Iorrio had drawn the conclusion in his mind that there would be no return to the Sheriff's Office. Practically half the Cobra Squad lay dead and the remaining members weren't exactly with it, he thought as he looked at the jittery thin kid behind the wheel. He probably should have walked away a while ago, but T.J. was hell-bent on finding the girl and now in taking care of the fisherman and his kid.

With Evans now gone, the best thing to do would have been to cut their loses and run. The storm probably gave them their best chance at getting away. After picking up the pieces and figuring out that the Cobra Squad was crooked, they could all be long gone in a far away country.

His dreams of opening his own gym back in Jersey, something he often thought about, had been dashed. But what about a gym somewhere else? Down in the Caribbean or South America? As Iorrio braced himself in the cab of the truck, in his head he could see the beautiful tan women in tight skimpy outfits, sweating at his commands. He knew enough Spanish to get by and he could just hire someone to take care of all the business aspects. That way he could focus on a carefree life away from kicking in doors and answering to someone else. He would be able to put in ample time in the gym to get bigger. He would have to leave T.J. behind; too much competition.

His mind was drifting farther and farther away from the slaloming truck and into the fantasy when he was snapped back to reality by Jackson's yelling at Stone to drive more carefully. Iorrio inhaled deeply and then exhaled in annoyance. He looked around and realized they were almost at the Green Bridge. He almost said something to T.J. about turning around, but decided not to.

Iorrio quickly swept the images of his gym out of his head and began to focus on the task at hand. He would have to end the lives of Jack and Katelyn if was going to get on with his own life.

"We're almost there. We have got to get this done," Jackson said to them. Jackson's mind was divided into two trains of thought: one was the tactical maneuvers the three would do in order to obtain their goal; the other was what he was going to do with Dawn Peterson.

It was not Jackson's fault that three of the seven members of the Cobra Squad were dead, it was Dawn's fault. It was not Jackson who was responsible for the death of Tom Underwood, it was Dawn's fault. It was not Jackson's actions that sealed the fate of Jack Foster and his daughter, it was Dawn's.

The way Jackson saw it, if she would have just kept her fucking mouth shut, none of this would be happening. So Jackson was not quite sure how he would make Dawn pay for all the damage and work she created for him, but he knew it would be bad.

The skiff zipped across the water and over to the dock. Jack ran up on it like he was going to ram it, but pulled back on the throttle and turned the wheel just in time to put the boat alongside of the dock.

The bobbing of the skiff had no affect on Jack's ability to walk around it. He strolled up to the front hatch, retrieved a line, fastened it to the cleat on the bow and wrapped it around one of the pilings. He strolled back to Katelyn and put his hand out to help her stand up.

Katelyn who had spent many hours on the water even in some not so perfect conditions did not quite have the sea legs her dad did. The bobbing of the boat caused it to bang into the pilings and did not give Katelyn enough of a stable platform; she almost went over if it were not for her dad's steadfast grip on her hand.

Jack led Katelyn to the bow and helped her up onto the dock, then pulled himself up. The wind was now gusting pretty hard. Katelyn steadied herself by holding onto the piling. Jack got up, stutter-stepped from a gust, but managed to correct himself.

"Come on Kat, let's get moving," he said as he took her hand.

Katelyn nodded and they sprinted down the dock unaware of the truck driving over the Green Bridge behind them.

The windshield wipers whipped back and forth as Darby and Brian strained to see the maroon truck ahead of them. They had feared they would lose the truck when there were some major winds on US 41, but thankfully, the truck continued north on the highway. Unintentionally, they were so far behind they remained undetected by the driver of the pick-up.

"You can't get any closer?" Brian asked impatiently.

"You don't think I'm try'n?" Darby snapped.

He didn't respond. He wasn't exactly sure that he wanted to catch the truck. He definitely wanted to see Jack and Katelyn safe; he just didn't want to have to face armed psychos in order to see it happen. Of course he was beginning to wonder what was really going on here. There was a dead cop at Jack's place. Then they go to some apartment to find out that Jack and Katelyn are at Tom Underwood's house. They get there and there's another dead cop. Then there was the one that Darby mention had been killed earlier. There seemed to be an unusual amount of cops dying and no sign of Jack and Katelyn.

"Darby, don't you find it odd that there seems to be a lot of cops getting killed and we haven't seen Jack or Katelyn."

Darby scrunched his brow and mulled over what Brian had just said. For whatever reason, the thought didn't cross his mind again, that Jack was the one on the rampage since he saw Foster's house. But now faced with the idea again, he wasn't sure; especially since it was one of Foster's own friends mentioning it.

"Do you think Foster is hunting down these guys?" Darby said as he braced to run into standing water.

"It doesn't really make much since to me, but then again I'm not really sure of anything right now," Brain said as he fell back into the seat after the impact. "I mean, I don't think Jack's that kind of guy. And I sure as hell don't think that Katelyn would be involved with anything like this."

158

"Then let's just stick with the plan of catch'n that truck," Darby said as he mashed the pedal once again. "Either way I've gotta stop them."

Brian nodded slightly in agreement. That might be what Darby needed to do, but he wasn't so sure that was what he needed to do.

The gusting wind caused the truck to rock back and forth. Jackson had one hand planted on the dashboard and the other on the door. The flapping wipers forcing drops of rain through the holes in the windshield were no longer a concern of Jackson's. He did not like this one bit. None of them did. Stone slowed down to a crawl up and over the bridge.

The piece of paper with the aerial photo of Aunt Gloria's house was heavily creased from being folded-up in Jackson's pocket. From time to time it would fold over causing Jackson to snap it open in frustration. "All right, once we're over the bridge, take your first left by the Shell station," Jackson said as he looked at the photo in one hand and keeping the other on the dashboard.

"If we make it over," Stone mumbled as he looked to the cloud-filled sky.

"Shut up!" Iorrio yelled. "Just pay attention and we'll be fine."

Stone looked over the bridge to the river. There he saw the bobbing skiff attached to a long dock. Quickly he followed the dock back to land just in time to get a glimpse of Jack and Katelyn dashing off of it.

"Holy shit! Holy shit! There they where! They just got off that dock! Do you see the boat tied to it?" Stone started yelling.

Iorrio lurched to the other side of the cab to see out the window. He did see the boat, but no sign of any people.

"Are you sure?" Iorrio asked as he squinted to see passed the streaking rain drops on the window.

"Hell, yeah! That's the boat I tell ya!"

"All right, we're obviously going to the right place. Just pay attention to the road so we can be sure to get there," ordered Jackson, still gripping the dash. Stone's jumping around had caused him to sink further into the seat with nerves.

With an evil grin Stone pressed the accelerator a little harder and the truck sped up. He could not wait to get there.

The wind and rain had begun to really rip. The tips of the waves rolling in the river were lifted off in a cloud of mist from the wind. Jack and Katelyn stepped off the dock and turned to run. Just a few yards away, Jack turned to look back at the skiff tied off. The rolling chop was pounding it into the dock causing it to boom like a drum. As they stood there, a gust snatched Jack's cap off his head and tossed it in the air. He turned to grab it only to see it skipping across the drenched grass. With his arm wrapped around Katelyn, they continued on toward the battered house-turned shelter for Dawn.

Katelyn nuzzled her face into Jack's chest as the two shuffled along. She continued to move because her dad kept pulling her along. Her jacket barely kept out the pelting rain and she just wanted to stop for a minute and rest, but she knew that wasn't possible. The couple hundred yards from the dock to the house seemed like miles as her legs were getting weaker with every step, till finally, she tripped.

They both went down. Jack caught them with his free hand from completely falling. Mud splashed up from the ground as Jack's hand plunged into it.

"Come on, baby, get up," Jack said as he tried to help her up, but all she did was cry.

"I can't. I just need a minute," she sobbed.

"Kat, we don't have a minute. Get up; it's not that far from here."

"Dad, please, just a minute to rest!"

Jack stood up "Give me you hand," he said sternly.

Katelyn raised her hand and Jack grabbed it and pulled her up. Then he bent over and slung her over his shoulder and started walking. The barraging wind and rain caused the grass and mud to plop off of Katelyn's jeans. Their combined weight cause Jack's steps to sink in the saturated ground and he almost tripped himself, but kept on until they made it only a few feet from the house.

"Kat, you gotta walk from here. We're right there," he said as he slid her off. Jack went to take a step and practically fell as his legs felt like rubber. He reached down and started rubbing his drained thighs.

"Are you all right?" Katelyn asked as she laid a hand on his shoulder.

"Yeah, let's get in there."

Hand-in-hand they walked up to the front door, which thankfully was out of the squalling winds. Jack banged against the door and yelled for Dawn.

"Dawn, come on and open up! It's me, Jack Foster. The storm is getting really bad again!"

Jack stood with his arms wrapped around Katelyn as they huddled together. Then he heard someone unlocking the door.

CHAPTER TWENTY NINE

As Darby and Brian made it to the top of the Green Bridge, they saw the maroon pick-up turn left. Darby's truck rolled at a crawl as he basically idled it. The rain came horizontal across them and the wind shook the truck.

Brian's heart was in his throat when, off in the distance, he saw something bobbing in the water. He squinted and looked past Darby.

A bead of sweat rolled down Darby's temple "What? What are you looking at?" he asked nervously, never taking his eyes off the road.

"Over there, on the water," Brian motioned with his chin. "That boat tied to the dock."

Darby tried to look with quick jerks of his head, but couldn't force himself to stop looking at the road long enough to see it. "What about it? So some dumb ass left his boat out. So what?" he asked, his knuckles white wrapped around the steering wheel.

Brain slowly began to nod, "That's Tom Underwood's boat. It's got that giant redfish on it."

No sooner did he recognize the boat, it was picked up by a wave and flipped into the side of the dock. The skiff was on its side pinned to the dock by the wind and waves. Then the dock shifted and slowly leaned into the water. Capt. Tom's pride and joy had taken on too much water. Her hull was cracked from being continuously rammed into the pilings to where she was tied and she was pulled under by the dock as it slowly disappeared under the white-crested chop of the river.

Chills ran up Brian's spine as he watched the eerie event unfold in a matter of seconds. Then the truck started to swerve as the wind caused it to hydroplane. Darby let off the gas right away and the tires grabbed hold again. The two looked at each other with a sigh of relief when a large gust came and slid the truck into the guard rail.

"Holy shit! Holy shit!" Brian screamed as he looked out the window to the sloshing water below. He locked his legs against the floor and grabbed the seat and braced his arm against the door.

Darby still had one hand on the steering wheel and the other planted into the roof of the cab. His leg began to shake as he pressed with all his might on the brake. Darby's breathing was fast and shallow as he waited to feel the truck flip over the rail.

The two sat motionless; the only sound was the tapping of the rain and the roar of the wind rushing by, which caused the truck to shake nervously.

Brian, realizing they weren't headed over yet, slowly turned his head to Darby "Get us the fuck off this bridge," he said barely over a whisper.

Darby remained frozen staring straight ahead. Another gust caused the truck to shake more.

"Darby, get us the fuck out of here!" now yelling through clenched teeth.

Darby took a long blink and a deep breath. Then he slowly pulled his hand down and gripped the steering wheel. Brian turned and looked straight ahead as he squeezed the seat so tight he thought he would puncture it.

Darby slowly released the brake allowing the truck to inch forward. Brian closed his eyes as he could hear and feel the side of the truck grinding against the concrete barrier.

Ever so slowly they made there way down the bridge. Once at the bottom they both let out a breath as if they had been holding it the whole time. Darby pulled the truck over and rested his forehead against the steering wheel. Brian rubbed his face in the palms of his hands. For that brief moment, they had forgotten what they were doing there in the first place.

Jack and Katelyn stood in each other's arms rocked from side to side as gusts of wind rushed by them. The door cracked and Jack saw a pretty young lady who appeared to have been crying.

"Dawn?" he asked, squinting from the spraying rain.

Dawn responded with a slow nod. Her face scrunched up as she began to cry again. Jack was about to say something when he saw movement off to the right of them. He turned to see the battered pick-up truck from Capt. Tom's place. His eyes widened as he saw the driver door open and a man appeared with a gun in his hand. He lunged forward pushing the door open, knocking Dawn to the ground, and threw Katelyn inside on top of her.

"Go, go, go; get inside!" Jack ordered as he reached back and drew his gun. As he brought it up on aim he saw the back cab door opening up and a large man exited holding a sub-machine gun. Then the driver fired and instantaneously wood exploded from the side of the house by Jack's head. Jack jerked his head and fired back. The two men ducked down as Jack's shots whizzed past them. When they looked up they saw the door slam shut.

Jack got to his feet and quickly twisted the deadbolt in the door. He turned to see Katelyn and Dawn standing together.

"Are you two all right?" he asked as he motioned for them to go.

"Why are they here?" Dawn screamed at him.

"I'm not sure how they found us," Jack said as he put an arm around each of them to move.

Dawn pulled away "Now they are going to kill us."

"No, they're not! Let's go!" Jack said as he took her by the arm and pulled her into the candlelit living room. There he saw an elderly woman knitting in a rocking chair. The old woman rocked and hummed a song, not acknowledging Jack or Katelyn. "What's with her?" he asked looking back at Dawn.

"That's my Aunt Gloria. She's not doing well."

"Kat, help her," Jack said motioning to Aunt Gloria. "You guys get upstairs," he said as he looked to the foyer.

Katelyn took Aunt Gloria by the arm "You need to come with me." Aunt Gloria looked at her confused.

"Aunt Gloria, these are friends of mine. They're here to help us," Dawn said as she went over, took her other arm and helped her stand up.

"What about Albert?" Aunt Gloria asked as the scarf she was knitting slid off her lap to the floor.

"Yes, they're gonna help him too," Dawn said as they walked to the staircase.

Katelyn looked passed Aunt Gloria to Dawn confused. Dawn looked at her and slightly shook her head.

Jack stood in the middle of the room looking around. "Kat, you better get that gun out," he said as they were halfway up the stairs.

"What about you, Dad?"

"I'll be up there in a minute. Find a room and get in there."

Katelyn nodded and they continued to ascend the dark staircase. At the top, it was pitch black down the hall. The only light was the low glow coming form the living room.

"Where do we go?" Katelyn asked.

Dawn put her hand against the wall "Just follow me," she said as she pulled Aunt Gloria along.

Katelyn held on to Aunt Gloria's other arm and went till she was no longer pulled along. Then she heard a high-pitched squeak as Dawn turned a door knob. As the door opened with a creak, a little bit of gray light eased into the hallway. Katelyn could make out the silhouettes of Dawn and Aunt Gloria as they turned into the room.

There were windows on two of the walls and a gray, hazy light filtered from around the shutters on the windows to reveal the cold damp room. The room was made up of a twin bed, a nightstand, a dresser, and a chair, which Aunt Gloria went over and sat in. The shutters rattled as the wind rushed around the house. Every so often there was a bang against the exterior wall from shingles being ripped from the roof of the neighbor's house.

As Katelyn looked around the room, Dawn walked behind her to shut the door.

"Wait, don't shut that," Katelyn said holding up a hand. "Leave it open for my dad."

Dawn paused and looked at Katelyn "What if it's not your dad who comes up here?"

Katelyn squinted here eyes "Leave it open. He will be up in a minute," she said sternly.

Dawn huffed and walked away from the door. "How old are you anyway?" she said as she plopped on the bed.

"I'm fifteen," Katelyn said as she pulled the revolver out of the fanny pack.

"Do you know how to use that thing?"

Katelyn looked down at the gun then looked back at Dawn, "You better hope so."

Jackson came around the bed of the truck crouched down. Iorrio and Stone were huddled together trying to stay upright from the wind as debris was tossed around them.

"Stone, you go around the back. Me and Iorrio will go in through the front." Jackson said, his face scrunched up from being pelted by the rain. Wait till you hear us inside and then come in.

Stone nodded slowly. He was not the least bit surprised that Jackson would stick with Iorrio. Nonetheless, he took off to the back side of the house. As he came around the corner he saw the massive oak tree that had fallen onto the house. He ducked down to look under the huge trunk to the back door, and then he looked up to where the oak had smashed a hole in the roof. Stone nodded as he holstered his gun and started climbing up the oak; his usual wry smile across his face.

The gusting wind jostled the hood on Jackson's jacket side to side as he and Iorrio made their way to the front door.

Jackson leaned in toward Iorrio "We go on three," he said holding up three fingers.

Iorrio licked the raindrops from around his lips and nodded. Jackson stood in front of the door with his gun pointed at the door. He held up a hand and began to count with his fingers; one. Every time he rocked his hand a finger would pop up from his fist; two. And with that, Iorrio reached up and grabbed his hand.

"T.J., fuck this man; let's get out of here."

Jackson's face was skewed as he looked at him, "What the fuck are you talking about?"

"There's something not right about this. Let's get the fuck outta here. This whole town; just grab our shit and leave the States."

Jackson slowly shook his head with the same skewed look.

Iorrio took a deep breath and let it out. "What the hell are we gonna do when this is over?" he said shrugging his shoulders. "Half the fucking team is gone and it's not gonna take long for someone to start poking around."

"You wanna take off now? Fuck that! We gotta finish this shit. You said it; this fucker has killed half the team. We can't let that shit go!" Jackson said as spit came out of his mouth.

Iorrio bobbed his head in agreement "All right, all right. But when this is done I'm outta here."

Jackson shook his head. "Whatever, let's get this done. On three," he said and began counting with his fingers once more.

With the candles blown out in the living room the only light Jack had to see by was the glow of the hurricane lamp in the kitchen. Try as he might, Jack couldn't hear much more than the roar of the wind bombarding the house. He wished that the gunmen outside the house would get blown away, but he was pretty sure, considering his luck thus far, that wouldn't happen.

Jack slowly backed up the stairs swaying his gun in the darkness. His heart was racing when he heard the crash at the front door. Wet air rushed into the house. At the very top of the stairs, Jack saw rain and leaves fly in from the foyer. He looked up the stairs and back down again, not sure what to do. If one would just peak their head through Jack figured he could pick him off. But nothing. What were they waiting for?

Jackson kicked the door in and Iorrio came in from the side into the foyer. He jostled the machine gun side to side looking for any signs of movement. Jackson held his handgun just above Iorrio's shoulder. The two crouched there, partially sheltered from the storm, waiting to hear the sound of Stone coming in from the back. Iorrio quickly glanced back at him, but Jackson could only shrug. After a few seconds Jackson tapped Iorrio to go.

Jackson began to grind his perfect teeth. Where in the hell was Stone? He couldn't believe he had to convince Joe not to run off and finish what they started. Now that fucking Stone has dropped the ball! It wasn't entirely impossible that the ex-jailer managed to off Stone. Hell, he had been doing a pretty good job at picking them off one at a time. Maybe it was a mistake to separate, but everyone going in together would have been like shooting fish in a barrel for him. The more Jackson thought about the situation the more he clenched his teeth. His jaw muscles were bulging out the sides of his face.

"What the fuck are we doing?" Iorrio asked nervously as he kept his focus straight ahead.

"I don't think Stone heard us," he hoped.

"Well how do we get his ass in here?"

Jackson was looking around for an idea when he remembered the distractionary device he had in his pocket. He reached down and pulled it out the side pocket on his black cargo pants.

Iorrio turned to see the jingling pin of the grenade being shook in Jackson's hand. Iorrio responded with a hardy nod. Jackson pulled the pin and tossed it into the living room and the two backed out of the house. Even with the roar of the wind and rain there was no mistaking the sound of the blast.

Jack had been patiently waiting to pick off the first one to walk through the door when he saw something come flying into the living room. He turned his head quickly to see it and then quickly tried to duck back into the stairs. His hands over his ears, he could feel the blast through his back against the wall. The gun clutched in his left hand didn't allow him to cover his ear all too well from the explosion. Jack worked his jaw up and down trying to get his ear to pop and stop ringing as he crawled into the dark hallway of the second floor.

This time Jackson and Iorrio didn't wait. Quickly they moved in, crouched low to the ground. They quickly scanned the living room. There was still no sign of Stone. The two worked together clearing the kitchen, dinning room, and the study on the first floor. They checked the backdoor in the kitchen, but there was no sign that Stone had ever made it there.

Jackson looked at Iorrio with a scowl, "Did you tell the kid to just take off? Like you wanted to do?"

"Absolutely not!" Iorrio said putting his hand up. "Listen, I was just saying we could have saved ourselves all this trouble and been outta here. That was just you and me talking."

Jackson looked at him sideways and nodded; then he motioned with his chin to go.

The wind steadily rocked the truck as Darby and Brian made there way down the road, but now it wasn't as intense as it was just minutes ago. Through the blinding rain and thrashing of the wipers Darby saw the maroon pick-up truck pulled off in front of a home.

"There it is up there." Darby said, crunched over the steering wheel trying to see out the windshield.

Brian took a deep breath and rubbed his hands together "So what's the plan?" he said. He started to pump his leg up and down as he looked to Darby.

Darby eased his truck in behind the other and put it in park. Brian shifted in his seat to face him, ready for instruction. As Darby searched for the answer he reached down and turned off the screeching wipers. Now the only sound was that off the forging winds that caused the truck to shake.

"I really don't know what to do," Darby said somberly. "We don't know who's in there or what the layout is."

Brian looked down at the seat and quietly nodded. He took a deep breath and looked up to Darby, "Well, I guess we just go in and play it by ear. Seems to have worked so far." He finished with a shrug.

Darby raised an eyebrow and tilted his head "There ya have it."

Darby turned to face him and put his hand out "You're a good friend to be doing this."

Brian looked down to Darby's hand and took it firmly "So are you."

Foster's friend? Darby never thought of Foster as a friend and he was pretty sure the same held true for Foster. But who else would be out here in the middle of this risking his life for him other then a friend? A friend like Richards. Is that what Darby had become?

A slight smile came across Darby's face "Thank you," he said with a nod.

Both men attempted to exit the truck, but it was not that easy to push the doors open against the rush of the wind. After the wind slammed Brian's door shut it took hold of him causing him to stumble toward the back of the truck. He caught himself on the tailgate before falling. His hat was sucked off his head and sent flying.

Darby's door slammed shut on his jacket and, as he tried to walk away, the tug against the truck and the wind knocked him back against it. As he was turning around to see what the problem was, Jason was pulling himself along the bed of the truck up to him.

"What's wrong?" Brian asked; his face was distorted as the winds smashed into him.

"I'm stuck," Darby said as he tried to twist around to see his jacket in the door.

Brian reached over and pulled the handle "Pull it now."

As Darby snatched his jacket out of the doorframe they heard a loud boom sound off from the house. The two turned with a startled jump in time to see two men enter the front door.

"Holy shit, there they are!" Darby said as he drew out his gun. He turned to Brian whose eyes were wide open, "You better get that gun out."

Brian reached under his jacket and pulled the revolver out of his waistband.

"Let's go," Darby said as he crouched down and jogged up to the front of the house.

Brian jogged behind him and was somewhat relieved by the slight cover the house provided from the pounding wind. He stopped next to Darby who was leaning against the house. Darby, whose gaze was fixed on the front door, turned to him. Brian responded by nodding while trying to catch his breath. Darby turned back toward the door and started walking. Brian squeezed the gun in his hands and followed.

After shimmying up the tree to the rooftop, it dawned on Stone that this might not have been a good idea with the winds steadily increasing with each passing minute. On the roof he found himself clinging to the branches of the oak just to stay up there. He inched his way closer and closer to the gouge in the roof. The leafless branches whipped around in the rampaging wind causing them to thrash his face and arms.

Stone growled as the branches lashed against him. He couldn't make it into the house fast enough, so as he felt the hole in the roof with his foot, he quickly attempted to slither down it, but as he got down to his waist, he heard a loud snap as the timbers in the roof gave way a little causing him to be pinned between the roof and the oak.

He let out a howl as the crevasse in the roof closed around him causing the splintered planks to poke into his lower back; but no one could hear him over the thundering winds gushing over everything. Luckily, the jagged wood did not penetrate Stone's vest, but with every squirm he made it seemed as if the hole closed more. Furiously and franticly he gripped a branch above him and tried to pull himself out, but it was of no use.

Then there was a thunderous boom from inside the house. Stone froze in anticipation of the roof collapsing. When it didn't, he began frantically looking around trying to figure out what was happening.

As Jackson and Iorrio made their way back into the living room Darby and Brian had just emerged from the foyer. At the sight of them, Jackson and Iorrio dropped back into the kitchen to take cover. Likewise, when Darby saw the two, he pushed Brian back and took cover behind the wall."

"This is the Sheriff's Office! Throw down your weapons and come out!" Darby yelled.

Iorrio looked to Jackson with his eyes wide open. Jackson responded with a shrug and shaking his head.

"We're with the Sheriff's Office too. I'm Sgt. Jackson with the Cobra Squad."

"I know who you are. Throw down your weapons and come out!" Darby ordered again.

Jackson scrunched his face and tilted his head. He popped his head out past the door frame to snag a look and then back. All he could see was part of Darby holding his gun up. Iorrio held his hand up and shrugged.

Jackson squinted his eyes, shook his head, leaned into Iorrio, and whispered "Slide over there and see if you can see anyone out the back door."

Iorrio nodded and crept over to the back door. He bobbed his head back and forth to catch a peak through the slits in the wooden shutters on the window. All he could see was the onslaught of Lynn. He turned back to Jackson and shook his head.

Jackson smiled and nodded, then waved him back over.

Brian stayed hunkered down behind Darby. His gaze changed from Darby to the power of Mother Nature to Darby and back again. His mind began to swirl like the winds around them. The orders Darby yelled seem to be coming from a tunnel. He could fell his temples throb as he stared at the gun in his hand. He flinched as Darby began yelling again. It all sounded garbled to him. He closed his eyes and clenched his jaw. Then he couldn't take it anymore.

"Where the fuck is Jack and Katelyn?" Brian screamed as he stood up behind Darby. His eyes flew open and his jaw dropped as he looked into the kitchen. In the back of the kitchen he saw Iorrio laying on his side pointing his machine gun at him.

As Iorrio squeezed the trigger, Brian felt himself being pulled to the ground. Burning brass whizzed by his face and one round grazed his shoulder. He dropped the gun and clutched his shoulder as he went to the ground. Plaster fell around him.

Darby shielded his face with his hand from the flying debris. Then he reached over and grabbed Brian, "Are you all right?"

Brian lifted his hand and looked at the little bit of blood on his hand and then at the rip in his jacket and nodded.

Darby reached down, picked up the revolver and handed it him. As he did, more gunfire rang out and more plaster flew about. Darby reached his gun out past the wall and blindly shot in the direction of the kitchen.

As Jack was making his way down the hallway he heard yelling. He paused and tried to make out what they were saying. He heard, "Sheriff's Office" and turned back around. Just as he began to peer out the stairway, shots rang out and Jack jerked back his head. More shots. Jack shook his head as he wasn't sure what was happening. None of the shots were directed at him. He quickly peaked out the stairwell again. He saw two men crouched in the foyer. One was firing into the living room and the other was huddled beside him with his hands around his head clutching a gun.

Wind and rain rushed past them as the one shooting pulled back to reload. Jack watched as the man dropped a magazine and inserted a new one. Jack squinted his eyes and shook his head. As rapid fire rang in from across the house the he realized it was Darby. Then he turned his focus on the man next to him. Richards!

Jack leaned down and scanned for where the shots where coming from. As he did the spray of brass continued to disintegrate the walls around Darby and Brian. He couldn't see the shooter, but he could see the brass casings skip across the floor in the kitchen. Jack held his gun out and double tapped two rounds into the kitchen wall.

As Iorrio laid cover for Jackson, two chunks of plaster exploded off the wall above his head. He turned his head with a jerk and looked at the holes in the wall and then frantically looked around.

The rapid fire of the machine gun halted and gave Darby notice that something was going on. He quickly poked out his head to catch a look. The only movement he saw was that of pictures flopping against the wall and a crocheted quilt flip off the back of the couch from the wind swirling through the house. Then he saw the door behind the couch slam shut.

Nervously, Darby dropped to one knee and held his gun on the door. He wasn't sure if it was the wind or one of them. As he was focused on the door he saw movement out to his left; someone coming down the stairs.

Darby swung his gun over and drew a bead on Jack as he was aiming at the kitchen. Darby lowered his gun and stood up. Furiously he waved Jack to get out.

Jack glanced over at Darby as he slowly sidestepped his way down the stairs. Keeping his gun up on sight with his left hand, he held up a finger with his right telling Darby to wait.

Darby shook his head no and continued to wave Jack on when his chest exploded. Darby stumbled back against the wind funneling through the door and fell into Brian. In his insistence to Jack, Darby didn't see Jackson pop up from behind the couch. But Jack did.

As Jack was bringing his hand back to his gun he saw Jackson pop up from behind the couch and shoot Darby center-mass. As Jackson was dropping his aim to shoot Brian, Jack fired center-mass on Jackson.

Jackson groaned in pain and reached over to where he was hit. He looked up and saw Jack on the stairs pointing his gun at him. He looked down at his hand and saw no blood and quickly raised his gun on Jack.

Jack fired again hitting Jackson square in the chest. Jackson jerked from the impact, stumbled back and fell out of sight behind the couch. Jack made his way down the stairs and over to the foyer. He glanced down at Darby struggling to breath in Brian's lap. Brian's hands were covered in blood. He looked up to Jack and shook his head in shock.

"Brian, we need to get him upstairs," Jack said reaching down to help pick Darby up, never taking his gun off the couch.

With Jack pulling on Darby, Brian got his feet underneath him and helped lift him. He slung Darby's arm over his shoulders and grabbed hold of his belt. Jack threw Darby's other arm over his shoulder and the two attempted to make their way over to the stairs with Darby in tow. Brian looked back at the revolver sitting on the ground and wondered if should grab it.

CHAPTER THIRTY

The carnage of wind and rain was taking its toll on Stone. The pelting rain made his face feel raw, as though he was being sand blasted. He couldn't believe that this was the way it was going to end, beaten by the storm. He thought that maybe he would die in the line of duty. He would be honored with a giant parade of squad cars from all over the state. The honor guard would be there, lifting there rifles and firing on command. The trumpeter would play a solemn, but powerful, "Oh Danny Boy" and tears would be shed.

But not now. No, now he was lodged between a big fucking tree and the roof in this Godforsaken storm. No doubt when they found his body an investigation would not lead to the honored funeral he had envisioned.

Stone slowly shook his head. Where the hell were Jackson and Iorrio? The two muscle heads must have been wondering where he was. Then he heard it. The popping of gunfire. The fight had begun between them and the old man and his kid. He balled his fists and began to beat on the trunk turned captor. He couldn't believe he was missing out on his chance to kill them.

Stone curled his upper lip and thrust his hand in through the hole and grabbed hold of his gun. He pulled it out and blindly began to fire into the room below until there were no more rounds left in the magazine. He continued to squeeze the trigger even though the slide was locked back, then he hung his head and dropped the gun. No one else in the house noticed Stone's shots with all the other gunfire.

From his vantage point Iorrio watched Jackson get shot, attempt to return fire, and get shot again. He watched as Jackson fell over and wriggled around on the floor clutching his chest. He sat there frozen with his eyes and jaw wide open. He sat there frozen in fear. Fear that he would be all alone. Alone to face the man who had now reduced the Cobra Squad to one.

But then Jackson stopped squirming side to side and rolled over onto his stomach. He planted his hands on the ground along the sides of his chest and pushed himself up. Then he got to a knee and looked over to Iorrio. Iorrio looked back him as if he just watched Jackson rise from the dead.

Iorrio scrambled to his feet and ran over to the door. He quickly stuck his head out and scanned for Foster or the others then ran over to help Jackson to his feet.

"Holy shit, I thought you were dead," Iorrio said as Jackson got to his feet.

Jackson looked at him sideways with a scowl. Then he reached up and pulled his vest away from his body and peered down it. "He hit dead center of the shock plate," He said as he rubbed his chest.

"Thank God he's a good shot, I guess," Iorrio said as he put a hand on Jackson's shoulder.

Jackson looked down at Iorrio's hand, then over to the foyer. "I got one of the ones at the door," Jackson said as he motioned over to the blood on the floor with his chin.

"Look's like they forgot something," Iorrio said pointing to the revolver. "Did they run out?"

"No, I think they went up the stairs."

Iorrio looked over at the staircase, "How are we gonna get up there without getting picked off?"

Jackson went to take a deep breath, but paused from the pain. "I'm not sure," he said as he exhaled. He looked down at the machine gun hanging by Iorrio's side. "How many rounds you got left?"

"Whatever's left in here," Iorrio said as he pulled the magazine out. "Looks like ten, plus I've got two more magazines." He loaded one of the full ones into the machine gun.

Jackson nodded. As he bent over to pick up his gun, a picture crashed into the floor beside him, but he didn't even flinch. He stood up, popped the magazine out, examined it and slid it back in.

The two men struggled under Darby's dead weight, but they managed to make it up to the second floor. Jack could feel Darby's breaths getting shallower. He holstered his gun and began groping the wall. He found a door, opened it with a squeak, no one in it. He shut the door and continued on.

"Jack, what are you looking for?" Brian grunted as they moved on.

"Katelyn is in one of these rooms."

Katelyn and Dawn heard commotion out in the hallway. They herded Aunt Gloria behind the bed and ducked down with her. Katelyn laid her arms across the bed with the revolver shaking in her hands pointed towards the door. Her heart was thumping as she watched the doorknob slowly turn.

Jack swung the door open and as he went to go in he caught sight of the revolver pointed at him and jerked back "Kat, it's me!" he yelled.

Katelyn jumped onto and across the bed and ran to the door. "Dad, thank God!" she said as a tear ran down her cheek.

Jack grabbed her and pushed into the room with Darby and Brian in tow. He stumbled and all four went to the ground.

"Who are these guys?" Dawn asked coming around the bed.

Jack and Brian rolled Darby onto his back, he wasn't breathing.

"Holy shit!" Jack said as he was cocking Darby's head back. He gave him two breaths as he started CPR. "Brian, you know how to do CPR, right?"

He nodded.

"… thirteen and fourteen and fifteen. Go!"

Brian dropped down and gave the two breaths.

"What happened, Dad? And why is Capt. Brian here?" Katelyn asked looking at the scene before her.

"… thirteen and fourteen and fifteen. He's been shot and I don't know," Jack said as he paused for Brian.

"Who the fuck are these guys?" Dawn yelled standing next to Katelyn.

Jack checked Darby's vitals "We've got to get him to the hospital. Now! Kat, you see what I'm doing?"

She nodded.

"Get down here and go; and remember to count."

Katelyn knelt down next to Darby and put here hands on his chest. Even in the gray-lit room she could see the blood stains on his shirt. Jack reached around her and positioned her hands.

"Go."

"One, two, three…"

"Harder, push harder," he said as he jumped up, ran over to the bed, and pulled the covers off.

There he saw Aunt Gloria huddled in the corner. She looked blankly to the ceiling and gave no notice of Jack or what he was doing.

Jack tore the sheet in his hands as he hurried back over to them. He started to pull Darby's jacket back and Katelyn stopped.

"Keep going!" Jack snapped as he continued to search for the entry wound. Unable to see in the dim light, Jack had to search with his hand and found the oozing hole in the side of Darby's chest. He folded over a strip of the sheet several times and placed it against the wound.

"Jack, how are we going to get him to the hospital? We're in the middle of a hurricane!" Brian asked as he readied himself to give breaths once more.

"Manatee Memorial is five minutes away."

Brian gave the two breaths "Five minutes away, yeah, on a normal day. You won't be able to make it over the bridge."

Jack looked down at Darby. "We don't have a choice. Sit him up so I can tie this around him," he said holding up a strip of sheet. "Kat, I need you to hold this here."

Katelyn reached down and held the blood-soaked rag against Darby's body while Brian lifted his shoulders up. Jack wrapped the strip around him, pulled the jacket out from under it, and tied it off.

"Brian, you two have a car or something outside?"

"His truck. The keys are probably in his pocket," he answered as he laid Darby back down.

"You guys gotta start CPR again," Jack said as he felt around Darby's pockets. "Dawn, grab those pillows."

Dawn was sitting on the edge of the strewn bed watching them work on the stranger. Between the noise of the storm and everyone trying to yell over the noise, Dawn was starting to lose it again.

"Dawn, did you hear me? Get those pillows!"

She grabbed two pillows, walked over, and handed them to Jack who snatched them out of her hands and propped Darby's feet up with them.

"He's dead," Dawn said standing over Katelyn.

"Shut the fuck up!" Brian snapped.

Jack grabbed a hold of Darby's wrist "He's lost a lot of blood. There's no time to waste; we've got to get him outta here."

Jack put a hand on Katelyn's shoulder and she stopped. He slid Darby's arm over his shoulders as he sat him up. Brian did the same on the other side. Jack counted and on three the two stood up with him.

"Dawn, get your aunt, we're getting out of here," Jack said as he drew his gun to his side. "Kat, go ahead and give them a hand. Brian, I know there was one in the kitchen, did you see any others?"

"Just the one you shot. The one in the kitchen has a big fuck'n gun," he said as he glanced down at his shoulder.

"You killed one?" Dawn asked as she made her way over to them with Aunt Gloria in tow.

Jack looked over at her and attempted to shrug with Darby's arm draped across his shoulders, "I think so."

"What did he look like?" she asked anxiously.

"We don't have time for this right now," he said as he started walking toward the door.

The group started down the dark hallway heading toward the light coming from the bottom of the staircase. They were just steps away from the stairs when rapid fire let out and plaster shot off the wall in front of them. Jack stopped immediately and held his gun up. Then another burst of fire rang out. This time the shots hitting the wall were angled more towards them.

"Go back! Go back!" Jack yelled.

Katelyn and Dawn hurried back into the room practically dragging Aunt Gloria. As Jack and Brian attempted to back pedal they tripped and tumbled to the ground. Darby landed with a thud and Jack landed on top of him. Jack attempted to look at Darby's face in the darkness. He was slipping farther away.

Jack was not sure why Darby was there in the first place or how Brian got involved in the situation. Hell, he wasn't sure how he got in this situation, either. But now he felt responsible for them. None of the good guys had died yet and he wasn't going to let it happen now.

"Get him in the room!" Jack yelled at Brian as more shots exploded across the wall. He got to his feet and crouched down against the wall aiming at the top of the stairwell.

Brian scrambled to his feet and grabbed hold of Darby's jacket and started pulling. As he pulled someone bumped into him and he turned to see Katelyn's face in the dim light. She didn't even acknowledge him; she just reached around him, grabbed some of the jacket and started pulling. The fact that she ran out there to help shocked Brian, and he found strength in her help. Together, they pulled Darby into the room.

Once they stopped he noticed the gun in Katelyn's other hand. She didn't resemble the little girl he had gone fishing with. He couldn't help but wonder what she was going through.

Iorrio had started out reaching around and blindly spraying rounds up the staircase allowing Jackson to come around. Jackson held his gun up and motioned Iorrio to come into the stairwell; and again Iorrio squeezed off more rounds as the made their way up. A couple of steps; more fire. A couple of steps; more fire. Reload; more fire.

As the shots got closer, Jack decided to take cover back in the room and quickly backpedaled into the doorway. He glanced down to see Brian and Katelyn preparing to start CPR once more. As he looked up he saw the barrel of the machine gun come around the bottom of the wall. He ducked into the room just as Iorrio's rounds met with the back of the hallway.

"I can't see shit down there," Iorrio said as he continued to take aim into the darkness.

Jackson pulled his flashlight out, clicked it on, reached around him and set it on the landing; lighting up the hallway. As Iorrio noticed the open door on the left, an arm swung out and fired two rounds at them. He quickly pulled back and then returned fire.

"What the fuck are we gonna do?" Iorrio asked as he glanced back and forth from the door to Jackson.

"I don't know," Jackson said wishing he had another flash bang.

CHAPTER THIRTY ONE

Rain collected and ran down Stone's limp form hanging in the ceiling making two streams; each poring off of his boots. The rampaging wind would cause him to rock side to side, back and forth. Stone tried to keep his arms in between his face and the rough bark of his captor. At 135 mph, the wind treated what was exposed of him like a paper doll and it only took one good rap of his head against the tree trunk for him to decide to make a barrier between him and the tree.

The sheer torture of the whole thing had driven him further over the edge. He was fairly sure he would die and wished that it would just happen already. But it hadn't. The storm seemed to last forever.

Stone planted his hands on the giant oak and pushed against it, arching his body as he strained. He let out a growl as he looked to the darkness above.

"Is that all you got?" he yelled skyward. "You haven't killed me yet, so fuck you!"

Just then he heard the snapping of timber off to the side. He squinted and looked through the pelting rain to see the neighbor's house begin to

179

crumble to the ground. Stone watched as the roof seemed to peel off like a sardine can top. His eyes grew huge as he realized the storm had hold of the mangle of lumber and shingles and was sending it straight at him.

Stone threw up his arms and let out a blood curdling scream as the massive projectile closed in on him.

Jack looked around the room for an escape. The only way out was the windows that were boarded up. Just as he was about to tell Dawn to see if the windows were an option, all hell broke loose. There was a huge thud followed instantly by the wall caving in. With the wall falling into the room there was no support for the ceiling which started to cave in.

He grabbed Katelyn, snatched her up and headed out the door into the hallway. Brian took Jack's lead and grabbed Dawn who stood in awe as she watched the wall come tumbling down on top of Aunt Gloria.

Jack fired down the hall as he dashed across it and through the closed door in front of him. He fell to the ground as crashed through the door and Katelyn landed on top of him. He quickly spun her off of him and aimed out the door only to see Brian and Dawn come stumbling in after them. Once in the room, Jack watched as the house continued to come down.

Iorrio was listening to Jackson telling him to continue on like they did coming up the stairs when an enormous boom rocked the house. He looked up to see Jack and Katelyn fleeing the room, but had no time to react because the walls began to slant as the house was coming down.

"Holy shit!" Iorrio yelled as the he looked down to see the stairway begin to twist. He pushed past Jackson to get down the stairs, afraid the walls would close in around them.

The two jumped out of the stairwell as plaster crumbled around them. Iorrio made it into the foyer as the wall collapsed next to him. He dove outside into the storm. As he turned to look back, he could see where the roof had impacted the house causing half the house to collapse. It looked as though the back wall of the house was still standing holding the roof at a steep angle. As he continued to turn and look, he saw Jackson. He lay motionless in the doorway.

Iorrio slowly got to his feet and stared at Jackson surrounded by the rubble. His lower body was covered by toppled doorway. The wind grabbed more of the neighbor's house and flung it next door crashing into the giant pile of debris. He scanned the rest of the mess for signs of life as the wind rocked him side to side. Nothing.

"It's over," he said as he turned and started to jog away.

Up in the second floor of the dilapidated house Jack shielded Katelyn in the crawl-space-like area they were huddled in.

"Are you all right?" Jack asked.

"Yeah, I think so."

Jack tried to look around in the pitch black. He felt the wall on one side and the ceiling that pinned them in on the other side.

"Can you crawl forward?"

Katelyn squirmed out from under her dad and felt the leg of a chair in front of her. Jack crawled backwards until his feet hit a night table behind him. He groped around to the side and felt the wrought iron of a bed frame. He reached under the bed and felt flesh.

Dawn screamed as Jack grabbed her arm.

"Dawn, is that you?"

"Oh, my God! What the fuck is happening?" she began to sob.

"Calm down, chick!" yelled Brian from under the bed.

"Brian, you all right?" he asked, shaking his head. Jack couldn't believe that they were both still alive.

"Other then being stuck under this bed I think so."

"Is there any way out over there?"

"I think so. I see some light and can feel the wind," Brian said as he kicked his foot out from under the bed.

"Well then let's get the hell outta here before the rest of this place comes down. Kat, crawl back to me."

Brian scooted out from under the bed and then into the space of the rafters at his feet. He lifted his head as much as he could to see hole in the roof and started kicking it to open it up more.

"Dawn, is he out from under the bed?"

"Yeah," she said with a sniffle.

"All right, slide over to where he was at."

She didn't move.

"Come on Dawn, we gotta get out of here."

Dawn took in a deep breath and wiggled her way over.

"Good, just stay with me, everything is gonna be all right," Jack hoped. "Kat, you feel the bed to the right here?" he asked as he got onto his belly to slide under the bed.

"Yeah, I'm touching it now."

"Is he out?" he asked Dawn.

"I think so."

"Well, then get out there; I'm right behind you," Jack said with a nudge.

Dawn followed the same path Brian had taken until she could see the opening. Once there she scrambled to get out as she could not take the small space anymore. Jack was not far behind Dawn, but paused every so often to make sure Katelyn was right behind him.

Jack was making his way through the trusses and was only a few feet away from the hole when he heard Dawn begin to scream. As he squirmed to reach around and draw his gun his elbow caught a nail poking through the roof. He jerked with a grimace and quickly snatched the gun.

"Kat, stay in here," Jack said as he quickly made his way to the hole.

Jack held the gun close to his face as he emerged from the hole. His eyes widened at the sight of Jackson holding Dawn by the throat.

CHAPTER THIRTY TWO

The once devastating hurricane, Lynn, now found herself subject to a greater force. As she continued on her trek over land, she began to weaken. The further she traveled, the more she met up with a prevailing front coming in from the north. In fact it was the powerful jet stream of this front that caused Lynn to turn inland. The once well-formed eye was now being swept across the state at a rapid pace, disintegrating into a large band of thunderstorms.

Blood trickled down Jackson's forehead as he laid motionless half buried by part of the house. As he tried to dive to safety from the toppling house, part of the door frame come down and cracked him in the head, knocking him unconscious. As he hit the floor so did the house around him.

He began to twitch as rain drops plopped on his face and he slowly came to. Jackson took deep breaths as he got to his hands. He slowly shook his head trying to lose the dazed feeling. He turned his head and looked back at the debris piled on his legs. With a grunt he pulled himself forward, dragging his legs out from under the mess and rolled over. Conditions had already begun to get better as the wind and rain had slowed down within the minutes he was unconscious. He was checking out his legs and looking around for Iorrio when he heard the pounding coming from atop the heap of house.

Jackson's nostrils flared as he inhaled deeply. As he got to his feet, he saw a foot poke through the roof and his lip curled as he let out a growl. Jackson took off running, scaling the piles of debris with leaps and bounds. As he got to the steep slant of the roof he used his hands and feet and climbed it like a crazed animal.

As he got to the gap, Brian was sliding out. When his head cleared the opening Jackson grabbed hold of him by his shoulders and yanked him the rest of the way out. A look of terror washed over Brian as he was face to face with the enraged Jackson.

Jackson hoisted him into the air by the front of his jacket. Brian punched him in the face but it had no effect. Jackson turned and tossed him down the slanted debris. Brian arched his body and landed on his back, causing his head to snap back. He slid on his back down the roof coming to a halt when his head rammed a large beam. He didn't move after that.

Jackson was about to go after him when he heard someone else coming through the hole. He turned to see Dawn's legs sliding out. He waited and as soon as she caught glimpse of him he grabbed her. Dawn let out a shriek and Jackson jerked her into him.

"You fucking bitch, you thought you could keep away from me!" Jackson snarled through clenched teeth. Spit flung out of his mouth hitting her in the face.

Her eyes huge, Dawn frantically shook her head.

"Bullshit," he said slowly. "Now I'm gonna send you to see your fisherman friend," Jackson said as he slid a hand around her throat.

Just then he saw someone else start to emerge form the hole. Jackson turned quickly to use Dawn as a shield. He started to stumble down but caught himself.

"Let her go!" Jack yelled as he began to come up. There was no clear fatal shot with Dawn in the way.

"Fuck you!" Jackson yelled as whipped out a knife from his belt. He was holding Dawn with his massive arm wrapped around her neck. He lifted his elbow exposing the lower portion of her neck and placed the tip of the blade there. "Throw down you gun or I'll kill her."

"You know it doesn't work that way. You kill her then I kill you."

"Jack, please!" Dawn began to sob.

"Hang in there Dawn. Throw down the knife. It's over."

"Fuck that," Jackson said making sure to keep his face shielded by Dawn's head.

"Well, it's your move. The way I see it you've got two choices; one, I kill you or two, you go to jail."

Jackson clinched his teeth causing the muscles in his jaw to flex. His upper lip started to quiver "Fine, have it your way."

Dawn let out a scream as Jackson began to push the tip of the blade into her throat. Blood began to trickle down her chest.

"Wait, wait, wait!" Jack yelled. His jaw muscles flexed as he cocked his head.

"What the fuck is it gonna be?"

"Hold on a minute!" Jack barked back. He knew he should be in control in this situation. Time was always a good thing. That was of course when backup was on the way. Jack's only backup was Katelyn. He glanced down to her. She was staring at him with her hands up. Jack blinked hard and turned back to Jackson and Dawn. He took one hand off the gun and scrunched his jean pocket. He felt the familiar shape of the Harpy. He slid his hand in and pulled it out and flipped the blade open with his thumb.

"Come on motha fucker, what's it gonna be?" Jackson yelled.

Her hands wrapped around Jackson's forearm Dawn begged Jack to do something in between whines.

"All right, all right; I'll throw down the gun and you let the girl go. We'll settle this, me and you."

A grin grew across Jackson's face "You and me, huh?"

"Please don't do it, Dad," Katelyn whispered.

Jack waved her off.

"Just shoot him. Just kill him. Don't do it, Dad."

"I throw down the gun and you and me finish it. I'm the one you wanted anyway."

"All right," Jackson said nodding his head.

"OK, I'm gonna drop the gun."

"Throw it past me. Throw it over there by that guy."

Jack looked over to see the lifeless body of Brian. He closed his eyes and let out a sigh. "All right," he said somberly and tossed the gun over by Brian.

Jackson saw the gun go by and land with a clank about ten feet shy of Brian's feet. He peaked over Dawn's shoulder to Jack's hands.

"All right, you saw the gun, now let her go."

"She can go. She can go straight to hell!" Jackson roared as he drove his blade into Dawn's throat.

Dawn's jaw dropped as she tried to scream, but nothing came out. Her eyes were fixed on Jack's and he could see the scream in them.

"No!" Jack roared and scrambled out of the hole.

Jackson tossed Dawn aside just as Jack was diving into him. The two locked and toppled down the roof, hitting a remaining portion of the second floor, flipping off and landing on the ground with a thud.

Both tried to gather their breath back as they scrambled to get to their feet. Jackson crouched down and held his knife and hand in front of him. Jack reached back and pulled his knife out of his back pocket.

Katelyn scrambled out of the collapsed roof as soon as her father bolted out. As she emerged, she saw her dad and another huge man roll off the house. As she attempted to climb down, Dawn's withering around caught her eye. Hesitantly, Katelyn maneuvered over to her.

Dawn was face down rolling back and forth clutching her throat.

"Dawn, what's wrong," Katelyn asked as she put a hand on her shoulder.

Dawn pulled a hand away from her neck and held it out toward Katelyn. Katelyn pulled back at first sight of the bloody hand, then leaned in and rolled her over. Dawn was gasping for breath as she clutched the bloody gouge in her throat.

"Oh, my God!"

Dawn grabbed Katelyn by the shoulder and pulled her in close to her face and mouthed something.

"What? I don't know what to do. I have to get my dad," she said as she tried to get up.

Dawn tugged on her sleeve, pulled her back down, and stared frantically into her eyes.

Katelyn looked into her eyes "What do you want?"

Dawn mouthed slowly again.

"Don't leave me," Katelyn whispered as she read her lips and then looked to Dawn's eyes again. Tears had welled up and rolled out of her eyes. Katelyn began to cry, "I have to get my Dad. He will help you." She tried to get up again, but Dawn wouldn't let go of her sleeve.

Katelyn looked away as she heard the ruckus of her dad and the bad cop. When she turned back Dawn stared blankly at the gray sky.

"Dawn?" she meekly asked.

Dawn's hand fell down as her grasp on Katelyn released. Katelyn put her hand over her mouth and rocked back and forth.

She sniffled real hard, "Good bye," and reached down and ran her hand over Dawn's face closing her eyes.

"I'm gonna cut your fucking head off," Jackson said as the two began to circle each other.

"For such a big, tough dude you haven't done such a good job yet," Jack said, egging him on.

Jack felt fairly equal in this fight. Jackson was much stronger and younger, but with all of Jack's training in the jail, his strong suit was hand to hand. He hoped to make Jackson as mad as possible so he would fight mad, not smart.

"This is the first chance we've had to meet," Jackson said as he flashed his smile.

Jack raised an eyebrow at the sight of his pearly-whites. "That's because you kept sending those punk bitches to do your work."

"Well, you know what they say, if ya want something done right, ya gotta do it yourself."

"*You* probably should have done it then, that way *you* might not have sent all those guys to their death."

Jack saw his nostrils flare and knew he was hitting the right button. "Are you supposed to be the leader of this bunch? I've seen better organized street thugs compared to you all. I mean how the fuck have y'all been able to survive on the streets? Probably hid somewhere and let the real police do all the work. Slackers come in…

"Shut the fuck up!" Jackson snapped. "I run the streets! Shit doesn't happen unless I say so! I take care of business!"

"Well, let's see it, *boy.*"

Jackson's face became distorted with rage "What did you call me?" he growled.

"Oh I think you heard me, *boy.*"

And with that Jackson came in slashing at him. Jack hopped back with each slash as to not get cut. Jackson swung at him and Jack sidestepped and pushed his shoulders. Jackson stumbled slightly, but as Jack discovered, he was much stronger than Jack.

Jack back pedaled "I'm still here," he said trying to control his breathing.

Jackson nodded his head, "Not for much longer." Jackson took off at a full sprint and bum rushed him taking them both to the ground with Jackson landing on top of Jack.

Jack reached in between them and ran the knife up from Jackson's gut to his chest, but all it did was rip his vest open. Jackson in return pulled back and tried to stab Jack in the throat. Jack was able to redirect his thrust with a backhand causing Jackson to stab the ground next to Jack's head.

With his other hand, Jackson pulled back and drilled Jack in the side of the ribs almost knocking the wind out of him. He pulled the knife out of the ground with mud dripping from it landing in Jack's eye. Jack closed his eye with a jerk and swung his knife into Jackson's shoulder. He could feel the arched blade grab and he ripped it toward himself gashing Jackson's shoulder open.

Jackson let out a roar as he reached over with the knife in his hand to feel the warm blood ooze out. He looked down just as Jack was coming at his throat with the bloody knife. He leaned back just as the blade whooshed by and blindly swung his own, slicing across Jack's chest.

Jack responded with a groan and reached back and punched Jackson in the throat. Jackson's eyes widened as he tried to choke a breath in and he slid off of Jack and tried to catch his breath. Jack quickly scrambled out from under him and to his feet. As he crouched low, he could see through a tear in Jackson's pants the scars from were the doctors had repaired his knee. Jack quickly did a leg sweep kicking Jackson in the knee. Jackson grimaced as he felt the contact and, dropping to his knees, tossed his knife as he reached for his knee.

Jack stood up looked down to see the slice in his shirt surrounded in a growing stain of crimson. He looked over to see Jackson trying to get to his feet while he gagged and coughed. Jack rushed in to try and finish him, but as he closed in, Jackson's hand came from his throat and rammed into the center of Jack's chest with a splat as it landed in the bleeding gash. Jack attempted to deflect the punch, but Jackson was much too powerful and connected with Jack's torso. As Jack staggered backwards struggling to stay upright, he tripped over debris falling onto his back.

Rage coursed though Jackson's veins as he looked over at Jack. He glanced down at his shoulder, let out a huff, and slightly shook his head. As he rubbed his knee, he was surprised that he didn't feel pain. The doctors did well, and so did Jackson, by exercising it constantly. He reached up and rubbed his throat as he tried to clear it, never taking his eyes off of Jack.

Jack was attempting to get to his feet as Jackson came marching up to him when the crack off gunfire sounded off. Jackson let out a moan and then started gasping for breath once more and reaching around to his back as he stumbled forward.

Jack looked up to the remaining portion of the second floor to see Katelyn standing with his gun in her hands. He looked down at Jackson on his knees in front of him struggling to breath. He walked over and kicked him in the chest knocking him onto his back.

"Are you all right?" he called up to Katelyn.

She nodded.

"Go check on Dawn."

Katelyn shook her head, "She's dead."

Jack looked down at Jackson rolling around. "What about Brian? Go check on him."

Katelyn nodded, turned, and sprinted away.

As soon as he saw Katelyn was out of sight, Jack dropped down on Jackson's chest with a knee knocking the breath Jackson was still trying to catch, out of him.

"You fucking piece of shit," Jack growled inches from his face. "I don't know why any of this had to happen, but I'm going to see to it that you pay for every bit of it." He put the tip of the blade against Jackson's neck. "I can't do it; I'm not like you," Jack said as he pulled the knife away. "But I'll see to it you get yours in prison."

Jackson blindly swung his huge arm over knocking Jack to the ground. Still struggling to breath he rolled over onto Jack and wrapped his hands around his throat.

There are several points to combat shooting. A firm grip with both hands, wrapping the non-gun hand around the gun hand. Shoulders rolled forward and arms locked at the elbows. The abdominal muscles slightly crunched. Knees slightly bent and feet shoulder-width apart. Inhale through the nose counting to four. Hold the breath for four seconds. Release the breath through the mouth counting to four. Line the sights on your target and slowly squeeze the trigger while exhaling.

Katelyn's shot was a good one. She inhaled through her nose, held it, released slowly and squeezed the trigger; just like her father had taught her. Her target was not more than fifteen feet away and the round found its mark right between the shoulder blades. Seeing Dawn die in front of her had caused a rage Katelyn had never felt before. She was not going to let that man kill her father. The shot, no doubt, would have been lethal if it wasn't for Jackson's vest.

Jack could feel himself starting to go out and frantically reached under Jackson and ran his blade up his gut again. This time the talon-like blade made it through the vest and caught on Jackson's sternum. Jackson's eye grew wide as he felt it begin to slice through his flesh. Jack pushed with everything he had left to drive the blade deep into Jackson's chest cavity puncturing his left ventricle.

Jackson's jaw dropped and he pulled his hands off of Jack. He reached down and felt the stump of the handle protruding from his torso. He held his hands up to see the bright red blood all over them. He slowly got to his feet, staggered back a couple of steps, then fell over crashing onto his back.

"Dad!" Katelyn yelled as she jogged over to the toppled wall. "Dad, he's still breathing."

As she got to the edge she saw Jackson lying on his back gasping for his last breaths and her father slowly getting to his feet.

"Oh, my God! Are you all right?" she yelled with her hands over her mouth.

Jack stood up, nodded, and gave a wave. Katelyn looked for a way down and then scrambled over to her father. He stood before her; bruised and battered, but still alive. She pointed to the blood all over his shirt.

Jack looked down "Looks like a rough night of shark fishing," he said as he looked up with a grin.

Katelyn crashed into him with a huge hug, then quickly pulled away "Brian, he's still breathing!" she said as she reached down and pulled him by the hand.

"We better get him some help," Jack said as she pulled him along.

Jack pushed to help Katelyn up to the second floor were Brian lay. As she was climbing up she heard a thud and turned to see Jack falling to the ground. Standing there was a demented man holding a piece of wood.

Stone screamed as the massive chunk of house came flipping at him. Amazingly, the giant oak that had held him prisoner had now turned savior by creating a gap between it and the flying timbers. Everything collapsed and Stone was freed. He managed to weasel his way through the wreckage to freedom.

Upon his escape, he saw the body of Jackson with the stump of a knife protruding from his chest. Then he heard the rustling of Jack and Katelyn trying to climb up what was left of the house. He reached down and grabbed a piece of wood and snuck up behind Jack; cracking him across the side of the head.

Stone reached up and jerked Katelyn to the ground "Get over here!" he growled.

Katelyn landed on the ground next to Jack "Dad get up!" she yelled, but he didn't move.

Stone stepped around to in front of her "He's gone," he said giving Jack a kick.

Katelyn reeled back and kicked Stone right in the balls.

Stone curled over dropping the board as he let out a gasp. Katelyn turn over and started to crawl away, but Stone fell on top of her. Katelyn screamed as she continued to kick her legs trying to get away.

"Oh, you fucking bitch!" Stone moaned as he grabbed her by the hair and pulled back. He reached over and flipped Katelyn onto her back. "OK, you fucking whore, I'm gonna teach you a lesson," he said as he reached down to undo his pants.

Katelyn started screaming and thrashing. She reached up and scratched Stone across the face. Stone yelled then reached back and punched her in the mouth, splitting her bottom lip open.

"Yeah, keep fighting, you fucking bitch," Stone said as he grabbed both of her wrists in one hand.

Tears streamed down Katelyn's face "Daddy, please help me!" she pleaded.

CHAPTER THIRTY THREE

Jack stood on the deck of his skiff with the sun shining above slightly to his back. There was a slight breeze, but it did not seem to disturb the surface of the water because it was like glass. He looked off into the distance to see an Osprey perched up in the mangroves watching his every move.

The reflection of the sun danced on top of the water like sequins. Then he saw something roll on top of the emerald green water creating an ever-growing set of rings on the surface. Jack crouched down and watched the swirls in the water from the fish pumping its tail. He looked to the end of the rod he was holding to see a small crab, opening and closing its claws, dangling from a circle hook. He flipped the bail, swung the rod back, then forward again releasing the line and sending the crab into the air.

The crab landed with a plop about two yards in front of the direction the swirls were moving. Jack flipped the bail back by hand and waited. Then he saw the line start to move out away from the boat. Jack reeled until the line was taut, then pulled back on the rod.

The reel screamed with a zing as the spool spun against the drag.

Then he could feel it, so Jack bowed down just as the monster mirror-like fish leaped from the calm water into the air. He marveled as the majestic tarpon swung its head side to side sending a spray of water in all directions. Then it crashed back into the salty bath and was off and running again.

A huge grin stretched across Jack's face as he watched the fish race on when he heard Katelyn screaming behind him. He turned, shocked to see her standing there tattered and screaming.

"What is it?" Jack asked. He looked back at the speeding tarpon. It was getting farther away. The line was still zinging off his reel.

"Daddy, please!"

Jack looked back at her again. Tears were streaming off her cheeks. "Kat, what is it?" He looked down at the reel to see he was about out of line when Katelyn let out a shriek. He turned with a jerk to see her.

Jack's eyes popped open. The side of his face was wet from lying on the rain soaked ground. His ears were ringing and his head throbbed with terrible waves of pain.

"Please, Daddy, help me!" he heard Katelyn cry.

He blinked slowly as he attempted to get to his hands. He rested on his elbows as he turned and looked to see Stone on top of Katelyn.

"Do ya want me to hit you again? Then stop resist'n," Stone said as he struggled to undo Katelyn's jeans.

"Please don't do this," she begged. "Daddy!"

"I told you…" was all Stone got out when he felt a weight land on him.

Jack got to his feet and fell on top of Stone wrapping his arm around his neck. Jack held on as tight as he could and rolled them off of Katelyn.

"Get outta here!" Jack garbled as Stone started elbowing him in the ribs.

Katelyn got to her feet and stood there as Jack lay on his back holding Stone on top of him. Stone started flailing his head back smacking against Jack's face. Jack tried to tuck his head in but every blow just echoed in his already fragile head. He was starting to go out again when he felt a weight jump on them.

"Stop hitting him!" Katelyn yelled in a fit of rage. She jumped on top of Stone flailing her arms landing punches on his face.

Stone put his hands up to try and block Katelyn's haymakers. It was enough of a distraction for Jack to readjust his arm; fitting Stone's neck in the crook of his elbow. He latched his hands together and started squeezing.

Stones hands became heavy and blackness closed in on his vision of the insane girl straddling him, punching him in the face. And then he was out.

Jack felt Stone's hands drop "Kat, Kat, he's done!" he yelled.

Katelyn continued to wail on Stone's limp body.

Jack reached up and grabbed one her arms "Kat, stop! Get off, I want to get out!"

Katelyn stopped and started sobbing as she slid off and sat on the ground. Jack slid Stone off and then rolled him over. He reached up and stuck his hand in the gash in his shirt and tore it. He put the strip in his mouth and pulled Stone's hands behind his back just as Stone was starting to come to. He fumbled with the knot and Katelyn jumped in and finished it.

"What the fuck is happening," Stone mumbled as Katelyn finished tying his hands.

Jack took off the rest of his shirt and tied up his legs, then turned and hugged Katelyn. The two sat there hanging on each other.

"It's over," Jack whispered in her ear.

"I hope so," she whispered back.

CHAPTER THIRTY FOUR

As people emerged and came back into the Manatee/Sarasota area, an overwhelming feeling of disbelief hung in the air. The sheer destruction left many without homes or power. War zone was commonly used to describe the conditions in which people began to try and put their lives back together. The everyday hustle and bustle that had been the way of the growing area came to a halt. Waiting in line at Wal-Mart was replaced with waiting in line at the Red Cross for simple supplies.

The search for survivors led to the discovery of Daniels curled up underneath the refrigerator that had toppled over onto the counter above him. Even given all that happened, the men that found Daniels thought it odd that he was handcuffed behind his back. A question detectives would like answered as well.

It would take several months for some semblance of normalcy to appear, which made it very difficult for detectives to work the bizarre case that Jack and Katelyn tried to lay out for them. As soon as their investigation focused on the Cobra Squad, it didn't take long for Daniels and Stone to start selling out each other. Additionally, the insider that pointed the corrupt group's sights toward Jack was discovered as well. At first, Jack was in denial, when he learned of Audrey Brown's involvement with the Cobra Squad, but as the evidence mounted, there was no question. As if there was not enough going on with the clean-up of Hurricane Lynn, now the Sheriff's Office had to do some internal cleaning as well. All of the arrests made by the Cobra Squad were in question and hundreds of files had to be re-opened.

Greed, lust, jealousy, and fear; they all seemed to be the driving forces behind the Cobra Squad's actions. The reason Tom Underwood was murdered, Jack and Katelyn ran and fought for their lives, and why Matt Darby and Dawn Peterson no longer walked the earth. Through years of working behind locked doors with society's rejects, after delving into cold cases of the worst man could do, Jack still could not believe how simple, yet complicated Terrance Jackson and his crew's motives were to kill him and Katelyn.

Jack was thrust into the headlines once again as the Sheriff's Office's dirty laundry began to air. This time Katelyn was dragged into it as well. A fact which Amy could not deal with. This coupled with their house being damaged in the storm; Amy decided it was time for a change. So with Jack's blessing, she and Katelyn moved out of state in the hopes of getting away from the mess. Escaping the mess wasn't easy though as Katelyn's testimony was needed and she was required to be in town while waiting to be called upon.

Jack's house was severely damaged and he lost a great deal of his belongings. He and Amy came to terms and agreed that Jack would move back into their old house once construction was completed. Until then he stayed in a trailer setup by FEMA. Which meant Amy and Katelyn had to stay in the trailer, as well while waiting to go to court. Grouped together in the small trailer seemed to solidify Amy's distain for Jack. Though she said little, it was apparent that this was all his fault and stemmed from the reason they divorced in the first place, the cold case unit. It was his success in the unit that put fear in the Cobra Squad. Jack wondered if Amy didn't blame him for the hurricane as well.

Katelyn testified and was quickly swooped away by her mother in hopes of never returning. Something Jack had feared ever since the divorce. But there was little he could do as he was once again trying to put his life back together; a task that would be made much easier once the trial was over.

Jack walked into the white sterile room and sat down. The crowd of the Jerry Springer show burst into screams and hollers on the TV mounted above him. Jack shook his head as he watched the stage erupt into a white-trash wrestling match then looked over at his friend on the bed. The only movement Brian made was the slight rise and fall of his chest.

Jack looked down at his watch then got up.

"How long you been here?" came a groggy voice

"Only a couple of minutes," Jack said as he sat back down.

Brian didn't answer; he just gingerly reached over and took a sip from a plastic cup.

"Jury came back with a guilty verdict today."

"Good," Brian said as he paused between sips.

"So what's the latest with you?"

Brian took a deep breath "Well, doc seems to think after some physical therapy I should be able to walk again."

Jack closed his eyes and hung his head. Then he looked up to Brian who was staring blankly at the TV. "You know I can't thank you enough for all you did. I'll do everything I can to help."

"Can you believe this crap? How did he *not* know he was sleeping with a man?" he said, never taking his eyes off the TV.

Jack nodded and stood up. He glanced at the TV as he stood at the foot of the bed then looked at a couple of nurses walking by the door. "Well, I should get going. I'll come back tomorrow if I have time."

Brian looked down to Jack "I don't care about tomorrow."

Jack dropped his head and nodded.

"Just make sure you make time to take me fishing when I get out of here," he said with a smile.

Jack's head popped up "Anytime Capt. Brian, anytime," he smiled back.

The door creaked as Jack pushed it open. He looked around the decrepit trailer. He dropped his keys on a small table, sat on the couch, ran his hands through his hair, and sat with his hands behind his head. Just then his cell phone started ringing.

He flipped it open and smiled, "Hello."

"I saw the verdict today."

"*And?*"

"Now it's over," Katelyn said with a giggle.

"Yes, now it's over," Jack nodded. "How are you holding up?"

"I'm OK."

"I went and saw Capt. Brian today," Jack said as he leaned back.

"And how's he doing?"

"Well, for a guy who was in a coma for a few months, I guess he's all right. Says he wants me to take him fishing."

"Sounds like he's feeling much better."

"Yeah, I guess so," Jack paused "I miss you, honey."

"I miss you, too, Dad. You should come and visit."

"Yeah, I'm not so sure your Mom would be too keen into that."

"Hey, it's not like you would have to stay with us; there's plenty of hotels in Pigeon Forge."

"Hmm, I have always liked the Smokey Mountains," he said as he rubbed his chin.

"You should really think about it, Dad."

"I will, honey, I will."

EPILOGUE

Two years later…

    The sun was shining bright above the small skiff just north of Long Bar. The woman on the deck had just cast a white-bait into a pothole in the grass. Jack stood on the poling platform and surveyed the waters for any sign of game fish. It was a perfectly calm day and he could see the slightest bit of movement in the water. But it also meant that it was steaming hot and beads of sweat rolled down Jack's temples.

    As he scanned ahead, he became distracted by the blonde on the deck that was slightly bent over in front of him. A wry smile eased across his face as he followed her legs up when he felt his belt start to vibrate.

    Jack looked down and snatched the cell phone off his waist, "Skinny Dip Charters, Capt. Jack, how may I help you?" he asked hushed.

    "Hey, Jack, it's David Roberts."

    "Hey, David, what's up?" Jack asked as he put the phone in the crock of his neck.

    "I just wanted to be the first to tell you, we got him."

    "Got him?"

    "We got Michael Iorrio."

    "No shit!" he said with his eyebrows raised. The woman on the deck turned sharply to look at him. Jack held his hand up apologetically. "So where did y'all find him?"

    "He was hiding out in Hoboken, New Jersey. He looks horrible, didn't put up a fight either."

"Wow, that is great news. I'll have to give Kat a call later and tell her."

"OK, then, I knew I had to call you right away. I'll let you go."

Jack started snapping his fingers at the woman on the deck. She looked back and he started motioning for her to reel up. "I do appreciate it, David. Yeah, I'm on the boat right now so I should let you go."

"No problem. Take care, Jack."

"Yeah, you do the same."

"I'm not paying you to talk on the phone," the woman said never looking back at him.

Jack laughed "You're not paying me."

The woman turned and looked at him over her sunglasses with a deviant smile.

Just then Jack's phone started to vibrate again.

"Skinny Dip Charters, Capt. Jack, how may I help you?"

"Hi, I'm Detective Travis Skinner…"

"Sara, over there! Three o'clock, fifteen yards, big red!" Jack whispered hard. "I'm sorry; who did you say you were?"

"Detective Skinner."

"Oh, hey, thanks for calling, but Detective Roberts called and already told me that they got him."

"Uh, I'm not sure what you're talking about. I'm with the Sarasota Sheriff's Office."

"Oh, sorry bout that."

"Mr. Foster, I need your help."

The End

Printed in the United States
84079LV00004B/70-72/A